Family Matters

Family Matters

Christopher Matthew

Hodder & Stoughton
LONDON SYDNEY AUCKLAND TORONTO

British Library Cataloguing in Publication Data

Matthew, Christopher
    Family matters.
    I. Title
    823'.914[F]   PR6063.A86
    ISBN 0-340-39437-4

To Sherry and Margaret

November

Friday, November 2nd

More than five and a half years have elapsed since I last
committed my innermost thoughts to the safe-keeping of my
diary. It hardly seems possible. So much has happened in that
time – the Falklands War, my marriage to Belinda, the rise of
Melvyn Bragg – and I can only curse myself for failing to jot
down my reactions to these and other events, as and when they
occurred.

It was, I think I am right in saying, Germaine Greer who,
during a particularly interesting edition of something like *Did
You See . . . ?* commented, apropos an Australian mini-
series on the founding of Adelaide, that everyone should be
his or her own historian. I couldn't agree with her more.
My life has been riddled with incident, drama, changes of
fortune, encounters with interesting people and insights
into the *condition humaine* – so much so that I hardly know
where to pick the story up again. It's one of a number of
problems with which both Wagner and I have wrestled in
our time.

Still, as he discovered when he moved onto the next cycle of
his Ring, one has got to start somewhere, and what better
moment to take up my pen once more than on the eve of the
arrival of my first born? I do not believe I am exaggerating
when I say that all my worldly success in the field of public
relations pales into insignificance in the face of this momentous event. Like Winston in 1940, I feel that my whole life has
been but a preparation for this moment.

Whether Belinda could be said to have inspired me in my

career to quite the same extent as Clemmie is, of course, a matter of opinion. Tim Pedalow is convinced that had one Mrs B. Bott not taken it into her head to plump herself next to one Mr S. Crisp in the restaurant of the Metropol Hotel during a winter weekend break in Moscow six years ago, my life would have turned out to be a good deal less interesting than it has been. But then, as Belinda is his sister, he is bound to be biased. I expect he wishes he could say the same thing re his first meeting with Vanessa now that his marriage has ended in such tears. Frankly, despite her friendly open features, her cheerful smile and her warm, marmite-coloured eyes, I cannot pretend that Belinda is Clemmie's equal in the looks department. Though admittedly bequeathed to her by her first husband, the surname Bott was a great deal more apposite than Crisp. Fortunately, however, I have always had something of a penchant for large women. It's possibly a reaction against Mother being so small. And actually B's legs are very much more slender and alluring than the rest of her might lead one to suppose – unlike her brisk, rather booming voice, which is altogether more in keeping with the general ensemble.

Mother says she reminds her of a Women's Royal Army Corps major who was billeted on her during the war and whose hair had also gone prematurely grey like B's. I cannot believe it is meant as a compliment.

Tim, needless to say, was unable to resist a cheap joke re it being as a direct result of the unfortunate business of our wedding night. I have explained to him until I am blue in the face that, had I known that Last Minute Places plc were not the respectable charter company Hugh Bryant-Fenn had painted them, I would never have dreamed of booking a night flight to Malaga through them, even at £117 a head. Also that the twin beds in the Kinnock Hotel near the airport are not nearly as narrow and unyielding as Belinda made out. Not to normal-sized guests anyway.

At all events, have long been of the opinion that handsome is as handsome does in this world, and what is an hour-glass figure compared with a *summa cum laude* from the Cuisine Folklorique School of Cookery, a way with a needle and cotton that is second to none, and all the makings of a perfect wife and mother?

I am sorry that she does not see eye to eye with me over the question of giving up the Brixton flat and moving to the country. In my humble opinion, being able to bring up children amid the woods and fields of Kent or Gloucestershire is rather more important than being within striking distance of Peter Jones. Indeed, I'd have thought that the journey from the High Weald to Sloane Square would be, if anything, marginally quicker and easier than it is from Valderma Road, SW9.

However, this is neither the time nor the place to press the point. It is a well known fact that women's personalities can change dramatically in the last stages of pregnancy. So, I am beginning to think, can men's.

Saturday, November 3rd

Slightly overslept and as a result was not able to get cracking on nursery until well after repeat of *Pick of the Week*. B was unnecessarily didactic, I thought, re the monkey mobile I had spent so much valuable time choosing in the toy department of the Army & Navy Stores. I do agree that the actual height of the mobile is not ideal. If I walked into the wretched thing once, I must have walked into it a dozen times. On the last occasion, one of the monkeys got hooked round my ear, as a result of which the Sellotape, with which it was attached to the ceiling, came away taking with it quite a large chunk of the brand new balloon-patterned paper. I have patched it up as best I can, using Pritt, but it'll never look quite the same again. Not that it'll worry the baby; unless of course he has exceptional eyesight.

After dinner, spent a fascinating hour browsing through an excellent little volume entitled *Names for Boys* by someone called Carole Boyer. Having announced that she couldn't bear self-conscious middle-class names like Justin and Peregrine, and what was wrong with good old-fashioned English favourites like George and Henry, Belinda ended up with a short list that included Flavian from the Latin, meaning "flaxen-haired"; Fenton, which means "dweller of the marshland"; and Zelig, an Old German name which apparently means "blessed". "In honour of Woody Allen, I presume," I said, but the allusion escaped her. Personally, I lean towards something with a rather more literary feel to it – like Auberon or Sheridan or even Kingsley or Melvyn. As Carole Boyer points out very sensibly, Christian names with three syllables often go well with surnames that have only one. Strictly speaking of course, Kingsley and Melvyn have only two, but sound as though they have more. She also suggests that if there is an unusual name which one likes but is uncertain about, one might perhaps pop it in as a second name and leave it up to one's son to use it or not as he wishes. Oddly enough, the name John Julius is one that has long featured high on my list of personal favourites. I haven't mentioned it to B as yet. I've got enough on my plate as it is with this wretched mobile.

Of course, if we should after all be blessed with a girl, then a certain amount of drastic rethinking will be needed.

Sunday, November 4th

When I mentioned something to Mother about B's unusual passion for housework, she said that it was all part of the nesting instinct. She could have a point, I suppose; although I must say I can't imagine that many blackbirds take kindly to their speckled spouses chucking out pairs of perfectly serviceable pyjamas just because they've gone home slightly at the elbows.

Hoped I might take her mind off the duster and broom and onto higher thoughts of nativity by tempting her to join me at Matins at St Mungo's.

As I reminded her, it's only a matter of time now before we'll be asking the Almighty to accept another small soul into His fold and perhaps it wouldn't be a bad thing if we were to put some spiritual spadework in on his behalf. She said, "Some of us already feel ourselves to be in a sufficient state of grace without having to prove it to the vicar."

I tried to explain to her about the inner peace that comes from listening to the familiar words of the prayers and singing the good old hymns, but apparently not well enough. In the event, I arrived to find that instead of Matins they had laid on something described as a "Family Service". Not only could I not follow a word of it, but the whole thing was couched in a sort of Civil Service jargon which the vicar bellowed through a loudspeaker system to the accompaniment of high pitched electronic squeals which drowned even the chattering of the children and squeaking of the large contingent of babes in arms. Made a mental note not to allow any of my children within a hundred yards of any church service until they are at least ten years old.

At teatime, B broke off from rearranging the medicine cabinet long enough to discuss the matter of possible godparents. I am sorry she should appear to view the whole thing in such blatantly commercial terms. Children are going to need all the spiritual guidance they can get in the next few years and I regret now that I did not follow up my idea of suggesting to the Ski Time people that they invite Sir Laurens van der Post to say a few words on the occasion of their launch party last year. As a Kalahari man, downhill skiing may not be altogether his cup of tea; on the other hand, he is nothing if not fully committed to the natural order of things, and the concept of a modern ski resort, built entirely of wood, deep in the French Alps might well have appealed to his sense of ecology.

Whether he and I would have hit it off sufficiently for me to feel able to ask him to accept yet another godfatherhood is another matter. Suffice it to say that Tim Pedalow does not carry quite the same intellectual and moral weight.

I quite agree that Beddoes, for all the years of friendship and flat-life we shared together, is simply not godfather material; nor is Hugh Bryant-Fenn. Philippe de Grande-Hauteville is charming enough but far too European for my liking. Theresa, on the other hand, is a strong contender for the female corner, especially now that she has taken up meditation. We'll see. It's early days yet.

Had just settled down with Melvyn and Oscar Kokoschka on South Bank at ten thirty when Vita walked across to the corner of the room towards the large pink elephant which B's mother sent us recently for the nursery, gave it a quick hump and then calmly bit its head off.

B said, "If I've said it before, I must have said it a dozen times, we are not terrier people – certainly not when the animal in question has such pronounced lesbian tendencies – and the fact that your mother had five on the trot and not a day's trouble from any of them is not, and never was, a valid reason for plunging eighty five pounds into yet another member of the breed." Must admit that Vita is a creature blessed with an unusually sharp tongue, not to say pair of teeth, and I am secretly quite surprised that she and B have not discovered a natural empathy.

B's relationship with Mother is another matter altogether.

Monday, November 5th

To Alexandra Palace dry ski slope at six thirty for firework and glühwein party for Ski Time. Quite a good turn-out considering Karen walked round London for three days with all the invitations in her shoulder-bag. Still, if TCP Public Relations are daft enough to hire a secretary with the surname of Brick, what can they expect? If she were not so pretty and eager to please, I'd have handed her her cards weeks ago.

Still, *Sunday Times* and *Observer* both sent people, which was something. I am not quite sure what sort of articles we can expect from a deputy sports editor's secretary and a picture desk assistant, but they have both promised to do their best.

A surprising number of people actually put on skis and ventured out onto the nylon matting, including yours truly. I am sorry the torchlight procession on skis was not more impressive. A couple of dozen flaming brands clasped aloft by some of the best skiers in the Burnese Oberland as they come swinging down the Lauberhorn is hardly the same thing as five so-called ski writers slightly the worse for wear stumbling across the lower slopes of Muswell Hill waving dim Ever Readies. On the other hand, the two girls in short skirts we had hired to ski around with trays of *vin chaud* on the end of their arms, looking like the roller-skaters in the Martini commercials, were a huge success. Was chatting to Maurice Valjean, the Ski Time marketing chap, when one of the girls came rushing towards me holding a tray with a note on it.

"It's for you-hoo," she called out in a facetious voice. It was a message to say that Belinda had suddenly gone into labour and had been whisked into hospital.

Everyone was most understanding and said that of course I must go straight away. Charlie Kippax even went so far as to offer to run me down there himself.

Unfortunately, was in such a rush to get away that I completely forgot I was still wearing my skiing boots and a full skiing outfit and in my rush to get away, I tripped on stairs, twisting my ankle painfully. Arrived at hospital to find I was quite unable to put any weight on foot and so had to hop up front steps with one arm round Charlie's shoulders. The nurse at the front desk looked up and said, "Casualty?" "No," I said. "Maternity."

I cannot imagine why she should have thought I was trying to be funny. I'm afraid I was rather sharp.

Eventually found way to B's room to find it had all been a false alarm and the latest plan was that she should have the baby induced in the morning. Was quite tempted to suggest I stay in overnight myself, but knowing how much these private wings charge nowadays, decided not even to sit down on a chair for fear of it costing me not only my bad leg but an arm too. Arrived home in a taxi to find that someone had seen fit to let off a Catherine Wheel using the right-hand post of the front gate as a fixing point. This is one November 5th that will certainly never be forgot.

Tuesday, November 6th

To the hospital at eleven carrying the biggest bunch of roses I could manage.

Why it had never occurred to me that red and white flowers in hospital might be associated in certain people's minds with

13

blood and bandages, I cannot think. But then, of course, women are notoriously more superstitious than men, hence the very small number of actresses who have successfully played Lady Macbeth.

Left bunch at porter's desk to collect on way out. Found B lying on side rigged up to a small machine monitoring her heart-beat, looking surprisingly cheerful and relaxed. What a wonderful support she is to me in times of stress. Nurse most sympathetic when I happened to mention my twisted ankle, and although I can quite understand she didn't have the time to look at it there and then, her suggestion that I should make an appointment to have it X-rayed and meanwhile not put too much weight on it could not have been more welcome. But then, that's private medicine for you. Cannot imagine anyone taking that sort of time and trouble in a National Health labour ward.

Rather shocked to find myself eyeing her with more than professional interest, but I daresay there is a perfectly good psychological explanation.

Was on my way for a bite of lunch when the gynaecologist, Armstrong, popped his head out of the sister's office and said, "I shouldn't go far if I were you. Things are likely to happen any minute now." Hurried back into room to find midwife and nurse rigging up contraption at side of bed and tying B's legs onto it in a raised, wide-open position. Then Armstrong arrived and began to tog himself up in a loose-fitting dark green outfit, rubber boots, cap and face mask.

Was looking round for my own set of surgical wear when he said, "If you wouldn't mind standing over there out of the way at the head of the bed and helping your wife with her breathing, I'd be most grateful."

I am not a man who indulges in foolish fantasies, but I cannot pretend that I was anything other than disappointed and slightly shocked that in a hospital of this repute, and at a critical moment such as this, I should find myself the only person in the room dressed in ordinary outdoor clothes.

I cannot seriously believe that Prince Charles was permitted to risk the safety and well-being of the future King of England by standing at his wife's bedside dressed in a germ-ridden worsted two-piece – even if it was one of Gieves and Hawkes' best.

Nor can I believe that he had any more spare time than I did to attend prenatal classes with his wife – unless, of course, Betty Parsons went round to Kensington Palace after work in the evenings and gave them private sessions on the drawing-room carpet. At all events, I can only hope for HRH's sake that he was able to play a slightly more significant role in the proceedings than clasping the royal paw and occasionally bending forward to murmur "push" in the royal ear.

After twenty minutes of puffing and panting, B announced that she had given her all and Armstrong reached for a pair of forceps. This was a welcome development from my point of view, since according to Paula Batty, if a birth involves complications of any kind, you can claim the cost of the whole thing back from the private health insurance people.

Was on the verge of asking Armstrong for confirmation of this technicality when suddenly he stood up holding a squawking, rather purple-looking baby which instantly relieved itself all over the floor. "There you are," he said, "a lovely bouncing son." To my astonishment I burst into floods of tears. Thought I could hear B tutting, but it may have been my imagination.

Later, when everyone had gone and the three of us were left alone at last, *en famille*, I attempted to give some expression to my feelings, but words failed me and in their place tears of pride and joy sprang unbidden once again to my eyes. B gave a weary smile and squeezed my hand in an unmistakable gesture of fondness and understanding. To compare her at that moment with Raphael's Madonna might be rather overstating the case, but I do not believe I have seen her looking lovelier or more serene since that historic April morning in Kensington Registry Office when I pledged her my troth.

Would happily have stayed on for the rest of the day, holding my son in my arms and talking silly baby-talk, had I not suddenly remembered something very important I had to do.

Gave them both one last kiss, and promising to be back in the evening, rushed downstairs, leapt into car and drove like a lunatic down the M4 to Eton. It's well known that if you want to be sure of a place for your boy, you must get his name down at birth, and I wasn't about to jeopardize his future with unnecessary shilly-shallying.

Disappointed not to be able to have a word with the headmaster himself, or even his secretary. I suppose I should really have made an appointment. However, middle-aged man I bumped into by Chapel steps couldn't have been more helpful. He was most interested to hear my good news, and even though I explained to him that I was not an old Etonian *per se*, he said he foresaw no serious problems in getting my son in in thirteen years' time; which house did I have in mind? When I asked him which he'd recommend, he replied that since I had no special preferences, I would probably do just as well to put his name down on the general list and get in touch with the school nearer the time. There was no hurry, as long as I did it before he was ten. The registration fee is apparently twenty pounds which I thought sounded a bit on the steep side, and said as much. He said, "You have to be prepared to pay to get the best these days." I said that, of course, he was quite right and enquired if he happened to *be* a housemaster, or merely a beak, as I believe they are known. He said, "Oh, I don't work here. I'm just a tourist."

Drove back to London in a mood of deep uncertainty.

So much has happened in the last few hours and my whole life has been altered in such a dramatic way that I feel I am probably not in the right frame of mind to go making important and far-reaching decisions of this nature at this stage. Struggled through terrible traffic to hospital, only to discover that B had just gone off to sleep. Was suddenly overwhelmed with such feelings of love for her that I could not resist tip-toeing towards the bed and planting a gentle kiss on her forehead. I suppose it could have been that that woke her up. Personally, I still blame the fool of a person who had to go and choose that moment to start testing his car thief alarm. All I know is that I seem to be one of those unlucky people whose best intentions are doomed forever to be misinterpreted.

Collected flowers from porter's desk and wended my way

home. Sitting now in these empty rooms over a solitary cheese omelette, it is hard to come to grips with the idea that I am at last a father, but I suppose I shall have to sooner or later. It is, after all, what being a man is all about.

Wednesday, November 7th

Woke exhausted, having sat up till two trying to compose an announcement for births column of *Telegraph*. B is keen that we should put one in *Times* as well but I have a feeling that's her parents speaking and they're not having to stand the bill.

The next thing I know, I'll have Mother wanting to take space in the *Kent Messenger*. Really, parents seem to think of nobody but themselves. Have made mental note not to fall into same trap myself.

Severely hampered in my attempts to hit right note by fact that we have not yet agreed on names. Was sorely tempted to bang something into print and present everyone, baby included, with a *fait accompli*. However, decided to canvass a little more opinion first, starting in the office.

Pamela van Zeller not a lot of help, as usual. How anyone with such a minimal talent for communicating with her fellow human beings could possibly have landed up in public relations is beyond me. I am all for simplicity in names myself, but surely anyone with the slightest social sense could see straightaway that Fred does not go with Crisp, and the fact that Richard Ingrams chose to call his boy by that name is unlikely to ease my own son's passage through life. I can only ascribe her choice to three years' worth of economics and the psychology of politics at the University of North Humberside. While I must applaud the fact that she came away with a first-class honours degree and turned down the offer of a research fellowship for the privilege of working under my personal aegis, I cannot help wondering if these redbrick places might not seriously consider introducing degree courses in common sense and imagination, with dieting, basic skin care and general self-improvement as optional extras. What's more, they could do worse than appoint Karen Brick as senior tutor. Although only a secretary, she has more charm, beauty and native wit in her little toe than Miss van Zeller could muster in a hundred years.

Should I perhaps consider asking her to be a godmother? It could be very useful for the little chap to have an easy entrée into the world of the lower orders.

One so-called friend I shall not be calling upon is Molly Marsh-Gibbon. As an occasional theatre companion she is second to none and better read than anyone I know; but I sometimes wonder if her elevator goes to the top floor.

When I rang her to tell her the good news, she said, "That'll teach you," and shrieked with laughter. I simply put the phone down on her.

To the hospital immediately after work pausing *en route* to buy a small gift for baby. Was rather sorry not to have taken Karen's advice and gone to Harrods' toy department, since Pakistani newsagent's opposite office rather low on stock. Finally chose small pink bear made of some sort of fluffy material. I don't think the dirty mark on its leg really matters; the shopkeeper assures me it's washable. Even so, I do think he could have offered some sort of token rebate. After all, I do buy my *Standard* there most days of the week.

B looking wonderfully maternal when I arrived, with baby dozing serenely in her arms.

Had no sooner picked him up than he screwed his face up and squawked loudly.

Took a leaf out of Princess of Wales' book by slipping little finger into his mouth with gratifying results for all concerned except B who demanded to know if I had washed my hands. When I said yes, but not since lunchtime, she flew into a terrible state and seized the baby from me, saying that if he were to die of some ghastly disease, which she considered highly probable in the circumstances, then she would hold me personally responsible. Left very much in dog-house, taking with me briefcase full of dirty nightclothes and matinée jackets and lengthy washing and ironing instructions. Roll on Friday when monthly nurse arrives to take charge. I only hope we shall still have a child for her to look after.

Thursday, November 8th

Have decided the only way to get this name business settled is by trying out the various possibilities one by one, a day at a time, and seeing which one we feel most comfortable with. In B's absence and by way of tribute to her efforts over the last few days, kicked off with one of her front-runners, Fenton. Funnily enough, it didn't sound at all bad; in fact, by mid-morning I was beginning to get quite used to the idea.

To Mazzarini & Block's at lunchtime to buy some wine. Have long promised myself that, were I ever to be blessed with a son, I would celebrate the event by laying down a few cases of decent claret which would be ready for drinking in time for his eighteenth birthday.

Spent useful twenty minutes in M & B's reception perusing their fascinating list. Block certainly knows his stuff. Was particularly interested in his comments re the 1978 claret. Apparently growers who picked early made wines that are often marred by a lack of ripeness and by the deadening effect of chaptalisation, whereas the late pickers benefited from the mid-October sunshine to make a wine that is complete and well-balanced in character. I can well believe it, but where exactly does this leave me? Was the Château Tronquoy-Lalande picked early or late compared with, say, the Château Latour du Mirail? Was the wine from Haut-Medoc more successful that year than the St Estèphe, and what exactly is the difference between the two, apart from the 34p? And if there is a difference, would I be able to spot it anyway? More to the point, would young Fenton, eighteen years hence?

And what exactly is chaptalisation? Would certainly have tackled Block on these basic points, had there not been quite so many pin-striped customers waiting behind me. In the end decided not to beat about the bush, and asked him straight out if he reckoned 1978 was a good investment. He said, "The top wines will keep well."

I do not know if the Château Verdun at £3.46 a bottle is considered to be in the premier league. At all events have bought three bottles to be getting on with. Block seemed rather surprised when I asked him if he wouldn't mind keeping a couple for me in bond for a bit while I took the third one home for a little private tasting. However, he said he'd be prepared to put them on one side until the middle of next week. It wasn't quite as long as I'd hoped, but time was pressing; ditto the man standing behind me. "Name?" said Block. When I told him Fenton Crisp, the name rolled so naturally and sonorously off the tongue that I wonder I did not jump at it the instant B brought it up. Was turning to leave when I happened to glance down at order book only to see that Block had written in large letters "Quentin Crisp".

Charlie Kippax wandered in around three for a general chat so took the opportunity to uncork the Château Verdun and ask his opinion. Quite why he felt the need to polish off three plastic tumblers full of the stuff before being able to deliver a judgement I can't think. I am no Cyril Ray but even I can spot a quality wine when I taste one, and I have a sneaking suspicion young Crisp may have good cause to bless me in the early years of the twenty-first century when he opens up a bottle or two for his eighteenth birthday party guests. Taste apart, it's a weighty wine, and by the time I set off for the hospital I was feeling quite woozy. Had I remembered to bring the clean baby clothes I doubt B would even have noticed, but somehow one thing led to another and before I knew what, I was on my way home with a flea in my ear and another pile of sick-stained baby clothing.

Am definitely having second thoughts about the name Fenton. Ditto about all this washing I'm doing without wearing rubber gloves. My skin is becoming quite rough.

Friday, November 9th

Wonder how the name Hunter Crisp would go down with all concerned. I remember Vanessa Pedalow once saying how people with thrusting-sounding names often seem to get ahead better than those who are more blandly named.

An astonishing thing happened shortly before lunch. Kippax popped his head round the door and said, "Steamy

Days". I replied that, on the contrary, I thought it had turned chillier recently.

"Steamy Days," he repeated. "Comic new set up in Norfolk. Redundant railway-carriages converted into *bijou* holiday cotts on disused railway-lines. Somewhere up near Sheringham, I believe. They've asked us if we can do anything for them. Unfortunately I'm a bit bogged down with this fizzy water junket to the Dordogne. Wonder if you'd mind talking to them? The chief ape there is someone called Hume Purkiss. A man presumably. Be a dear and take him to lunch at Botticelli and see what he wants, will you?'

Talk about chickens coming home to roost. I haven't seen Hume since we were Trojan servants together in a college production of Anouilh's *Tiger at the Gates*; but I've certainly heard a lot about him. Who hasn't? I have often wondered over the years why he, of all the unlikely people, should have turned out to be such a whizz kid. I can only suppose that he was born with a special nodule somewhere at the back of his brain that has been denied to the rest of us. Got Karen to ring Botticelli and book table for one fifteen.

Left early for hospital. Hunter still looking healthy and very much alive, despite finger incident. Commented on this fact, to be told that it was no thanks to the coolies who had sat there in their Taiwanese sweat shops turning out pink fluffy teddies whose eyes fall out the moment they see a new baby. Couldn't help thinking that the chances of a three-day-old swallowing a plastic eye were fairly remote, but kept a low profile on the subject and merely said that I would take it back to the shop and kick up a stink.

"A kick up someone's bottom would be more appropriate," said B. What a strange mood she seems to be in these days. I have heard that some women can suffer from post-natal depression, but post-natal rattiness is a new one on me. But then so, of course, is post-natal everything.

Were it not costing me two hundred pounds a day, I might seriously consider suggesting she stay in over the weekend and rest. Still, the monthly nurse arrives first thing in the morning and she will doubtless be able to take the pressure off both of us. I feel sure that once B is home she will see things quite differently. Is it my imagination, or did she tell me the nurse's surname is Thatcher?

Dog bit teddy's whole head off during *Nine O'Clock News*, which saves me a journey. Unless, of course, I now have to go to the vet.

Saturday, November 10th

To Paddington to collect monthly nurse – a blatant misnomer if ever I heard one. The word "monthly" implies she comes once a month whereas she is in fact staying for a month. 'Month-long' might be slightly nearer the mark.

At all events, she couldn't have chosen to arrive at a more inconvenient railway terminal if she had tried. Given the sort of traffic one has to put up with on Saturday mornings these days, it was almost inevitable that I should be held up somewhere along the line. Apologised as best I could for keeping her waiting, to which she replied, "The early bird catches the worm," and tapped me gently but surprisingly painfully on the right wrist.

Decided to avoid congestion in Park Lane by slipping through Park, only to find myself at the back of a very long queue, two abreast, waiting to exit at the top of Exhibition Road. Tried to reverse with view to U-turn but found I was already blocked by three or four cars behind. Was congratulating myself on keeping my temper when she tapped me again – on my good wrist – and said, "I could have told you the Park is always bad on Saturday mornings. When I was working for the Roskills, we always used to go via Park Lane. But then, of course, they did always send a car for me."

She is called Hilda Thatcher. I can't say I am surprised. To the hospital, following a snacky sort of lunch, to fetch B and Hunter – alone and again slightly on the late side.

At last moment, fool of a dog slipped through half-open front door and leapt onto passenger seat. Could not spare time to boot her out. Besides, at moments of stress it's good to have someone in the car to chat to. Arrived to find B already dressed in loose-fitting, flowery dress and packed and sitting on the edge of the bed with Hunter wrapped in a white shawl on her lap.

Gathered up bits and pieces and went to collect rather pretty assortment of chrysanths and freesias that Mother had sent via Interflora. B said, "I thought we'd leave the cut flowers for the nurses." I noticed she wasn't feeling so generous with her parents' azalea. Rather an emotional send-off for staff and patient alike, although in B's case tears turned quickly to irritation when she discovered a) how far away I'd parked and b) that I'd brought Vita with me. "If this baby dies of some dog-borne disease, I shall hold you personally responsible," she said. Attempted to point out that in African countries, children are invariably exposed to livestock within moments of being born and that amongst nomadic tribes, it is not uncommon for babies to be born on the hoof, as it were. I went on to say that the world is full of germs and that the sooner Hunter got used to them, the greater would be his resistance in the long run.

"Who?" she said.

I explained my plan for trying out names.

She said, "Well, you can forget that one for a start. I'm not going to have a child going around sounding like some sort of nuclear submarine."

I pointed out that I wasn't entirely sold on it myself and that I was hoping we might discuss it in the car. She said *I* could discuss it in the car if I wanted; *she* was going home by taxi. Tried to talk sense to her but might have been addressing brick wall. In the end, compromised by sending Vita home in taxi. Driver curiously unsympathetic when I tried to explain about her not being very keen on people swinging too fast round bends, so much so that I had to slip him an extra fiver before he'd agree to take her at all. All the more irritated, therefore, to get stuck in appalling traffic in Park Lane and arrive home to find V sitting in taxi outside the flat and meter registering double the amount I'd anticipated. Explained my problem to driver who merely shrugged his shoulders and said, "You should have gone through the Park like I did."

What should have been a joyous homecoming made all the stickier by the fact that in the excitement I had forgotten to get in a supply of nappy liners, as requested. So, instead of seeing my son being put to bed for the first time in his new home, had to battle my way through late shoppers in Boots, only to arrive home to find Miss Thatcher had brought some with her just in case.

"Forewarned is forearmed, that's my motto," she said. It would be.

In the circumstances, was quite surprised when she allowed me to hold the baby for a few minutes before "putting him down", as she calls it. A more unfortunate phrase it would be hard to imagine. Perhaps she has a veterinary background. Was so terrified of standing up too suddenly and catching his little head on the sloping ceiling above his bed that I didn't look what I was doing and gave my own head a nasty crack instead, very nearly dropping child in process.

Later, had just settled down to watch Saturday arts programme on BBC 2 when Miss T marched in, took one look at Russell Davies and said, "Oh, so you're not watching Juliet Bravo then?" Attempted to make a little pleasantry by pretending that in fact it was an episode of JB about an investigation into a case of fraud involving a well-known BBC 2 arts presenter. She said, "I don't mind. It's just that when I was with the Roskills it was a well-known thing in the family that Saturday night was Nanny's Juliet Bravo night. But then, of course, I *did* have my own room; and my own television set." I am not a man who takes against people he has never met, but I am bound to say that the Roskills are currently making a rather poor showing in my personal Top of the Pops chart. To bed rather earlier than usual with a slight throbbing in my head and the name Russell Crisp very much on my lips.

Sunday, November 11th

I suppose I must have dozed off at some stage last night, but I can scarcely believe it. I never realised babies were capable of so much noise and for such long periods at a time. Or that they needed to be fed at two o'clock in the morning. Am beginning to wonder if breast-feeding is all it's cracked up to be.

B's parents to lunch.

Am still at a loss how to address them. With the best will in the world, even after seven months of marriage, I simply cannot bring myself to call them Claud and Alyson; and since I call Mother "Mother", I would feel very odd indeed addressing some comparative stranger in the same terms. Broached the subject with Major Pedalow over a La Ina dry sherry before lunch, and explained my predicament. How, as the husband of his only daughter and the father of his, so far, only grandchild, *should* I address them? He thought for a moment. "I think Major and Mrs Pedalow would fit the bill," he said.

Slight chill after lunch when I made a casual reference to Russell who was at that moment reclining in Alyson's arms. "Did you say Russell?" said the major. I said that, as names went, it was still very much at the drawing-board stage. "We once had a gardener called Russell," he said.

To Clapham Common for a walk later which was slightly marred by the fact that Alyson trod in some dog dirt on three separate occasions. Our own animal did not behave in exemplary fashion either. At one stage she attempted to mount a black labrador. By a bizarre coincidence, the animal's name was Violet. The major said, "If that was my dog, I'd have it doctored. Settle it down a bit." I replied that castration was not in this case a viable option, since Vita is a bitch.

"Could have fooled me," he said.

They left soon afterwards with an invitation to visit them in Gloucestershire as soon as possible, which I have a feeling did not include Yours Truly. As we were waving them away from the pavement, a couple of youths walked behind us, casually chucked a Kentucky Fried Chicken carton and a half-eaten portion of chips over our privet hedge and ran off up the road. The major said, "I hope this is only a temporary address." It was the only time I felt like agreeing with him all day.

Monday, November 12th

To office rather later than usual thanks to unexpected arrival of local council midwife. Pointed out that she was a little on the late side since the baby had been safely delivered five days previously. She explained that these visits are standing procedure nowadays and are intended merely as a check on the baby's progress. I said that I supposed there were some young couples around with a sadly underdeveloped sense of responsibility towards their infants, but that of course there was no danger of that in the case of private medicine. "The nanny society may suit some," I said, "but not those of us who have our own nannies." It was unfortunate in the circumstances that she should have discovered that Melvyn is suffering from a mild attack of nappy-rash. Ditto that she happened to be black. We are having enough trouble with our credibility in the eyes of the world over South Africa without adding to it with silly little slip ups of this nature.

To Botticelli for lunch with Hume Purkiss. It's funny to think that this was the very restaurant where Bryant-Fenn humiliated me all those years ago in front of Tim and Vanessa by claiming to be the restaurant's PR man and fobbing me off with a bogus invitation to take some friends along for a free meal. And now here I am working for the firm that is currently handling its account!

Arrived slightly earlier than I had expected and sat over a spritzer and a small plate of *amuse gueules*, happily recalling those golden days of youth that Hume and I were privileged to share together. Although not perhaps one of my closest friends at Oxford, he was certainly very much a part of the social and intellectual world in which I moved and many's the time we've chewed the fat over a pork pie and a pint with Joyce and Eliot in the garden of the Turf. Whatever became of Joyce I wonder? Her legs were very much her downfall, if I remember rightly. Eliot, I know, is something in the City – though not half as big as Hume. Even as an undergraduate he was very much of an entrepreneur and to judge by his various well-publicised exploits in the world of high finance, his early promise has been amply fulfilled. Surprised when he walked through front door to see that he was looking, if anything, even younger than I remember. Ditto that he walked straight past me in the bar and, although standing only a few feet from me, informed the manager that a Mr Cripps was expecting him. I called out, "Hello, Hume." He turned and looked at me as if I were a complete stranger. Of course he remembered me in the end, though not without a little prompting on my part, and apart from the veal chop with rosemary being on the rather tough side, we spent an agreeable couple of hours together, talking old trains and travel in general. I cannot see any reason not to add him to our client list.

Was busily trying to remind him of the hilarious incident concerning the tights and the protruding nail during that legendary matinée of *Tiger at the Gates*, when who should come lumbering into view but Hugh Bryant-Fenn, of all people, obviously angling for a free lunch. I'm afraid I had no alternative but to send him packing. Doubtless he will see this as a personal snub and a revenge for my own shabby treatment at his hands in the same restaurant all those years ago. I'm equally certain that nothing I say to the contrary will persuade him otherwise, so I shan't waste my breath. They say you should never spurn the people you meet on the way up in case you meet them again on the way down, but of course there are exceptions to every rule.

Tuesday, November 13th

Melvyn noisier than ever last night. When I did finally get off at around two thirty, I had such vivid dreams about not being able to sleep that I woke more exhausted than ever.

Miss Thatcher, on the other hand, arrived for breakfast looking as fresh and serene as if she had just come from a fortnight's cruise in the Caribbean. Am more convinced than ever that she is related to the Prime Minister. Possibly quite closely.

As if her presence were not sufficiently intrusive, she has now begun to introduce her curious brand of nursery jargon into our family life. Only this morning, I overheard B chiding M for "wizzling" all over her clean skirt. Heaven knows what euphemism we must learn to use from now on to describe our number twos. Much of breakfast taken up with fruitless attempts on my part to revive our long-running debate re moving to the country. But quite honestly I might have been addressing a tube of toothpaste for all the enthusiasm I aroused. Miss Thatcher said, "Anyone who is tired of London is tired of life."

"A man," I corrected her.

"Women too," she said.

I may well have to take matters into my own hands. B is nothing if not empiric, and I feel sure that, were I to present her with the right house in the right part of the country, she would go for it like a shot.

A slightly inconsequential day at the office, at the end of which I found that all I had achieved was a memo to Carlo and Angelo at the Botticelli re the Christmas lunch, and another to Ski Time proposing a fondue party in the Cheddar Caves. I have always been a great believer in taking the product to the people, and the West Country is an area with a potentially large skiing population. I shall be interested to hear Valjean's reaction.

Wednesday, November 14th

An historic day indeed. Not only is today the birthday of the Prince of Wales, King Hussein of Jordan, Dame Elisabeth Frink, Aaron Copland, Lord Ramsay and Harold Larwood, but it also happens to be the wedding anniversary of Princess Anne and Captain Mark Phillips. I feel I ought to be sending various telegrams. I certainly would be, if such things still existed. Is it my imagination or did I hear someone use the phrase "big potties" just before bath-time this evening?

Thursday, November 15th

Did Auberon sleep rather better last night, or are my cotton-wool earplugs more effective than I thought? Put this question to Hilda, as we must now learn to call Miss Thatcher. She said, "What the ear doesn't hear, the heart doesn't grieve over," and plunged the nappies into Napisan.

Bought *Country Life* on way to office, only to find that it was the London number, and full of advertisements for substantial period houses in Chelsea and Holland Park and penthouses in Eaton Square. Was on the point of chucking it away in disgust when my eye was caught by a very pretty Georgian rectory which Hampers & Co have on their books at Clifton Botting in Hampshire. Though not perhaps quite as close to the M25 as one might wish, and therefore not offering the easiest possible access to Heathrow and Gatwick airports, this outstanding Grade II listed house is set in a delightful secluded position on the edge of the village and enjoys fine views over the surrounding countryside. Not only does it look from the colour photograph to be exactly the sort of house in which I have always envisaged bringing up a young family, but it also offers exactly the right amount of accommodation (five bedrooms) and has a one-and-a-half-acre garden and a detached coach-house with potential for conversion. Though the possibility of our having Mother to live with us sometime in the not too distant future is something which I have yet to broach with B, a possible granny annexe must inevitably play a significant part in my thinking. Surprised to see there was no mention of price. Rang Hampers immediately upon arrival at office and spoke to very nice man called Anthony Stanford-Dingley who said he would be only too delighted to send me details and that, as he rather quaintly put it, they were "looking for offers in excess of £275,000". This is slightly more than I had in mind, since although the flat must be worth a great deal more than the £28,500 I paid for it in 1981, and I'm sure Hugh Bryant-Fenn was correct in predicting that Brixton was the next up-and-coming area, I somehow doubt that prices have improved quite as much as tenfold. Nor is £20,000 a year the most princely of salaries.

On the other hand, nothing venture nothing gain in this world. The only way to make a lot of money these days is by pulling off deals, and although I have never seen myself as the natural successor to the likes of Harry Hyams in the property market, everyone has to start somewhere, and this could well prove a turning-point in my fortunes. Have decided for the time being not to mention the house to Belinda. It's early days and there's no point in getting her excited unnecessarily.

Friday, November 16th

I have heard it said that dogs can get very upset by the arrival of a baby, but I doubt that many take their neuroses to quite the lengths ours does. Barking at the postman through the letter-box is one thing: leaping up, seizing the letters the moment they appear, hauling them onto the mat and attacking them as if they were rats is quite another.

It was particularly unfortunate that the animal should have chosen to launch her campaign of jealousy and general dissatis-faction in this way with what was obviously a most beautifully presented brochure of the Clifton Botting house. Even more so that its incisors should have punctured the main glossy colour photograph at the very spot above the front door where the sundial sits that's reputed to have once been the property of Lady Jane Grey. Never mind. Not even the worst canine ravages could destroy the grace, beauty and symmetry of this charming house. I'm bound to say that I am not a great fan of the ruched blind or the canopied bed, and while I am totally in favour of making the best of period plasterwork, I do not believe that gold necessarily shows it off to its best advantage. Still, these are minor points. Everyone who buys a new house must expect to undertake a modicum of cosmetic refurbish-ment, and I can almost feel the good stout handle of the four-inch Harris nestling in my palm already.

Rang Hampers as soon as I got to my desk and have arranged a viewing at eleven tomorrow morning. Stanford-Dingley said that he wouldn't be able to join me in person on this occasion as he has been invited to shoot in Wiltshire. However, he has arranged for someone from their local office to be there. Stupidly, I forgot to ask the name of the owners. Not that it could possibly make the slightest difference. I know there is a school of purchaser that believes in becoming personally involved with its vendors. Nevertheless, "*caveat emptor*" has always been my policy in these matters, and since on this occasion I happen to be the *emptor*, then it is I who am very much in the driving-seat and any attempts to establish a personal relationship on either side, however well-meaning, might well result in serious embarrassment all round.

Am so excited at the prospect of returning to my roots and becoming a countryman once again that I found I could scarcely bend my mind to anything else all day. Even Valjean's curiously testy comments on my Cheddar Caves suggestion could raise little more in me than a sigh of resignation.

Pamela adopted a smug "told-you-so" expression which she wore for the rest of the day and very nearly drove me, for the first time in my life, to contemplate striking a woman. As we were leaving Kippax's office after a particularly inconsequential meeting re the Botticelli Christmas lunch, she said quietly, "Not only do you appear to have cheese on the brain but on your suit too. Or is it sick?"

Attempted to explain to her about the problems inherent in winding a week-old baby, but she simply walked away, still wearing that same very silly look. I wouldn't at all mind bringing her wind up, I don't mind saying.

Saturday, November 17th

Up early and to work with bucket and shammy on Polo. Grey metallic paintwork never as easy to buff to a gleaming finish as good old gloss, but light application of Turtle Wax certainly added an extra *je ne sais quoi*. Decided against hoovering interior in favour of some brisk dustpan and brush work.

Belinda unnecessarily suspicious, despite my assurances that my visit to Hampshire was strictly business. She said, "Business? On a Saturday?" I replied that, in the rather Bohemian world of arts and communication, people are not like machines which can be switched on for five days and off for two. The creative process is continuous and open-ended, and if a client is suddenly inspired to call a meeting and kick some new idea around, then one has to be flexible enough to take this sort of thing in one's stride. As a result, left later than anticipated and inexplicably light on brownie points. After a surprisingly trouble-free journey, arrived at Clifton Botting shortly before eleven. It's a pretty little village, very well kept and full of elderly men with shopping baskets and golden labradors, and ladies in headscarves clambering in and out of Rover 2600s. There's a large village green with a cricket pitch in the middle, a pub called the Barley Mow, a village store-cum-post-office, a greengrocer's, and a delicatessen-cum-off-licence. I couldn't have felt more at home if I had tried, and when I asked a man with a shopping basket how to get to the Old Rectory, he not only gave me detailed instructions, but actually smiled and made an amusing comment about the weather – something which, of course, would never happen in Brixton.

Drove to Rectory and fell in love with it on sight. Particularly liked the fact that it stood well back from the road, behind a genuinely old redbrick wall. Unfortunately, was so taken by architecture that when I drove through the gates I completely failed to notice the protruding piece of metal in the middle where they met, which caught me a nasty bang as I went past and punctured my rear offside tyre.

Immediately drew up on gravel forecourt and was about to get out to assess extent of damage when front door opened and out leapt a large Dobermann Pinscher. It came bounding towards me, obviously completely out of control. Attempted, too late, to jam on the brakes, but unable to secure any purchase on the freshly laid gravel, skidded for a few yards before it leapt onto the bonnet, paws scrabbling wildly, continued on across the roof, down across the hatchback and off again.

Was examining deep grooves in otherwise immaculate metallic paintwork when a man's voice behind me, said, "If he had to do it, he couldn't have chosen a nicer victim." Swivelled round to find myself face to face with my old boss and father of my erstwhile fiancée Amanda, Derrick Trubshawe. Had it been anyone else, I would have had no hesitation in letting him feel the sharp side of my tongue. But of course, breeding will always out, and within seconds I was smiling politely and saying it couldn't matter less and that, anyway, it was a company car (not true, as it happens) and how was Enid, I hadn't seen her for ages. What with all the shock and excitement, I had completely forgotten that, of course, they were divorced some years ago. She had not remarried, but was living happily in Esher with the leader of a Dutch pop group called Hans. "Hans knees and boompsadaisy, I call him," said Derrick.

I laughed and said that I hoped Amanda at least was flying the flag in the marriage stakes. He replied that that was not on the cards since she had joined a silent order of nuns in Northumberland and had refused to see anyone for three years.

Not surprisingly, when we finally got round to viewing the house, I was quite unable to concentrate, and returned to London with a splitting headache and a bill for bodywork that could easily run to fifty pounds or more. It was only when passing the Richmond Rugby Ground that I realised that the young man from Hampers hadn't turned up. I shall definitely have something to say about that when I ring them on Monday morning. Sheridan in filthy mood all afternoon and was sick all over my new trousers.

Sunday, November 18

To Kent to show John Julius off to Mother. For one who has known what it is to bring up a small child and never misses an opportunity to comment on the failure of modern parents to come up to her own high standards, she seemed curiously ill at ease when B finally consented to hand JJ over to her care. She held him with all the grace and confidence of an Austrian ski instructor who has managed to catch the greasy pig on New Year's Eve. When I remarked that he didn't seem terribly happy, all she said was, "A smacked bottom, that's what he needs." B said loudly, "He needs nothing of the sort," and went to take him away. Unfortunately the shawl got caught in mother's Siamese cat brooch and there was very nearly a nasty accident. Not an auspicious start to a grandparental relationship. Attempted to lighten proceedings by explaining that

one of the reasons we had finally plumped for the name John
Julius was that we knew that she had always had such a soft
spot for Lord Norwich on *Face the Music*.

"I did have," she said. "He's not the only fish in the sea
though." She paused, then said, "Magnus is a very nice name,
I always think."

I did not say anything and neither, I am glad to say, did
Belinda, even though Mother refused to call JJ by his name for
the rest of the day, preferring to refer to him as "your son".

"Your son," she declared, as we were leaving, "is quite a
character. I'm only sorry you'll be too old to enjoy him." I
honestly sometimes wonder if she knows who she's talking
to.

Monday, November 19th

John Julius seems definitely to have settled down at night, and
so have I. Did not even wake when B got up for two o'clock
feed.

The post brings an invitation from Tim Pedalow for B and
me to take part in something called the "Scratch Messiah". It
takes place in the Albert Hall on Friday next. Rang Tim first
thing to find out more. He explained that one simply turns up
on the day and sings. There's a professional orchestra con-
ducted by someone called Willcocks, and the soloists are also in
the business, but the massed thousands get no rehearsal time
beyond what they choose to put in at home. The Watkins
Shaw is the edition they use. This is extremely unfortunate,
since I am only familiar with the Ebenezer Prout which we
used when I last took part in this great oratorial feast at school
in the late fifties and which I keep in a treasured place on a
bookshelf in the sitting-room.

I must admit it is some time since I last got it down and ran
through the score, and when I did so this evening after the
household had gone to bed, I found I could remember very
little of it indeed, especially since at the time I was a treble and
knew nothing of the tenor part which is what I plan to be
singing on this occasion.

Curiously enough, though, I found that certain bits of the opening recitative – "Comfort ye My people" – followed by the aria, "Ev'ry valley" etc did seem surprisingly familiar, so much so that I could not resist trying out a phrase or two.

Had just got into my stride with the bit about her iniquity being pardoned and was about to tackle tricky section re "The voice of him that crieth in the wilderness" when the door flew open and in marched B asking what on earth I thought I was doing making that terrible noise and did I realise that I had set the dog howling which had in turn woken up the baby? It makes one realise the sort of reception poor John the Baptist must have encountered. To bed feeling more sympathetic than usual with the early Christians and in a strange way quite religious.

Tuesday, November 20th

I spoke too soon. Our worst night ever with JJ. Am not surprised B is not feeling up to Friday. More to the point, am I? Either one does things properly in this life or one doesn't. The human body, as I see it, is like a musical instrument: keep it in tune and it will perform wonders; left out of practice, it will become flabby and inefficient. And although I am always the first to lend my light but curiously effective tenor to a really good Christmas carol or an Easter hymn of rejoicing, and rarely miss the opportunity to sing along with a Mozart opera on a long car journey, I cannot pretend that my voice is quite up to the standard it was when I last performed this Handelian masterpiece.

Have therefore decided to take a professional singing lesson. Not having a list of teachers at my fingertips, turned to that faithful old standby, the Yellow Pages. Looked up "Singing Tuition". "See Music Schools", it said. Though a great believer in going straight to the top, I rather doubt that the Royal College of Music or the Guildhall are prepared to take people on for an hour or two at a time. There is a list of "Music Teachers", but since there are only four names on it, cannot help wondering if these really are the very top people in the profession. I suspect the *maestri* prefer to maintain a rather low profile.

Cannot pretend I have ever been a keen reader of the music and opera columns in the better newspapers, but today found myself tackling a long review of Missa Solemnis with unusual zeal. Was most interested to see that this latest performance was done with a choir of less than forty voices and am not surprised therefore that it lacked some of the grandeur that was the keynote of Klemperer's performances twenty years ago. On the other hand, it seems that the conductor showed a real grasp of the music's architecture as well as genuine Beethovian vitality. I only hope this chap Willcocks will be similarly blessed on Friday night in the Albert Hall.

Was running through a few reedy scales in the privacy of my office after lunch when Karen popped her head round the door to ask if everything was all right. I replied that it would be if only I could do something about my breathing. She said, "Have you tried Contacts?"

Replied that I did not actually have a cold as such, and that even if I did, I would not dream of trying to fight it off with patent medicines. She laughed and explained that Contacts is a show business directory, full of useful names and addresses, and that if I was interested in learning how to sing, she was sure I'd find no shortage of teachers. Charlie Kippax had a copy in his office. What a gem that girl is. I begin to see now why so many men marry their secretaries.

Spent a fascinating twenty minutes browsing through ads. Was particularly struck by services offered by Betty Askew – "of Hollywood, Canada and now London". Her name definitely rings a bell, but why? I have never been to Hollywood or Canada. Have an idea Ashford may be the link. Cannot imagine what "one-voice stereophonic method" might possibly be when it's at home, or whether it's of any use to me. However, "diction, breathing and relaxation" definitely very much in need of fine tuning, so rang her at her home in Redcliffe Gardens and have booked an hour-long lunchtime session tomorrow. Twenty guineas seems little enough to pay for the privilege of singing unto the Lord a glad song. Decided not to mention it to B for the time being. No particular reason.

Rang Hampers late afternoon and told Stanford-Dingley about failure of young man to show up on Saturday. Also about extensive damage to car. All he said was, "Apart from that, what did you think?" Replied stiffly that I thought I'd better see what I could get for the flat first, and put the phone down on him. Am not quite sure what sort of reaction I was expecting, but it was certainly something of a rather more grovelling nature.

Wednesday, November 21st

Had planned to devote morning to drafting fresh proposals to Ski Time re regional presentation in light of Valjean's typically Gallic and over-dramatic reaction to my Cheddar Caves idea, but could scarcely put pen to paper for thinking about my singing lesson. And is it any wonder?

Ars longa, vita brevis est. Or is it the other way round? One thing that certainly isn't at all *brevis* is trying to find a taxi around lunchtime these days. Finally arrived at Redcliffe Gardens rather later than anticipated and extremely out of breath – hence my inability to do full justice to "Comfort ye". However, Betty Askew could not have been more under-standing, and told me that I have got into the bad habit of breathing from my chest and ribs, and that henceforth I must learn to breathe from my diaphragm. By way of demonstra-tion, she placed my hands over her midriff and told me to feel the way it expanded and contracted like a pair of bellows while her chest and shoulders remained completely still. I expressed polite interest, but frankly, with a woman of her proportions, even the most distinguished professor of anatomy would have felt obliged to take her word for it. Am also not entirely convinced that words like "iniquity" sound better if sung through open, locked jaw, and the idea that one's head amplifies sounds, sounds pretty far-fetched to my way of thinking. I said laughingly, "I suppose that's what's meant by one-voice stereophonic." "No," she said.

Frankly, it all smacks rather too much of Hollywood for my liking, and possibly of Canada too. On the other hand, her

37

suggestion that one can loosen one's throat muscles by going round feeling wide-nosed and humming a lot could well pay off, if my efforts *en route* back to the office are anything to go by. Am wondering if Fischer Dieskau minds being stared at on tube trains. Had been hoping to watch a Channel 4 programme this evening on open-heart surgery. I feel sure it would have afforded me a fascinating insight into the workings of the human chest. However, made foolish mistake of slipping into kitchen after *This Is Your Life* to make myself a tuna-fish sandwich, and got back to find Hilda firmly established in front of *East Enders*.

"Seeing how the other half lives?" I enquired, my voice tinged with irony.

"Many a mickle makes a muckle," she said.

The maddening thing is, I know she got the phrase completely out of context, but I'm blowed if I can think what it should be. We have her for at least another fortnight.

Thursday, November 22nd

Rang Clapham office of Loomis Chaffee first thing to ask if they would be interested in sending someone round to look at the flat and give me some idea of its current market value. Was it my imagination or did a faint note of disappointment enter the girl's voice when I mentioned the address? If so, it struck me as very poor PR.

I realise that, as London estate agents go, they are, socially speaking, very much in the first division ("The Radley College of the estate agency world," Tim once called them), and that their bread and butter is the £150,000 Victorian family house in the Clapham/Wandsworth Common area; but surely no agent, however beautifully spoken, can afford to turn his nose up at any business these days? I said to the girl, "I think you'll find the garden flat *vaut le détour*, as they used to say in the Michelin Guides."

"I think we'll be the judges of that," she said. Thinking back on it, I suppose that six o'clock was not the ideal time to arrange for their Mr Hankey-Barber to call. Breast-feeding and business do not always go hand in hand, especially when one has neglected, through pressure of work, to forewarn one's wife, for whom moving house does not head the list of priorities anyway. While Julian Hankey-Barber was outside casting an eye over the kitchen cupboards, I attempted to explain to B in a quiet way that this was by way of being an academic exercise.

"The only person who needs any academic exercise round here," she replied in an unnecessarily loud voice, "is you."

I don't *think* he heard. Still, I daresay in his line of business the occasional interfamilial chill is pretty much run-of-the-mill stuff.

After he had finished, took Julian through to the sitting-room and went to pour him a large whisky and soda.

"What do you think then?" I asked him casually.

He asked me in return how much I had paid for it.

Have long been of the opinion that one's estate agent is very much on a par with one's doctor, and that unless one is prepared to be thoroughly candid with him, one is unlikely to be given an honest diagnosis. I said, "About thirty-eight, or thirty-nine. I forget exactly." I added, "Of course, that was two or three years ago now."

He hummed and said, "If I may say so, I think you paid rather over the odds."

I said, "Possibly, but of course this is very much an improving area."

"I can't imagine where you got that idea from," he said. "There has never in my experience been a very thriving market in fear and suspicion". I replied that if it were not for people like Alan Bennett and the *Sunday Times Insight* team, where would Camden Town and Islington be these days? There may not be much of a market in fear, I went on, but what price initiative?

"In the case of your flat," he said, "about forty-three, forty-four at a push."

I couldn't believe my ears.

I said, "But if what you say is true, that means that in real terms the property has actually dropped in value."

39

He said, "You're very welcome to try another agent, but that's my professional opinion."

I said I'd give it some serious thought and put the top back on the whisky bottle.

When he had gone, B said, "Well?"

I said, "I don't honestly think this is his cup of tea."

"Or his whisky and soda apparently," she said.

To bed at nine thirty with the "Messiah" score and a mug of hot lemon and honey to help relax throat muscles. Interested to see that in his excellent introduction Prout writes: "It is well known to those who have studied the subject, that double dots were never, and dotted rests very seldom, used in Handel's time, and that consequently the music, if played strictly according to the notation, will in many places not accurately reproduce the composer's intentions." I shall be interested to see which way Willcocks veers in this regard.

Friday, November 23rd

Woke at five to find I had developed the most appalling sore throat. To the office stuffed to the eyeballs with Veganins and my mouth numb from sucking anaesthetic pastilles. Obviously I didn't dare risk putting more strain on my larynx than was absolutely necessary, so cancelled a Botticelli meeting and locked my office door. Left shortly before lunch and went home to rest.

Hilda volunteered the information that Mrs Roskill, a keen member of the Notting Hill Gate Orpheus Choir, always gargles with a little port whenever she has any trouble with her voice.

Slipped out to off-licence later and explained situation to Mr Skewes, who said that although he had never gargled with port, he felt sure the Val de Lobo 1984 at five pounds fifty would fit the bill more than adequately.

Gargled immediately upon return, though obviously did not spit afterwards.

Improvement to voice so drastic that I applied two more medications during Six O'Clock News and another as I was changing. Just to be on the safe side, wrapped bottle in brown paper bag and set off with it tucked inside raincoat.

As I was leaving, B called out, "Sing up, Placido."

Pretended not to hear.

Arrived outside Albert Hall to find place swarming with people. Finally located Tim at Door H with his new girlfriend, Caroline – a dumpy, rather red-faced creature with short fair hair and a loud mouth. Also Philippe and Theresa de Grande-Hauteville and a small, rather older couple in glasses with matching grey hair. Philippe asked how things were going in the publishing world. In the fifteen years I have known him, he has never quite managed to work out what I do, nor I he. I think he is a picture dealer: that, or a property developer. Theresa looking rather drawn, I thought. Tim handed out tickets and explained that the hall had been divided up into large blocks according to voices. Tenors were up on the left, just below the organ.

Wondered, as I sat there revising score for last time, whether Prince Charles felt half as nervous as I did when he performed with the Bach Choir a year or two ago. The more I think about it, the more I realise we have in common: husbands, fathers, singers, life-enhancers. Disappointed to note from programme that Willcocks had elected to cut several numbers, including "His yoke is easy and His burthen is light" at the very end of part one. A great mistake in my view. Though admittedly not one of my favourite passages, the sentiments contained have always struck quite a chord with me. Happy to see, however, that "Surely He hath borne" still very much in.

The man sitting on my right, a small Welshman with a shock of gingery hair, remarked, "I see you're singing the Prout," and added, "I hope we're not going to have any trouble."

"Not if we've all done our homework as carefully as I have," I said.

Had assumed there would be a few minutes' rehearsal before actual thing, and was astonished when Willcocks, neat, elegant, and silver-haired, marched in, picked up his baton and without so much as a by-your-leave, launched into overture.

"That's too fast for a start," murmured the Welshman.

"Comfort ye," sung very well by solo tenor though personally felt he could have attacked "The voice of him that crieth in the wilderness" with more conviction.

My own rendering of "And He shall purify" also not quite as positive as I had hoped, owing to getting lost among Sons of Levi.

The Welshman said, "I don't mind people who can't read music following those who can, but I do object when they're a beat behind."

I can't imagine who he was referring to.

During interval, was treating throat to restorative swig of port, taking care to conceal bottle in brown paper, when suddenly spotted Welshman staring at me from other side of crowd. Made offering gesture, but he turned and scuttled away.

Second half rather more of a personal triumph than the first. Have rarely felt more spiritually and artistically in accord with anyone than I did that evening with Willcocks. In fact, hardly needed the two safety swigs I gave myself during second interval.

Eventually, became so carried away by soaring music and sense of oneness with my fellow performers that during Amen Chorus became quite dizzy with the sound and underwent what I can only describe as a religious experience.

I quite agreed with the Welshman that it was most unfortunate that I should have been the only one in the entire building to break the dramatic silence before the final "Amen" with such a loud and positive affirmation of faith, but as I pointed out, although the passage is quite clearly marked *adagio*, there is no mention whatever of everyone stopping altogether, and that if anyone was to blame it was Ebenezer Prout.

He said, "Prout has many things to answer for, but alcoholism is not one of them."

If there is one thing madder than a Welshman, it is a Welshman who, without any evidence to support it, thinks he is Stuart Burrows.

At supper afterwards at the Bordelino, Tim said, "That man who shouted out at the end of the Amen Chorus must be feeling pretty stupid."

42

I said, "Funnily enough, he was standing right next to me. I think he must have been drinking."

"That made two of you," said Tim.

Everyone roared; but then, of course, most of the early Christians had to put up with a certain amount of mockery at one time or another.

Saturday, November 24th

A better night. Even so, woke feeling slightly headachy. Tension from last night, I daresay. One can hardly expect to work oneself up to such a pitch of creative energy without paying for it.

Rang Betty Askew shortly before lunch to tell her how well it had all gone and to thank her for her help and encouragement, without which none of it would have been possible. She was obviously rather touched.

I said, "By the way, I've been meaning to ask you; did your father by any chance ever own a small tobacconist's shop in Ashford?"

"I don't think so," she said. "As far as I am aware, he was always an income tax inspector in Dundee."

How very odd. I suppose she was telling the truth.

Sunday, November 25th

An astonishing thing happened this morning. Was in the middle of winding John Julius when the front door bell rang. It was Harbottle from No. 28 wanting to know if I'd be interested in taking over from him as co-ordinator of the local Neighbourhood Watch Scheme as they are moving to Clapham.

I couldn't quite work out who had suggested my name, but they certainly could not have come up with a better candidate if they'd tried. I have always taken a keen interest in police work, and I doubt there's a single broadcast of *Crimewatch* that has escaped my attention. Am only sorry that in all that time since the series started there has not been a single case in which I have been able to assist the police in their enquiries. Perhaps I shall now be in a position to break my duck at last. Whether the co-ordinatorship carries with it the privilege of being allowed to accompany the local police in their panda cars or on the beat, I am not quite sure. It was not apparently a question Harbottle had ever thought to ask. I'm surprised. I'd have thought that anyone with the faintest sense of social responsibility would be only too eager to examine the problems of inner city deprivation at grass-roots level. It is certainly an opportunity that I welcome with both hands. I am proud and privileged to have been asked, and told Harbottle so in no uncertain terms.

"Thank goodness for that," he said. "If you hadn't said yes, I can't imagine who we'd have turned to. We'd really have had to start scraping the barrel."

Interested to learn that they have sold their house quietly through Rawlinson Smith Jamieson's London residential office in Mayfair. I said that I did not realise people like that dealt with properties in areas like this.

Harbottle said, "There are properties and properties."

Am not quite sure I followed his drift, but will definitely give RSJ a ring on Monday morning and see how the land lies.

Was on my way to paper shop when Vita slipped her lead, rushed ahead and became involved in an ugly argy-bargy with a Yorkshire Terrier outside the butcher's. Rushed up road, seized animal by scruff of neck and lifted her high into the air. Unfortunately, teeth still firmly embedded in Yorkie which flew up with her. Just my luck that the owner had to go and be West Indian.

Attempted to defuse situation while man was struggling to wrest Yorkie from V's jaws by pointing out that it always takes two to make a fight, but he was not to be appeased.

"If I catch your dog out again without a lead," he said as he finally clutched the pathetic bundle of fluff to his chest, "I'll cut its throat. Yours too. You have my word for it."

I said, "I happen to have close personal dealings with the local police, and I'd advise you not to start taking the law into your own hands or you could find yourself in very serious trouble indeed." And I walked away.

Cannot pretend that I was not rather nervous that he might come after me, but in my experience if you speak to these sort of people firmly and sensibly, they quickly come to their senses and realise it's more than their lives are worth to go trying any rough stuff. Am also reassured to know that from now on I shall be in a better position than most to understand this kind of anger and how to deal with it.

By a curious coincidence, *Death Wish* was on TV tonight starring Charles Bronson. It makes you wonder sometimes.

Monday, November 26th

Rang Rawlinson Smith Jamieson first thing and spoke to a Mr Nick Sartorian who couldn't have been more polite or more charming. Was naturally disappointed to learn that he did not feel ours was quite the sort of property that would benefit from Rawlinson's particular style of marketing. Had we thought of instructing someone like Loomis Chaffee? he asked. They had a very good reputation south of the river and had been known to take on some very unusual properties indeed. Reminded him that his firm had been happy enough to take on the Harbottles' house only two doors away up the road.

"Would that be No. 28?" he asked.

I said that it was.

"Ah yes," he said. "I remember now; there were rather special circumstances there."

When I asked him what the nature of these circumstances might be, he replied that he did not feel it would be right or proper for him to discuss a client's affairs without first receiving permission. He said, "Let's just say there are properties and properties." I suppose I could have taken the matter further if I'd felt so inclined. Names could have been mentioned; connections hinted at. But frankly I have better fish to fry. For all his ping-pong ball accent and expensive suiting, he is only an estate agent, and frankly two and a half per cent of fifty odd grand is an awful lot to pay for the privilege of being patronised. In fact, am seriously considering keeping the money in my pocket and handling the whole business myself.

First, though, I must do a little cosmetic work on that damp patch at the back of the broom cupboard.

Tuesday, November 27th

Arrived at office to find letter from Valjean suggesting we scrap regional idea and concentrate instead on running a really good press trip to Les Vals 2000 in late Jan/early Feb. That's fine by me. It is many years since I last pitted my skills against a field of deep moguls and punched my way down a black run, and although I daresay my technique may need a little fine honing, I can think of no better way of reviving the spirits and preparing oneself for the rigours of a long February than by treating oneself to some healthy sunshine, crisp mountain air and vigorous exercise.

Would, of course, be even more excited at the prospect if I thought that there was the slightest chance of B joining me on the T-bar, but presume she will be far too tied up with JJ to even consider it. Next year perhaps.

Still, it won't be all beer and skittles for me anyway. As far as I am concerned, this will be very much a business trip, and in my experience, work and pleasure make uneasy bedfellows.

Started to make out possible list of invitees. Got as far as Selina Scott, Anneke Rice and Sue Cook and gave up. Spent rest of morning drafting out ad for flat to go in posh Sundays this coming weekend. It reads:

ANGELL TOWN, SW9. On the road to Kennington. Garden flat of great elegance and charm in quiet, leafy road in rapidly improving backwater of south-west London. Short walk Victoria line tube and 2 mins drive to rural reaches of Clapham Common. Immac. drawing-room with original features; 2 beds; compact bathroom; attractive kit/breakfast room leading onto mature, south-west facing patio garden. £49,950. Viewing highly recommended.

Am naturally reluctant to publicise our telephone number, even in the quality press. On the other hand, am only too aware of value of impulse purchase and feel a box number could be a definite turn-off. Stupidly decided to try it out on Pamela van Zeller who read it through carefully and said, "Sounds just the sort of thing Ron and I are looking for. Whose is it?"

When I told her it was mine, she stared at me in utter disbelief and burst into loud shrieks of laughter.

"You must be joking," she said, handing it back. "If you're not careful, you could be had up under the Trades Description Act."

Said nothing, but when she had left, changed "Immac." to "Imaginatively decorated" and phoned *Sunday Times* classified. Spoke to nice woman who said I had until five o'clock on Thursday evening to place ad, and that if I cared to read it out, she'd give me some idea of how it might best be displayed and what it would be likely to cost. Felt slightly foolish spouting details down phone, but when I got to the end, she said she thought it sounded really very nice indeed, with plenty of good selling points – so much so that she felt it warranted a display, with a nice border, a bold headline which I could either write myself or leave to her to suggest. She also recommended putting the telephone number at the bottom.

"One insertion should sell it without too much difficulty," she said. Could hardly believe my ears.

"Who needs estate agents?" I said with a laugh.

She did not laugh and neither did I when she told me how much display costs.

Fifty-six pounds a centimetre, if you please. And you have to take a minimum of three centimetres.

She said, "I think we should be able to fit that into three centimetres."

I pointed out that that would come to £168.

"Yes," she said, "but of course it would take it to the top of the classification."

The only alternative, I gathered, was a simple lineage ad which would cost nine pounds fifty a line. At roughly six words per line, my ad would run to about a dozen lines which would cost about £115.

I asked her if lineage sold as well as display.

"Not as a rule," she said. "But then you have got some very, very good selling points."

Said I'd think about it and ring her back. Decided finally she must know what she's talking about, and plumped for display.

Over *spaghetti carbonara* at the Bordelino, Belinda finally agreed that in principle the flat was not going to be big enough for all of us and the pram, and that since it was only a matter of time before John Julius would be crawling, the sooner we found somewhere with a proper garden and a lawn the better. Decided not to press her on country house at this stage. A good general does not expect to win a campaign until he has fought all the battles.

Wednesday, November 28th

Rang ad through to classified first thing. Had stupidly forgotten to take name of woman I spoke to yesterday. However, new girl, if anything, more enthusiastic than first.

"You're quite right to choose the display," she said. "You've got a real winner up your sleeve there."

"I realise that," I said. "The point is, have you?"

None of us is so good at our jobs that we cannot benefit from being kept on our toes.

In the evening, Tim brought Caroline round for a quiet dinner *à quatre*. I should have thought that a man who so blatantly sports an Old Etonian tie could have found himself someone with a little more style. She seemed to me to be even redder in the face than on the night of the "Messiah" and definitely more raucous. If the quantity of gin and tonic she poured down her throat was any indication of what she had consumed earlier, I can't say I'm surprised. I only hope Tim is not serious about her. I do not relish the prospect of my family escutcheon being besmirched by crude alcohol.

Tim's behaviour also not above reproach. If he left the table once with a muttered excuse about his waterworks, he must have left it half a dozen times. Each time he came back looking extremely pleased with himself and wearing a very silly expression indeed before very quickly reverting to silence and an expression of deep boredom. I am no doctor but I shouldn't be at all surprised to learn that his wallet is full of recently furled fivers, and his pockets with traces of white powder. If so, his behaviour put me in an exceedingly awkward position. As a Neighbourhood Watch official, I would be clearly duty-bound to inform my police colleagues of his unlawful activities. At the same time, I would not like to give anyone the impression that I had, wittingly or otherwise, permitted the law to be broken in my own house.

Decided there was no future in shilly-shallying and that brutal honesty was the best policy.

While Belinda and Caroline were outside in the kitchen making coffee and shrieking their heads off, I said quietly, "I hope you don't mind my asking, not only as a brother-in-law, but also as a friend, if you are in the habit of sniffing?"

"As a matter of fact," he said, "I am. However, I will tell you only on condition you tell me whether or not you break wind whenever you eat Brussels sprouts."

I still cannot make up my mind if he was being serious, or whether in fact we have a junky in our midst who has not yet faced up to his addiction.

At all events, am definitely having second thoughts about putting John Julius down for Eton. Privilege carries with it a heavy burden of responsibility, and any school that fails to instil this in its pupils cannot expect to win the confidence and approval of normal, clean-living folk.

Thursday, November 29th

Was chewing fat in the pub at lunchtime with Kippax re modern education when he happened to mention the fact that the distinguished athlete and onetime junior education minister, Christopher Chataway, had had no qualms about sending some of his children to the local comprehensive and that, as he understood it, the operation had been a great success. Have

49

always understood that comprehensives were places that did not believe in discipline, where the children more or less decided what they wanted to do and what they didn't, and if they felt like sloping off for the day, were at perfect liberty to do so. Or am I muddling them with something else?

Called Karen in on pretence of dictating a Botticelli letter, sat her down and said that I realised it must sound silly to her, but I honestly had no idea what life was like at a modern comprehensive.

"It's no good asking me," she said. "I went to Benenden."

To the registrar's office in Marylebone Road during lunch hour to register John Julius's birth; and not before time. It's curious to think that at the most private and emotional moments of one's life, such as the birth of a child or the death of a relative, one is obliged to entrust the most intimate details into the safe-keeping of complete strangers. Was all the more embarrassed, therefore, when I could not remember whether B's birthday was August the 18th or 19th.

"Don't worry," said the registrar. "At least half the husbands who come in here suffer from the same problem."

B sounded quite amused when I rang her on registrar's phone to enquire; but one can never tell with women. Tiny human errors like this are not easily forgiven, or forgotten.

Friday, November 30th

Morning spent writing out invitations to Botticelli Christmas lunch on December 20th. Could have gone in for something gimmicky, like the pop-up paper turkey we tried a couple of years ago, with the message about the event being "stuffed with fun", and the paper hat and balloon concealed within the bird's carcase, but feel that this would not entirely fit in with restaurant's attempts to go up-market. If we wish to attract the top food and wine writers we must give the impression that ours is a *maison sérieuse*. The trouble is, the top people spend so much time eating out in order to fill their columns that the prospect of yet another meal must make them feel quite ill. However, I think that our straightforward, formal invitation

50

makes it clear that this is one gastronomic event that no-one will wish to refuse. The embossing is a touch of genius. I only wish I had thought of it before Pamela.

Have also written off to Fortnum & Mason, Harrods etc for a quote on a hundred of their best Christmas crackers, although the personally initialled Daytaday diaries with the imitation gold corners may preclude anything really luxurious in the way of paper hats, jokes and trinkets.

December

Saturday, December 1st

Woke in unusually cheerful mood. The Botticelli invitations are all ready for the postbag, the plans for the skiing trip are under way and my ad is on the point of being run through the presses in Docklands. John Julius's cradle cap is definitely showing signs of clearing up and Hilda has gone off to spend the weekend with her sister in Horsham. What better moment to take a few snaps of the little fellow? All sorts of people have written congratulatory letters asking which one of us he looks like and wondering if it might be possible to let them have any photographs.

Have had some outstanding successes recently with little Olympus XA: notably my recent series entitled "Autumn in Richmond Park". Portrait work not perhaps quite up to a standard where I feel I can bring it out when friends come to dinner. Belinda says it's my fault for getting everybody in position and then "fiddling about" rather than taking the shot straightaway. Have tried to point out on several occasions that what she likes to refer to as "fiddling about" is what the Snowdons of this world call focussing and "stopping" up or down.

"Stopping altogether in your case," she said once, since when I have not attempted any more serious photographic conversations. Wives and husbands who do not share their marriage partners' passion for creative endeavour are like foreigners who cannot speak the same language.

Quite surprised, therefore, that B should have agreed so readily to my idea of compiling a modest portfolio of JJ with and without his mother. Having got him washed and powdered and dolled up in his long white nightdress, she disappeared into the bedroom to prepare herself for her Madonna role. While she was there, decided to fire off a quick roll of JJ lying in his crib. It was only after I had taken half a dozen shots that I suddenly noticed he was blinking rather more than usual, and before I knew what, he had burst into floods of tears. At this moment, the awful thought occurred to me that perhaps one is not supposed to photograph babies using a flash-bulb. After all, their eyes must be very tender at that age, and when I consider how dazzled I am whenever anyone uses a flash on me, the effect on a new-born child's pupils could well be highly damaging. Was it possible that through sheer thoughtlessness and stupidity, I had blinded my own child within a few days of welcoming him into this world?

Terrible images rose up before me of this innocent child crawling around bumping into the furniture; then, of a small boy at prep-school age, stumbling around with a white stick and dark glasses when he should be out on the rugger field playing for the Under-11s; of a room piled high with editions of the children's classics in Braille; of a young man unable to step outdoors unless accompanied by a golden labrador; of an elderly man sitting in an armchair in St Dunstan's, who had gone through life never having known the joy of a parent's face, or a sunset over the Mediterranean.

Seizing fluffy pig, I waved it around in front of his eyes, praying fervently for some kind of reaction, but he was by now crying far too loudly for the test to prove conclusive one way or the other.

Suddenly remembered an old British film I had once seen many years ago in which Richard Todd had lost his sight and Phyllis Calvert had passed a lighted match backwards and forwards in front of his eyes. Threw camera carelessly down onto floor and rushed to kitchen to find a box of Bryant & Mays. Had just lit one after third time of trying, and was bending over crib when B walked in wearing a loose floral affair of the sort popularised by Sarah Keays.

Needless to say, she had to go and get the wrong end of the stick. When I explained what had happened, she said, "If what you say is true, Cecil Beaton would have condemned most of the Royal Family to a lifetime of piano tuning. Now then, where do you want me to sit?"

Spent the next five minutes shakily posing her and JJ in a chair in front of Mexican bark painting only to find that when it came to it, the flash wouldn't work anyway. Obviously it had smashed when I dropped it on the floor. As if I didn't have enough extra expense on my plate.

While we were watching Paul Daniels, the dog pulled off a trick of her own by swallowing an entire J-cloth. She sauntered into the room with a fragment of the pink material hanging out of one corner of her mouth like a little pink tongue. I rushed forward to seize it, thinking to draw the whole thing out, as though cleaning a .303 barrel, only for the creature to nip behind the sofa and polish off this curiously unappetising snack before I could get a hand to it. In a state of near panic rang the vet, who said there was nothing to worry about and that the cloth would almost certainly work its way through the animal's body in the normal way.

Was not reassured. Gave dog an extra long walk in hope that digestion might suddenly have started working overtime, but whole system apparently completely blocked.

To bed, rather later than anticipated, where I lay awake trying to recall school biology lessons on inner workings of rat, and failing. Still, every cloud has a silver lining, as Miss Thatcher would undoubtedly have pointed out, had she been here, and as a result of latest drama, have not given my son's eyesight a second thought.

Sunday, December 2nd

John Julius would have to wait until Miss T is away before deciding to launch into a bout of insomnia. I hope he's not the sort of child who derives pleasure from annoying people. I can see him finishing up working in a VAT office in Croydon.

B most unsympathetic, and pointed out that it was not as though I had to do anything about it. She'd been up three times in the night, including the two o'clock feed. But, of course, that's not the point. As anyone who has ever stood on the sidelines during a rugger match knows very well, being a spectator is always far more exhausting than being a competitor.

Finally fell fast asleep halfway through six o'clock stint and woke with a splitting headache at nine thirty. Lay there for a moment or two, savouring the warm embrace of the king-size cotton until I suddenly remembered the ad. Leapt from bed, threw on clothes and rushed up to newsagent's only to find that Mr Patel had been short-changed by his supplier and that I had missed the last *Sunday Times* by a matter of minutes. Fortunately happened to spot a few on a shelf in his back room, so crinkled a fiver in my pocket and suggested he might be able to see his way to helping out a fellow media man. At this, he wobbled his head, gave a sly grin and said, "Oh Mr Crisp. One of these days you'll get me into the hot soup." He slipped the note into his pocket, disappeared through the long strips of multi-coloured plastic into the back room and came back brandishing a thick wadge of newsprint. I thanked him very much, slipped it under my arm and hurried home. Made coffee and settled down to hunt for ad when suddenly realised I was looking at last week's newspaper.

Tore back up the road and shook Mr Patel metaphorically by the throat. He shook his head, sighed deeply and said, "I told you we didn't have any copies left this week but you were so persuasive."

My powers of persuasion appeared to have waned a little in the intervening half an hour, since nothing I said or did or threatened would make him give me back my fiver.

"Let's just call it a down payment on your next month's paper bill," he said. Since I have no receipt and there were no witnesses to this unfortunate transaction, I can only pray that he is as much a man of his word as his forebears were a century ago in the heyday of the Raj.

Was on my way home again, with dog pulling hard on lead, *Observer* tucked angrily under my arm, when I happened to spot a copy of *Sunday Times* poking carelessly out of a nearby letter-box. Have long been of the opinion that brand loyalty does not add up to a row of beans where Sunday newspapers are concerned, and slipped in through front gate with view to swapping my *Obs* for his *ST*. Was just bending down to effect changeover, when front door opened and a deep voice enquired if it could help me. Looked up to realise with shock that owner of voice also owner of Yorkie that V savaged a week or two ago. Tried to explain that, as a media man, I merely wished to see how much space the *ST* had devoted to this social security hoo-ha compared with the *Observer*. Far from being appeased, a look of undisguised fury darkened his face even further. Turned to see Vita doing big potties slap outside the gate.

Had no alternative but to gather up offending material, using Business section of my newspaper, and beat a dignified retreat. Quite clearly, there's no talking to some people.

Was turning into my own front gate when it suddenly struck me that there had been no sign whatever of his beastly little yapper. I suppose this means I can now expect a huge vet bill through the letter-box any day now. Possibly for euthanasia.

Got in to find B eating a bowl of Grape Nuts and reading *Sunday Times*. When I asked her where on earth she had got it, she said, "Outside the tube station, of course. You were gone so long, I thought you must have forgotten, so John Julius and I popped down in the car." Slightly disappointed that she'd made no apparent effort to look for my ad – though how she could possibly have missed it, I can't imagine. The woman in classified could not have placed it nearer the top of the page if she'd tried, and the bold border made it positively leap out of the page. The fact that it was slap next to an ad for a so-called "sensational studio" in New Cross at the same price can surely only enhance its appeal; nor can I honestly believe there are many would-be purchasers who would see "compost bathroom" as anything other than the glaring typographical error it so obviously is. Am wondering if one qualifies for some sort of discount in cases of this sort or whether the onus is on the advertiser to get out the big stick and draft a solicitor's letter.

Would happily have offered B a much needed break by running JJ up to Clapham Common for a quick circuit in the pram, but obviously could not leave phone unattended for a second. So, while she enjoyed a restorative breath of fresh air, I had to make do with part one of the new D. W. Griffith biography and an old black and white Cecil Parker comedy on Channel 4.

B's comments re my taking food out of baby's mouth and tipping it into the greedy maw of Rupert Murdoch made to look very silly indeed when, in the middle of the Ladies' Giant Slalom from Bad Gastein, a man rang from Peckham to say that he had seen the ad, thought it sounded just what he was looking for, and that he would be round within the hour to have a look. He turned up shortly after seven with a friend. I cannot pretend that a pair of freelance plumbers with rings through their ears are absolutely my idea of the perfect successors to this little home of ours in which we have known so many happy hours. On the other hand, it's people in cash businesses like that who have the money these days and, unlike B, I was not at all surprised when he offered not only the asking price, but in cash.

B highly sceptical, as usual. Personally, I prefer to look on the bright side. Lady Luck is a fickle tyrant, and when she takes it into her head to turn her face in one's direction and bless one with the warmth of her smile, one should accept her bounty for what it is, and not immediately start finding all the reasons why it is bound to turn out to be a Trojan horse.

I am only thankful Miss Thatcher is not here to offer us the benefit of one of her little saws.

Monday, December 3rd

Another tearful night all round, so on way in to work bought a copy of Spock. Astonished to find how expensive it is, even in the paperback edition. Still, I daresay twenty million readers can't all be wrong. Looked up "crying" in index to find no less than eighteen possible causes, ranging from wind and ear pain to intestinal obstruction and intussusception, whatever that may be when it's at home. Decided to go straight for "common causes in early weeks" which alone take up *seven pages*. Am still none the wiser. Could it be, as the doctor suggests, that "he has outgrown the breast milk supply"? Or that "the breast supply is decreasing"? If so, it is surely hardly a possibility I can raise with his mother.

A safety pin through the skin may well be something that happens only once in a hundred years, but happen it can, and why should not Mrs Crisp, for all her practical common sense, be the one responsible for this rare phenomenon?

I do not believe we have spoiled our child (though I cannot speak for Miss T in this regard), nor do I believe him to be hypertonic. The Crisps have never been a family given to neuroses and I see no reason why one of our members should become so now.

Am wondering if it isn't a simple matter of fretfulness. Living in this part of London is enough to make anyone fretful, as I know to my, and B's, cost.

Spock says that no-one really knows what the cause is in this instance, but it is nothing serious and will pass in time, although it is hard on parents while it lasts. As far as a remedy goes, he suggests rocking him gently in his cradle, playing him some quiet music or taking him out for a ride in the car. Funnily enough, this last suggestion is not quite as outlandish as it may at first appear. I know of several creative people who swear by a quick midnight spin in the car as a way of unlocking the flood-gates of inspiration (or at least I know *of* them), and a run down to Brighton and back in the wee small hours could very well produce some much needed thoughts on the Botticelli Christmas lunch, as well as providing everyone with a decent night's sleep.

Rang B to tell her that help might be nearer at hand than we thought, but phone engaged. Tried several times during morning with ditto results. Finally got through just before lunch to find that people had been ringing all morning in response to *Sunday Times* ad. This was exciting news and gave me cause to wonder yet again where the estate agency business would be today if more people had the courage to take the bull by the horns and go it on their own. It makes sense from every point of view. Why they don't, I can't imagine. After all, who is likely to be the more effective salesman: the man who is trying to make two and a half per cent commission or the man who is trying to save it?

Slightly surprised to hear that none of the callers so far have expressed an interest in taking the matter further by making an appointment to view the property. *Tant mieux*. We already have a firm cash buyer and B has better things to do with her days than entertaining an endless string of time-wasters and nosy-parkers.

Could not resist mentioning our good fortune to Pamela, who said, "Just as long as you haven't opened your front door to a couple of burglars." I said I couldn't imagine what she was talking about.

She said, "Oh, didn't you know? There's no easier way for a villain to case a potential hit than by picking out a few possible targets from the posh Sundays, then posing as a buyer and having a good nose round."

I replied that if that were the case, the *Sunday Times* and *Observer* property advertising would have been closed down by the police years ago. Not surprisingly, that rather took the wind out of her sails. Still, I suppose I should be grateful to her for reminding me of my somewhat lax attitude towards security in the garden flat, and before going to bed tonight, I may well just slip one of the heavy armchairs across the front door. Better to be safe than sorry. Oh dear, I'm beginning to sound just like Miss Thatcher.

Can it really be less than a week to go now until she packs her bags and moves on to wreak havoc on another happy family? I can hardly believe it. As I was leaving for the office this morning, I distinctly heard her saying that my shoes could do with a polish. So could her brain.

Tuesday, December 4th

Woke to loud ringing at front door. Peered through curtains to see postman standing outside holding interesting-looking package. Unfortunately, in my anxiety to get to the door, completely forgot about armchair and in semi-darkness went hard into it, stubbing my toe very badly indeed and barking one shin. Pitched forward, ending up with nose in nether quarters of Vita who had taken it upon herself to spend night curled up on cushions. By the time I had recovered and pulled chair away from door, the postman had moved on up the street. Rest of morning spent agonising over possible contents of package and whether I should make special journey to post office during lunch-hour rather than wait for redelivery in a couple of days' time. Rather shocked to find I am totally incapable of coming to any firm decision. I had not realised that fatherhood brought with it quite so many unexpected and unwelcome side effects, both mental and physical. Or is this just another sign of incipient middle-age? The awful thing is, I can't decide that either.

Wednesday, December 5th

Have suffered from the nagging feeling all day that today is someone's birthday and that I should have sent off a card to someone; possibly even a present. But who? Perhaps it is nothing more than guilt at the fact that while B is out and about every day, usually at Peter Jones, stocking up with enough Christmas presents to last the next three years, I have not even begun to think what to give her or John Julius. Mother also a worry, as usual. A nightie looks definitely on the cards. Feelings of *angst* increased by fact that I have heard nothing further from Peckham plumber. Had expected that he would have been on the phone by now, possibly arranging for a surveyor to come and visit us. Unless, of course, Pamela was right and he was up to no good. In which case, why hasn't he followed up his research with swag bag and jemmy?

To Banham's on way home from Botticelli meeting to ask for rough quote on modest but effective security system. The assistant said he couldn't possibly give me a realistic idea without sending someone round to look the place over first.

Is it my imagination, or did I read a story somewhere about a member of a gang of thieves joining a firm of security experts to extraordinary effect? Have told Banham's I'll be in touch.

Am reminded that we still haven't come to any serious

conclusion re suitable choice of church for christening. St Mungo's is far too cold and ugly, and the vicar so hideous that he might easily traumatise the child and turn him against religion for ever, if not the human race. Personally, I favour somewhere far more old-fashioned both in terms of architecture and the way of doing things. All this "let's-do-the-show-right-here, kids" attitude may suit these free-and-easy *Guardian* types who seem to be colonising south of the river these days, but frankly, I have always been a good old "thee" and "thou" type. If the original prayer-book was good enough for King James, it's good enough for me. There's nothing guaranteed to make a man ponder the meaning of things more than the feel of a well-worn prayer-book nestling in the palm of the hand; and to have to flounder through amateurish, dog-eared pamphlets in pursuit of some trendy young vicar who talks to everyone as if they were backward children is merely to distract and irritate the contemplative mind.

As for this constant hand shaking with all and sundry which is so much part and parcel of modern Christianity, frankly the more people keep to themselves these days, the better will be our chances of stamping out these sexually transmitted diseases we hear so much about.

If it were up to me, I'd aim for somewhere like St Peter's, Eaton Square, or Chelsea Old Church: at any rate somewhere reasonably central with decent local parking. Am only sorry I have never had the opportunity to worship in either of these churches myself. I will definitely try and make a point of attending Matins at one or both of them before the event.

Incidentally, I wonder if *anyone* can be christened at the Queen's Chapel at the Savoy, and, if so, whether it's that much more expensive than anywhere else?

Thursday, December 6th

Woke early and immediately remembered that it was Beddoes who had had a birthday yesterday. Not that I could have done anything about it. We have been rather out of touch since he left his EEC job in Brussels and moved to America to join the business consultancy people in New York. Had he returned to England, I would definitely have pencilled him in as a god-father. Morally, of course, he is completely beyond the pale; on the other hand, one does not share a flat with someone for as long as I did with him, without retaining some feelings.

Still not a peep from the so-called plumber – or anyone else, come to that. Am in no mood to shilly-shally and as soon as I arrived in the office, drafted out a second ad for *Sunday Times*, couched this time in rather more self-deprecating tones, à la Roy Brooks. To wit:

> Idiosyncratic PR executive and ex-ad agency receptionist seek adventurous buyer with highly developed sense of imagination and humour who fancies the idea of a slightly scruffy but cosy basement flat in fashionable SW9. 2 bed-rooms – one to suit crouching dwarf; decoratively tired but comfortable sitting-room big enough to accommodate a full-sized billiard-table; charmingly old-fashioned bath-room; kit/din rm that has to be seen to be believed; small patch of concrete at the back which we laughingly call our garden. At £48,500 we're robbing ourselves blind. See for yourself by calling etc etc.

If Brooks could have intelligent, professional types rushing up to Islington and down to Pimlico in the sixties, I should certainly be able to interest one or two like-minded people in Brixton in the eighties.

Rang *Sunday Times* classified and got rather superior young lady who appeared to think I was having her on. I said that the fact that it had produced such a positive response in her was extremely encouraging, since readability was my number one objective.

"Oh," she said, "it's some sort of literary joke, is it?"

I tried to explain that the style was quite deliberate, and that it was a sort of pastiche of Roy Brooks.

"Brooks?" she said. "Isn't he something to do with films?"

Decided to cut cackle and said that however she may try to

persuade me to the contrary, I definitely wanted lineage, not display.

"In the circumstances," she said, "I couldn't agree more."

So that's all right, then.

Friday, December 7th

A full month has passed since our son and heir made his entrance onto the world stage, yet at no stage has my wife shown the slightest sign of wishing to resume what they refer to in text books as "normal marital relations". Hence the fact that I am still here at my desk in the sitting-room, writing up today's diary entry when by rights I should be curled up in bed in the arms of my life's companion and helpmate, enjoying a contented night's sleep.

Had in fact planned that the day should end in quite different fashion; indeed had signalled my intentions quite clearly by hopping into bed dressed only in pyjama bottoms. Had lain there for several minutes with the top sheet pulled ostentatiously down to mid-chest level, enjoying new Alan Coren paperback despite freezing temperatures, when B put down her *Daily Mail*, took off her glasses and said, "Sorry; you'll find some clean pyjamas in the airing cupboard." I said, admittedly in a rather facetious tone of voice, "We could both find something we want much nearer at hand than the airing cupboard;" to which she replied, "There's nothing I want at this time of night but my beauty sleep." And she switched out her bedside light, rolled over and pulled the sheet up over her ear exposing my chilled torso even further. I daresay a more brutish type would have interpreted this as some sort of challenge and forced his attentions upon her willy-nilly. I wonder sometimes if I am not too sensitive for my own good. I had always understood marriage to be a caring partnership in every sense, but perhaps I am hopelessly out of touch. I am certainly very cold.

Am seriously wondering if I might not write a book entitled *The Misery of Sex*. Well illustrated and frankly written, it could be a huge bestseller.

Saturday, December 8th

Only one more day beneath the Thatcher heel and we can begin to enjoy real family life at last, not to say some decent television programmes. At breakfast she said, "Of course, the Roskills gave me quite a little party the night before I left them for the last time."

Pretended to be deeply absorbed in free Masters of the Universe vinyl place-mat offer on the back of the cereal packet.

Later, while washing out a matinée jacket, she made a second reference to the Roskills' legendary generosity.

I said, "Funnily enough, Hilda, we were thinking of taking you out for a slap-up dinner at Le Gavroche tonight, but we felt sure you wouldn't want to miss *Blankety Blank* or the last in the current series of *Juliet Bravo*."

Couldn't help noticing as I was reading *Telegraph* in loo that they have postponed *Juliet Bravo* and *Blankety Blank* in favour of some big international football match. Said nothing to Hilda and hid newspaper behind cistern.

To Post Office, at last, after mid-morning coffee to collect undelivered package of last Tuesday. Queued obediently with half a dozen others in small stuffy room for fully twenty minutes, only to discover it was a mail order catalogue for the people in Flat 2.

Harbottle looked round after tea for official handover of co-ordinatorship of Neighbourhood Watch Scheme. Not that there was a lot to hand over except for a few remaining copies of circulars from the local police station reminding house-holders of need to lock windows and doors, avoid poorly lit streets and report any suspicious-looking behaviour to duty sergeant. Also a number of stickers to put inside front win-dows to say that the owner is a member of Neighbourhood Watch, plus minutes of obviously not very well-attended meeting at No. 28 when Scheme was first introduced to area. Small wonder people like me have never felt sufficiently inspired to subscribe. A new broom is long overdue, and good communication is essential if one wishes to stand the slightest chance of calling the citizenry to arms against the evil elements in our society. The more I think about it, the more convinced I am that they could not have picked a better man to spearhead the attack. As trappings of power go, this meagre file of papers is possibly less impressive than some, but that is not to say that the task I have undertaken and the burden of responsibility that goes with it are any the less heavy for that.

After JJ had been "put down" for the night, as Miss Thatcher will insist on describing this most moving moment of the child's day, we invited her into the sitting-room for a farewell amontillado. As she sipped genteelly at her glass, her eyes suddenly filled with tears and before we knew what, she had launched into a little speech, to the effect that the last month had been one of the happiest of her life and she would never forget us. And then blow me down if B didn't say what a joy and a comfort she had been to us and how we didn't know how we were going to cope without her, and suddenly we were all falling on one another's neck and making elaborate plans for her to come back and see us again soon.

Quite how the Thatcher family manage to turn disaster into triumph and deep disapproval into approbation and affection is one of the greatest mysteries of the twentieth century; but despite one's better judgement, one has to admire it. When she had regained her composure, Hilda said to me, "You're a very naughty boy," and tapped me playfully on the cheek. When I asked her why, she said, "You told me it was *Blankety Blank* and *Juliet Bravo* tonight when all the time it was England versus Romania. You know how much I love football. You're a terrible tease." As a product of a rugger school, and one for whom soccer has always seemed a soft and ungentlemanly game, and having mentally circled *Clive James in Lhasa* in my *TV Times*, my heart sank.

I said, "I was going to tell you but . . ."

"You lost the paper behind the cistern," she said, and went off to the small bedroom to pack.

And I thought King Lear was hard done by.

Sunday, December 9th

Sunday Times ad could not have stood out better. Knowing the number of people who still look back with affection to the great days when Sunday wasn't Sunday without the Roy Brooks property ads, I shouldn't be at all surprised if my little pastiche doesn't get picked up by one or two of the more intelligent gossip columns. Amusing little items like this are very much their bread and butter. If so, it will be very much one in the eye for the estate agency world. At all events, I think we can reasonably expect to have a large number of discerning, educated buyers beating a path to our door in the next few days. Indeed, was in the middle of giving John Julius another routine eye test after breakfast by jiggling teddy up and down on the edge of the crib when the front door bell rang. In fact it wasn't a potential purchaser but a large bearded bobby who introduced himself as PC Arthur Dunwoody, our "home beat officer". Quite why I felt the necessity to make a feeble joke about an unpaid parking fine, I can't imagine. I do not make a habit of parking on yellow lines, unlike some members of my family whom I could mention but won't, and now that I have become an ex-officio member of the police force, I would certainly not be foolish enough to play silly devils over a parking ticket, even if I were unlucky enough to receive one. Perhaps I just have a guilty conscience, though I cannot for the life of me imagine why.

At all events, managed to laugh it off, and Dunwoody and I quickly got down to the serious business of crime busting. He is very keen on this business of neighbours keeping an eye on one another's houses; ditto of people marking certain items of property, using a special property marking kit. It is unfortunate that the kit is not available at present, owing to the fact that someone has borrowed it from his office without permission. However, he has promised to let me have it as soon as possible. He concluded by saying that Neighbourhood Watch is a challenging project for us all and, if successful, will not only prevent crime but improve the quality of life in our neighbourhood and eventually in the whole of the London area.

I said that I quite agreed and that, in my view, the only way one can be sure of pointing people in the right direction is by example, starting at the top. PC Dunwoody said he couldn't agree more and suggested I might care to start by cutting down my hedge.

"There's nothing guaranteed to please a burglar more than the sight of a nice tall length of privet," he said. "The greater the cover, the more he likes it." I said that while I appreciated his point of view, one also had a responsibility to balance pragmatism with ecology. Quality of life in the inner city areas of Britain today sprang as much from an abundance of green foliage as it did from peace of mind and a sense of security.

PC Dunwoody said, "If I may say so, sir, what we are dealing with here are nasty little tearaway opportunists with sticky fingers and an eye to the main chance, not a bunch of do-gooding David Bellamys."

I said that I would give his suggestion serious consideration. Also the idea of having a real alarm put inside the plain red box above the front door.

As he was leaving, he said, "Don't forget to pay that parking fine."

I think he was joking, but you can never tell with police-men.

When he had gone, B, who had obviously been eaves-dropping from the bedroom, marched in and said that in her view there was nothing to consider, and that the sooner I got cracking with the shears, the easier she'd sleep at nights. Alternatively, I said, she could do the hedge and I could run Hilda up to Paddington.

"Certainly," she said, "provided you'll also feed the baby, change him, cook the lunch and finish doing the shopping for the weekend."

Had already made significant inroads into left-hand section by the time Hilda had finally gathered all her bits and pieces ready for the off.

As she was getting into the car she said, "Prevention is always better than cure."

"What will be will be," I replied with a wave.

"Look before you leap," she said and disappeared up the street and out of our lives, hopefully for ever.

Quite how I managed to misjudge my footing to such an extent while stepping off the ladder I can't think. I never did like aluminium. You never get silly accidents like that with a decent length of well-crafted English ash. Luckily, I didn't have to wait too long in casualty, and the Trinidadian doctor who attended me assured me that light sprains of this nature usually clear up very quickly – for what his opinion is worth.

Funnily enough, despite the pain, I feel the quality of life in the Crisp household has definitely taken a turn for the better already.

Monday, December 10th

To the Botticelli, leaning heavily on a stout stick kindly lent by Charlie Kippax. Once again I am reminded how useful it is to have as one's boss a man whose office is crammed with every possible item to cope with every possible eventuality, from malt whisky to jump leads.

Everyone at restaurant very enthusiastic about my formal invitation card for the Christmas lunch, and it came as quite a surprise, not to say a disappointment, when Carlo and Angelo both launched into a noisy account of how they want the highlight of the party to be a huge cardboard cake covered with imitation white icing, which will be wheeled in immediately after the *piccatine alla Botticelli* and placed in the middle of the room, whereupon Carlo will shout "*Buon natale a tutti!*", or words to that effect, and Angelo's shapely daughter Simona will come bursting out of the top dressed in a skimpy Santa Claus outfit and distribute small gifts to all the guests, in the form of signed remaindered copies of their cookery book "Mangiamo!"

I said that I quite agreed that Simona is *bellissima* and that if anyone represents the joy of Christmas and the rebirth of innocence, she certainly does. I also promised them that the reference to Venus Rising From the Foam had not escaped me and that of course I appreciated the connection between the painting and the restaurant. Unfortunately, so anxious was I to reassure them of the brilliance and inventiveness of this

68

sensational ploy and the eagerness with which every journalist present would immediately rush to his or her typewriter to tell the world of this great event, that all my arguments re the advisability of actually putting the stunt into effect and instantly transforming a distinguished gastronomic event into a vulgar bunfight fell on deaf and extremely foreign ears.

Left mentally and physically extremely shaky, the matter still far from resolved.

A particularly nasty snarl-up on Waterloo Bridge meant that I had no time whatever to get home and slap a quick coat of paint over the damp patch at the back of the broom cupboard before the first respondent to our latest *ST* ad was standing outside the front door, finger on bell.

B an unusually ungracious hostess, to my way of thinking, especially in view of the man's obvious Indian origins. I can quite understand that being a wife and mother takes it out of you, particularly if you are no longer in the first flush of youth, but honestly, at this rate, we may seriously have to consider recalling Miss Thatcher to the fray. Fortunately, Mr Isaacs did not appear to notice anything amiss, so intent was he on peering behind every chair, rapping every exposed piece of woodwork and examining every length of piping with the intensity of a Cambridge scientist on his way to a Nobel Prize. He also asked a large number of questions concerning the electrical wiring and what he kept referring to as "the common parts", whatever they may be, and scribbled down pages of comments in a small notebook.

Still, it was quite obvious that he was very keen on the place, and that although our way of decorating and furnishing is possibly a little sophisticated for someone of his simple background and florid tastes, this is a flat that would suit him very well indeed. In fact, so delighted with everything did he seem that I even showed him the damp patch in the broom cupboard. He gave a little grunt but did not comment. Finally, he put his notebook away and said, "When I read your advertisement, I could not believe that any flat could be quite so bad as you described it, but now I see it, it is far worse than I'd imagined. It needs completely rewiring, the plumbing is very poor and the woodwork needs replacing in most of the rooms.

I could perhaps offer you £39,000 for a quick cash sale, but even then, I'd be a fool to myself."

And all this delivered in a marked Indian accent, complete with head wobbling.

Luckily, B was in the bedroom at the time. "Thirty nine thousand?" I said in a low voice. "Are you mad? You sound just like an estate agent."

"I am an estate agent," he said.

Was by this stage totally mystified. However, did not feel inclined to let Mr Isaacs see this. I have always been a great believer in Anthony Eden's principle of playing one's cards close to one's chest, smiling disarmingly and keeping one's lines of communication open, so have said I'll consider his offer. No point in cutting off one's nose to spite one's face.

Three other people came during the course of the evening to no great effect, including a rather common couple called Turner. He claimed to have been in the same house as me at school. I can't say I remember him. At all events, his comments re the nasty patch on the balloon-patterned paper on JJ's ceiling quite uncalled for.

Was sorting through some old correspondence later when I came across a stiffly worded reminder to B from police re some long overdue parking fine. Had no alternative but to put on my official hat and read riot act, as a result of which we had words. Am wondering how Sir Kenneth Newman would have coped in a similar situation.

Tuesday, December 11th

Fortunately, the Crisps are nothing if not resilient. We have always been a family who believe in riding above life's little setbacks and irritations. Onward and upward is our motto – or it would be if we had our own coat of arms – and I spent an extremely profitable half an hour this morning ringing around possible day schools for JJ, including a couple of comprehensives. Was strangely impressed by the headmaster of one, who spoke so enthusiastically about his school, his job, his pupils and his hopes for the future of education in this country that I found myself wondering why I have even bothered to consider private schools in the first place. Will definitely make an appointment to look round place in New Year. His name is Utkinson-Hill. I'm quite sold on the school already. "I expect you know Christopher Chataway," I said before ringing off.

"No," he said.

Never mind, we can't know everyone. Besides, how refreshing to be dealing with a system of education where personal connections and old school ties count for nothing.

Wednesday, December 12th

Philippe and Theresa de Grande-Hauteville to supper, bringing with them Yves, now aged five and a half. Could not help expressing surprise that he hadn't been tucked up in bed with his teddy hours ago. Theresa said, in a rather silly, superior voice, "Oh don't be so boringly English. The whole reason we've been left standing by the rest of Europe is that on the continent they treat their children in a sensible, adult way and we treat ours like dim domestic pets. To my way of thinking, the more children are exposed to grown-up conversation and grown-up life, the quicker they'll develop into interesting individuals with minds of their own, capable of playing their parts in the Europe of the twenty-first century."

"Like the Luxembourgeouis, I suppose," I said.

Not surprisingly, she immediately changed the subject.

Needless to say, Yves behaved extremely badly throughout the entire evening, throwing his food around, disrupting the conversation with loud squawking and generally drawing attention to himself. I suppose one can hardly blame the child, but I do blame his parents for not giving him a sharp smack on his fat little bottom and packing him off to bed for the rest of the evening.

After tonight's performance, I can only feel relieved that we have not yet finalised our godparents list. At this rate, it's going to be a very short list indeed.

Thursday, December 13th

I suppose I should be relieved that at least it isn't Friday. Even so, as black a day as I can remember in a long while. With only a week to go, I have not yet received a single reply to my Botticelli invitations from anyone who counts for anything in the world of serious food writing. Hugh Bryant-Fenn has accepted, needless to say, but then he'd go anywhere to get something for nothing. He's particularly strong on openings. As someone once remarked, "Bryant-Fenn would go to the opening of an envelope." Still, I ought not to complain. If it wasn't for freeloaders like him, people like me would be out of a job.

Is he the right sort of material for a godfather, though? I certainly would not want a child of mine to go through life thinking that he need never put his hand in his pocket.

Had hoped that by now I would have heard from a few heavyweights, the *Observer*, for example, the *Standard*, *A La Carte*, *Gourmet*, etc. I realise we are in the thick of the office party season, but *quand même* . . .

Is there no loyalty left in Fleet Street? Have I spent the last three years building up friendships with some of the biggest names in journalism only to have them flung back in my face like old gloves? More to the point, has Karen forgotten to post the invitations *yet again*? Heads may roll.

Friday, December 14th

Whole day spent signing office Christmas cards. While I agree that no-one could fail to be amused by a card depicting Charlie Kippax dressed as Father Christmas, trying to sort through a heap of parcels with the names of our accounts on them, I still feel that *Black Grouse in the Snow* by Archibald Thorburn would have lent an air of *gravitas* to our message of Christmas cheer that is all too often lacking in our profession. Our own "Adoring Angel" (detail) by Lippi, in aid of UNICEF, very much nearer the mark. I think we were right not to go for the printed address. Ostentation is no part of Christmas.

Several more acceptances for Botticelli, but only one from First Division and that to refuse. I foresee a heavy day on the telephone on Monday. On the other hand, the post brings particulars from Hampers of what looks and sounds like an absolutely enchanting house called Pear Tree Farm in Suffolk, only a stone's throw from Ipswich and the A45.

A charming period house, set in about 2½ acres of mature gardens, grounds and paddocks. Hall, dining-room, morning-room, sitting-room, four bedrooms: plus adjoining cottage which offers an additional living-room and two bedrooms. Believed to date from the sixteenth century, this potentially most attractive farmhouse retains much of its original charm and character and offers great scope in providing a spacious country property.

All right, so it's in need of "restoration and modernisation", but then what period property isn't? And okay, so it needs a spot of rewiring and the roof could use a new tile or two, but quite honestly there's nothing that can't be improved out of all recognition with a lick of paint, a slap of plaster and a few strategically placed night storage heaters. Actually, to judge from the colour pictures, it doesn't look nearly as bad as the agents make out. The land alone must be worth the £89,500 asking price.

Have rung Stanford-Dingley at Hampers and made an appointment to see the place tomorrow morning at nine thirty. He has promised that their local chap will definitely turn up this time. I'll believe that when I see it. Funnily enough, that's exactly what B said when I told her I thought this could turn out to be one of the property bargains of the year. I don't know; I'd always been under the impression that married couples were supposed to be travelling along vaguely the same lines. Or have I completely missed the point? Or should I say points?

Have carefully put all clothes for tomorrow's trip – wellingtons, Babour, cap, thick cords, roll-neck etc – in sitting room in order not to disturb B tomorrow morning. Have also placed alarm clock in strategic position on bedside table for quick and easy access. Am quite excited already. Thank goodness someone in this family has a sense of adventure.

Saturday, December 15th

The only serious drawback to alarm clocks is that one is awake half the night waiting for the wretched things to go off. Finally slipped away to Land of Nod at what seemed like about five o'clock, only to be blasted into consciousness again a minute and a half later by urgent jangle of bell. By that stage, was in such a deep sleep that I had completely forgotten I'd placed clock carefully next to glass of water. In my anxiety not to wake B, swung arm quickly across in direction of table, catching water *en passant* and soaking everything within range of approximately five feet, including new Alan Coren and pile of *Sunday Telegraph* mags I'd been storing up for a rainy day. (No joke intended.) Instinctively swore loudly, leapt out of bed, switched on light and started mopping up.

By the time I left the house at six thirty, every member of the family wide awake and giving vent to feelings in various individual ways. Still, every cloud has a silver lining, and half an hour later I was whisking up a traffic-less Leytonstone High Street and out onto M11. By the time I passed Bury St Edmunds, a glorious sunny day was dawning and twenty minutes later I drew up outside Pear Tree Farm. Quite why I had been so convinced it would take me three hours at least to get there I can't imagine. Still, it gave me plenty of time to have a good nose around before the Hampers man turned up.

What can I say?

The instant I set eyes on Pear Tree Farm, I knew for certain that at long last I had found my true spiritual home and that this was where I was going to live out my days, surrounded by my family and the beauty of the English countryside. And that was despite the badly disintegrating roof, the nasty cracks in the shabby outside walls, the obviously rotten woodwork and the completely overgrown garden.

As I stood there in the pale winter sunshine, gazing out over the fields that stretched away into the distance as far as the eye could see, I suddenly found myself recalling the words of Joseph Smith, founder of the Mormons upon first seeing the Great Salt Lake at Utah: "This is the place!"

Life seems to be throwing up religious experiences at almost every turn these days, and often in the most unusual places. But then, of course, that's God for you.

Indeed it is some measure of the Christian feelings the place aroused in me that though the Hampers man was twenty-five minutes late, I never even thought to draw attention to the fact. At first sight, the interior appeared to be even worse than the outside; but the more I looked at it, the more I began to wonder whether, despite the peeling walls, the uneven floors, the holes in the roof, the dust, the dirt and the damp, one is really going to be facing quite as big a refurbishment job as one might at first suppose. Provided the basic structure is sound and the owner is prepared to accept a cash offer of, say, eighty-five, who knows . . . ?

According to the Hampers chap, the house belongs to a couple of doddery sisters in their nineties who live in a nearby old people's home and haven't been near the place for years. They hardly sound to me the types who are going to strike a particularly hard bargain.

At all events, have decided to play cards close to chest for time being and get someone to carry out a basic structural survey and give me an independent valuation.

Funnily enough, Paula Batty's husband Roland used to live in Ipswich; he may well know of someone who'd be prepared to do me a decent professional job without charging an arm and a leg for it.

Drove back to London, humming snatches of Elgar, interspersed with 'To be a farmer's boy'. Who knows it's what John Julius may very well turn out to be.

Decided at this stage not to risk putting B against the whole project by seeming too keen, so when she asked whether I'd had a good day, I simply replied, "So so," and immediately changed the subject.

To bed early with an apple where I read five chapters of

Cider with Rosie, a book of which I have hitherto never managed to get past page one.

Sunday, December 16th

An astonishing thing happened. Turned on TV shortly before lunch for no particular reason to be confronted by none other than my old flatmate Beddoes, of all people, holding forth in Washington on the subject of US foreign policy in the Middle East. Underneath him were the words: WHITE HOUSE ADVISER ON FOREIGN AFFAIRS. Frankly, I'd have thought that the only "foreign affairs" on which he was an expert would have been of little value, or interest, to the Reagans.

On the other hand, as B wittily pointed out, he could hardly know *less* than the President; and although in terms of character and moral outlook, particularly *in re* his dealings with the opposite sex of all nationalities, he is about as ideal godfather material as ex-President Marcos, there is a lot to be said for a young man having someone streetwise, wordly and filled with rat-like cunning whom he can turn to for the odd tip in years to come.

B obviously impressed by Beddoes. She said, "To hear you talk, anyone would think you spent five years of your life sharing a flat with Martin Bormann. In fact, he's rather good-looking, extremely bright and obviously enormously successful. I'm not surprised you're always knocking him. You're obviously jealous of him and have been for years. I've never met him, but despite everything you say, I think he'd be a very good godfather."

Did not see any point in disillusioning her, and said that I was glad she saw it my way.

Sat down straight away and wrote to him accordingly c/o The White House, Washington, DC.

B also agreed with me that there is probably nothing that Tim can bring to godparenthood that he cannot already offer as an uncle, and with her rather reluctant approval have also rung Bryant-Fenn and invited him to join the team. He seemed genuinely pleased and flattered to be asked, although when I mentioned a few possible dates for the christening in early January, he said there was a faint possibility that he might have to ask someone to stand proxy for him since he had been invited, as contributing editor of *Relationships* magazine, to join a small party of psychological journalists that some obscure firm of travel agents in Essex is getting up to visit a couple of the more fashionable French ski resorts.

I said, "But you have never put on a pair of skis in your life."

"True," he said, "but then I'm interested in what happens after the skis have been taken off, aren't I?"

Poor old Hugh. For all his success, he is still desperately in need of constant reassurance. It's difficult not to admire his enthusiasm and industry. But then, of course, he hasn't got anything else in his life on which to expend his energies. One of the great joys of *la vie familiale* is being able to get one's priorities right at last and realising that there is more to our existence here on earth than knocking out thousand word articles at £150 a time for magazines that don't even make it to the dentist's waiting-room.

Still, if nothing else positive came out of the conversation, at least I have learnt one or two tricks for making one's home seem rather more attractive to a potential buyer than it might otherwise appear. According to Hugh, these include switching on all the lights, turning the heating up, having a few fresh flowers round the place, getting one's wife to put on something bright and cheerful and have her face made up and her hair done nicely, and making sure that the moment a buyer steps through the front door, his nostrils are assailed by the odour of delicious home cooking.

"A lot of people swear by a nice leg of English lamb," said Hugh. "But actually you can't go far wrong with home-baked bread."

When I mentioned this to B, she said, "What does Hugh know about it? He's never sold a property in his life or owned one. He's far too mean. His permanent address is Junket Cottage, Freebyland."

I said that, though this may be true from a purely factual point of view, it doesn't mean that his advice may not be thoroughly sound in principle. After all, he must have learnt a thing or two from the "Man-About-Town" column he used to write for the Lenwade Properties in-house magazine. Besides, since no-one who came to look round the flat last week as a result of my latest ad has yet made an offer worthy of our consideration, we certainly have nothing to lose by giving it a try.

B said, "I'm just about prepared to put up with you trying to save a few bob by being your own estate agent and driving round the English countryside looking at houses we couldn't possibly afford to buy or to live in even if we could; I suppose I can just about accept the fact that men have not the faintest conception of how women feel after they've had a baby and what hard work it is being a nurse, washerwoman, cook, daily, chauffeur and personal secretary and valet twenty-four hours a day, seven days a week, and how irritating it is to have total strangers forever wandering in and out of one's bedroom and bathroom and kitchen at the most inconvenient moments, who have no intention whatever of buying the place. But if you think that, on top of all that, I'm going to change into a snappy cocktail number, reach for the mascara and the hair-dryer, and roast a joint of meat every time the front door bell rings, you've got another think coming." And with that she burst into tears, snatched JJ up from the floor and disappeared into the bedroom, slamming the door behind her. She's a funny old stick and I do love her, but really she does have a tendency to overreact sometimes.

As I said to her, following a largely monosyllabic lunch, if the going gets tough, she only has to ask me and I'll be delighted to help out at any time of the day or night.

She said, "I'd have thought you'd be sensitive enough to the situation by now to know when I need help without my having to ask you."

I said I was very sorry if I didn't come up to scratch and that I would certainly try and be a bit more helpful in the future and why didn't I take the baby out for a walk while she had a little lie down?

"The trouble with you men is that you're so damned martyrish about everything," she said, and once again stormed out of the room.

I honestly give up.

Had been planning to ring Theresa and ask her to be godmother, but am seriously beginning to wonder if having a god*mother* is either desirable or neccessary.

Am also wondering if this après-ski jaunt of Bryant-Fenn's is something I should have suggested to Ski Time. It's rather up their street. Or should I say up their Alp?

Monday, December 17th

It's quite obvious we're not going to get any more serious replies to last week's ad, so after dealing with mail (two more refusals for Botticelli), rang Julian Hankey-Barber to say that, after much heart-searching, I had decided that Loomis Chaffee would be the ideal people to sell the flat and perhaps he'd like to drop by later in the day and talk over some preliminary marketing thoughts I'd had since we last met. He said that, by an odd coincidence, he had to see a house in Dulwich at five, and perhaps he could call in on his way home to Chelsea.

Rest of day spent on telephone working through Botticelli guest list. Apart from the features editor of *What's Cooking?*, I have not come up with a single name to set Carlo and Angelo dancing on the tables with delight. I suppose as a last resort, could always paper the house with people from the office. Karen looks as though she could do with a square meal, and Jim from accounts is always game for an outing. Unfortunately, none of them is going to fill a single column inch.

Julian turned up, finally, at seven – just as B had tucked up JJ for the night, needless to say – and had a quick look round to remind himself of the basic geography, as he put it. He was most optimistic, and said that he was sure he could "knock it away" without too much difficulty at £42,000, or somewhere near it.

I reminded him that the last time we'd spoken, he'd talked confidently in terms of forty-three or even forty-four.

"Ah yes," he said, "but that was nearly a month ago. The market's gone very quiet since then and probably won't pick

79

up again until well into the New Year. We could hang on for a bit, I suppose, but frankly, if it's a quick sale you're after, I'd honestly recommend you lower your sights a little. As I said before, people aren't exactly queueing up to live down here and there's no point in putting potential punters off more than is absolutely necessary." I may not be as *au courant* with the London property scene as some, but I somehow can't believe there are many examples of prices plummeting, even at this time of the year. Still, I presume he must know what he's talking about, although I must say I was surprised he didn't react a little more positively to my suggestion of an ad or two in publications like *Portrait*, *The Magazine* and *Boardroom*. I'm also anxious not to lose the Suffolk house through unnecessary shilly-shallying and have instructed him to go ahead and prepare particulars. Also pointed out that I may well consider instructing a joint agent if he doesn't get results within a month. I am a great believer in keeping these estate agents on their toes.

B still curiously indifferent to my efforts to better my family. I do see that trying to decide whether to give the body lotion to Paula or Vanessa is a worry, but surely one that must pale into comparison with our future happiness and well-being? Or have I got it all wrong *yet again*? At least B's decision to take JJ off two o'clock feed can only improve matters.

Tuesday, December 18th

Am now so used to waking up at two that I woke anyway and couldn't get back to sleep for over an hour.

Mother rang first thing to confirm that we would all be down in time for lunch on Christmas Day, and to say why didn't we stay for the night and set off for the Pedalows first thing on Boxing Day morning? Reminded her that they always had their Christmas meal in the evening, and that since we had agreed months ago that we would have lunch with her and dinner with them, to alter the plan now would be a bitter disappointment to the Pedalows and nothing short of marital suicide for me.

Mother said, "I wonder you're bothering to come down at all. You obviously can't wait to get to Gloucestershire."

I replied that, on the contrary, we were very much looking forward to seeing her, and that as far as we were concerned, lunch with her would be the centrepiece of Christmas Day. However, as I was sure she understood, now that I was a family man, my loyalties were perforce divided.

"Yes," she said. "Eighty twenty."

I said that that was a complete exaggeration and that, were it not for the fact that the Boxing Day shooting party was something of a Pedalow family tradition, we would almost certainly be returning home first thing in the morning on the twenty-sixth.

Mother said, "Christmas Night with Morecambe and Wise used to be something of a Crisp family tradition, too."

I reminded her that Eric's untimely departure from the stage had rather knocked that particular tradition on the head.

She said, "I know someone else who needs knocking on the head."

I know I should feel sorry for her, living on her own like that, especially at this time of the year, and my Christian conscience has never been more severely wrung, but with the best will in the world I cannot help feeling that even Our Lord would have a few sharp, well-chosen words to say to someone who used emotional blackmail as shamelessly as she does. Even the turkey found itself being used as a lever at one point. Since the unfortunate creature is presumably even now wandering innocently around some farmyard, gobbling away contentedly to itself, totally unaware of its forthcoming *rendez-vous* with Mother's Aga, it is surely not too late for her to order a smaller bird, abandon the cold meat stage for once and go straight for the *fricassée* on Boxing Day.

I suppose I can't really blame Nigel and Priscilla deciding to emigrate to New Zealand like that. I'm quite sure they need every accountant they can get in Rotarua, and since, even at the age of thirteen, James is never happier than when pushing people about, I daresay he will make an ideal sheep-farmer.

They could never have guessed that, after all those years as a bachelor, I would suddenly up and marry and leave Mother in the Yuletide lurch. On the other hand, I do think the cat has a great deal to answer for. From the moment Nigel and Priscilla introduced it into her life that Christmas Eve seven years ago it has treated Mother, and indeed everyone else who has ever dared to come into the house, in a disgracefully cavalier fashion. If it were a creature with any sort of breeding at all, it would have learnt long ago to repay the many kindnesses shown to it by its owner with a modicum of companionship.

Mother said, "So that's it then, is it? You're definitely leaving after lunch. You're not staying the night."

"No," I said.

"Right," she said. "Just as long as I know. It's just that I didn't want to accept the Barrington-Hills' invitation to dinner, only to have to cancel at the last moment because you decide you can't face the journey." I was thinking of buying Mother a new radio this year, but now she can definitely put up with the nightie after all. Possibly in Bri-nylon.

Wednesday, December 19th

This new nightly régime has completely worked up my mental time-clock. Last night, woke at four to realise that with less than forty eight hours to go before the Botticelli lunch, only a third of the people invited have bothered to reply.

In normal circumstances, would not inflict Pamela on any journalist I know for fear of frightening them off altogether, but on this occasion her brusque, rather military manner may be just what's needed to chivvy up the last few regional stragglers. I handed her the list of defaulters, having carefully earmarked the big guns, who require special handling, for my personal attention.

Returned to my desk, only to find that every single food writer on my list was either in a meeting, on the phone or out of the office. Left messages for as many as possible and spent the rest of morning sending out complimentary packets of cheese fondue mix to a hundred or so deserving journalists on behalf of Ski Time.

By twelve thirty, none of my people had rung back, so went

into Pam's office to see how she had been getting on, only to find an empty chair. Was composing a stiff note on electronic Brother when Pamela strolled in and announced coolly that all the people on her bit of the list were definitely coming, and would I mind if she left early to have lunch with her boy-friend Ron and did some Christmas shopping afterwards?

In the circumstances felt I could hardly refuse her request.

Unfortunately, being an account director carries with it rather weightier responsibilities than those of a mere executive, and even though I am acutely aware that I still haven't the faintest idea what I am going to give B for Christmas, I put all personal considerations aside and spent the afternoon at Botticelli going through menu with Emilio in the kitchen and making last desperate – and as it turned out unsuccessful – attempts to get through to so-called top food writers on my list.

Carlo and Angelo, not surprisingly, rather depressed to hear that so few of the big names would be coming. Carlo patted me on the shoulder, shook his head sadly and said, "Life is full of disappointments. We aim for the moon, but all too often we must be satisfied with the stars."

"Stars are not everything," said Carlo. "Just so long as everyone has a good time."

"And they write about us in their newspapers," said Angelo.

In the circumstances have agreed that we might as well go ahead with the lady-in-the-cake-idea. I can't imagine that the majority of the names on the guest list would know the difference between *paglia a fieno alla Venusiana* and a tin of Heinz spaghetti hoops. As long as they go home feeling they've had plenty to drink and a few laughs, they'll be perfectly happy.

Home at half past eight to find that the dog had disembowelled John Julius's favourite furry hedgehog and swallowed the squeaker. Immediately rang the vet who was out delivering a dray pony, but spoke to very nice girl who said there was no need to panic, the object would almost certainly make its way out in the usual way, and that when I take the animal out for its morning vacation (I *think* that's what she

83

said), I should remember to pay particular attention to its stools.

I said that I was not in the habit of paying them any attention whatever and did she mean that I was to carry out a post-mortem on them, as it were, there and then in the gutter?

She said, "A cursory examination should be sufficient."

I said, "And what if the squeaker hasn't made it through?"

"Dogs have surprisingly strong stomachs," she said.

I only hope mine will be able to match it.

Thursday, December 20th

Whereabouts of squeaker still very much a matter of conjecture, owing to serious abdominal disorder of my own. I detect Emilio's hand in this – a cruel irony, since by eight o'clock this morning, it was perfectly obvious I was in no fit state to go to the office, let alone the Botticelli lunch.

The thought that, with Charlie Kippax taken up with the big mineral water promotion at the Centurion Hotel, the whole affair now rested in the inexperienced hands of Pamela van Zeller, merely added fuel to the fires that wreacked my stomach.

Unfortunately, rather more pressing personal matters prevented me from getting on the telephone quite as early as I would have liked, and it was nine thirty before I finally found the strength to dial the number. Appalled to find Pamela not in yet.

"I think she said something about stopping off to have her hair done," Karen told me. "But really there's nothing to worry about. Everything's under control. You rest up and keep warm and leave it all to us." Three-quarters of an hour later, my so-called assistant condescended to start earning the princely salary that TCP Public Relations is obliged to pay its most junior employees nowadays.

I started to explain that although I had said I would deal with all the names that had asterisks against them, there was still some doubt about one or two of them and perhaps she could give them all a final call, just to be on the safe side, when she interrupted to say that she had done all that yesterday and they had all accepted. I said that we were obviously talking at cross purposes since I had made it quite clear that she was to handle the chaff and leave the straw to me.

"I know," she said, "but I could see you had a lot of other things on your plate, and knowing how difficult it is to get a decision out of these people, I decided it was time to force the issue."

When I asked her to explain, she said, "It's quite simple. I told them that if they came to the lunch, we'd give them a hundred pounds each, cash in hand. Of course, they all agreed like a shot."

For once in my life I was rendered completely speechless.

She said, "That was all right, wasn't it? I mean, you did want all the top names to come, didn't you?"

I had just launched into a brief and pithy speech on the subject of professional ethics, when she again interrupted me by saying that since I was obviously not in a fit state to think clearly about anything, why didn't I pop back to bed with a cup of Bovril and a slice of dry toast and she'd call me later and tell me how it had all gone. And with that she rang off.

In normal circumstances would have got straight on to Charlie, but on this occasion, the less said the better.

Fell back into bed where I tried to compose an explanatory letter to the Press Council, another to Charlie offering my resignation, and a third to the police confessing to the brutal murder of an assistant public relations executive. Failed dismally on all three counts, fell into a fitful sleep and had a vivid dream of Pamela leaping naked out of a huge pile of ten pound notes.

Woke in a sweat and with the realisation that I had forgotten to tell Pamela to tell Carlo and Angelo to cancel cake item.

Looked at my watch to find that it was two thirty, which was exactly the time we'd arranged for the kitchen doors to open and the cake to be wheeled in. On the off-chance that the timetable was running slow, rushed to the phone and rang Botticelli.

Absolutely no reply. My first thought was that something

had gone terribly wrong: there'd been an affray and the vice squad had been called. The fraud squad, more likely. Perhaps there'd been a ghastly fire, or everyone had been poisoned by the veal.

Finally the phone was picked up by someone whose voice I didn't recognise. Tried to explain who I was and what I wanted, but he said he was very sorry, he couldn't hear a word, there was a private party going on and if it was a booking I wanted, would I ring back later. At that moment, there was a bellow of laughter and the sound of champagne corks being popped. The man called out, "Hang on, I'm coming", and the phone went dead.

Lay in bed for rest of afternoon, quite unable to concentrate on *Afternoon Theatre* play about witchcraft or *Bookshelf*, until finally at five Pamela rang. Apparently it had all been an enormous success. Everybody had said that it was some of the best Italian food they'd eaten all year and they all agreed that the cake had been a masterly stroke.

I said, "So they really did all come, did they?"

"Who?" she said.

"The big guns," I said.

"Of course," she said.

I said, "And the money? What did you do, slip it into the press pack?"

"What money?" she said.

"The money," I said. "The hundred pounds. You did tell them not to breathe a word to anyone, didn't you?"

At this, she burst out laughing.

"You didn't seriously believe all that stuff, did you?" she said.

"It was meant to be a joke. You sounded as though you needed cheering up."

I said, "In that case, how did you get them all to come?"

"Oh," she said, "It was nothing to do with me. It was a pure stroke of luck. Apparently they were all due to have lunch at Le Moulin-à-Vent, but there was a fire in the kitchen and it had to be cancelled at the last moment, so they all decided to come on to us. But then that's PR for you. You lose some, you win some."

86

I still can't make up my mind whether to give her a raise or the sack. At all events, I'm beginning to wonder if there is a place amid the rough and tumble of the modern commercial world for the man of principle.

Friday, December 21st

The first decent night's sleep in weeks and medically speaking, an altogether more satisfactory start to the day, both for me, and for Vita; though how an object the size of, and with the awkward contours of, that squeaker managed to negotiate all the twists and turns of any animal's digestive system is nothing short of a miracle. Am seriously thinking of applying for it to be entered in the *Guinness Book of Records*; perhaps even contacting the producer of *Blue Peter* or the Esther Rantzen programme; except that, knowing the items they have on that sort of show, I daresay I'd have to teach the animal to blow the squeaker as well.

Arrived at the office slightly later than usual to find that several people had already rung and left messages of thanks and congratulations for lunch.

When Pamela came in, I said laughingly that if I didn't watch out, I might find she'd snatched the Botticelli account from under my nose. She said, "Anything's possible in this business." I noticed she didn't laugh. Roland Batty rang to say that he had spoken to a Mr Jarvis of Price Feltwell who had said he would be very happy to carry out a full structural survey for me on Pear Tree Farm and would eleven o'clock tomorrow be convenient?

Called Hampers chap who said that was fine by him, and that since he himself would be shooting all day over at Thetford, he would arrange for Jarvis to pick the key up from his office.

Have said that in the circumstances I wouldn't mind going down there myself.

"You can, if you want," he said, "but really, it's not necessary. I've seen Mr Jarvis' survey reports and they really do tell you everything you need to know."

I replied firmly that I didn't doubt Mr Jarvis' professional standards for a minute, but I'd like to go anyway.

"Suit yourself," he said.

Have rung Jarvis and confirmed.

At lunch-time, we all gathered in Kippax's office for a Christmas "snifter", as Charlie put it.

What with the Botticelli lunch and Charlie's triumph with the mineral water account, we had plenty to celebrate.

Was strongly tempted to take up Kippax's offer and join him, Nightingale and Hebblethwaite for lunch at his club, but decided the old tum could do with a twenty-four-hour sabbatical and spent a happy lunch-time isolated in my office with a beaker of Bovril from the machine and a possible guest list for the Ski Time press trip to the French Alps in late January.

The *Bon Viveur* chap rang from Wilmslow to say how much he'd enjoyed the lunch and what a pity it was that more restaurants didn't indulge in the occasional *coup de théâtre*.

He added, "That girl of yours has got a marvellous figure."

I explained that Simona didn't work for me; she was the daughter of one of the proprietors.

"I don't know anything about any Simona," he said. "This girl told me quite distinctly her name was Pamela, and she was about to take over from you on the Botticelli account."

Since I have always thought of Pamela as being on the decidedly lumpy side, I am still not entirely convinced we are talking about the same person. Would certainly have wasted no time getting to the bottom of this mysterious matter had B not rung to say that Julian Hankey-Barber had been on to her to say that he was sending a Mrs Dabitov round to look at the flat. She sounded very keen indeed and there was a good chance she might make an offer. Did she seriously want me to go ahead with the bread-baking idea, and if so, could I come home early, because she hadn't got any of the proper ingredients and John Julius had got a slight temperature and Mrs Dabitov was due at three thirty?

Had not imagined that when one got married and had children, one was expected to take on the role of mother's help, delivery-boy and general dogsbody – all unpaid – in addition to working one's fingers to the bone at the office.

Left the office at two thirty in a taxi, picking up packet of home-bake mix at the Light of Allah Delicatessen, Video Club and Takeaway Tandoori *en route*.

Got home to find B on her way to the doctor with JJ bright red in the face and squawking loudly in his carrycot.

When I asked her what I was supposed to do about the bread, she asked how I could even think about such trivialities when our son might be dying from whooping cough or scarlet fever.

Tried to point out there hasn't been a case of scarlet fever in Britain for thirty years, but by then she was already halfway to the car.

Rushed in, carefully read instructions on packet and, after several bosh shots, threw something into the oven, turned it up to "high" and set to work with Hoover. Suddenly remembered about flowers, so dashed down to Floral Dance and came back with small, over-priced bunch of mixed chrysanths.

Had just got them into pint beer mug when front door bell rang and there was Mrs Dabitov, looking like a smaller version of Flora Robson. I said, "Oh there you are. I was expecting you twenty minutes ago."

"Valderma Road isn't easy to find," she said. "Where's the lavatory?"

I asked her if she wouldn't prefer to see the bedroom first, or perhaps the sitting-room?

"I need to use it," she said.

Seized the opportunity to rush round and turn on all the lights. Also threw Beethoven's Sixth on gramophone.

If she was seriously interested in making the garden flat her home, she had a funny way of showing it.

Two minutes later, we were standing by the front door again, having looked round the whole flat.

"Well," I said, feeling that some sort of *rapprochement* was called for. "What do you think?"

"I think," she said, "there's a very funny smell in this flat. You haven't got mice by any chance, have you?"

It wasn't until after she had left and I had gone round turning out the lights that I remembered the bread. Rushed to the kitchen and threw open the oven door, to be confronted by the most perfect loaf I think I have ever seen.

The curious thing is, it hardly smelt at all. Perhaps we *have* got mice.

John Julius has certainly got a cold.

To bed early, feeling even more exhausted than at this time yesterday.

Saturday, December 22nd

Up considerably later than on my last visit to Suffolk. As a result, got stuck in the most terrible traffic in Seven Sisters Road and arrived at Pear Tree Cottage to find Mr Jarvis already hard at work, standing in the garden swinging his moisture meter in a menacing sort of way. Barely had time to get out my notebook before he had begun.

"Right," he said. "Well, for a start, that chimney needs repointing and proper lead-flashing. The timber framework obviously needs doing, so basically we're talking about a complete new roof. The dormer window's a bit of a joke frankly. It's cockeyed and the cheeks have gone. Rainwater goods next: that's gutters, drainpipes, and so on. Well, there aren't any on this side, and there's nothing to hang the guttering on, even if there were any . . ."

On the way round to the front, he hacked at the base of the well with his heel and removed a layer of loose rendering.

"Ah yes," he said. "Thought so. Now that crack could simply mean the lintel's dropped. But in fact, as you can see, the footing's gone and the corners have dropped. The wavy walls might be nothing more than a charming period feature. Or they might not."

As we made our way indoors, I said, "The basic structure looks sound enough, which is the main thing."

Mr Jarvis said, "Do you think so?"

We made our way into what is described in the particulars as the sitting-room. He pointed at the rough panelling that ran along the bottom of the walls. "Hallo, hallo," he said and pulled at one of the boards which came away in his hand.

"Thought so," he said. "Someone's been filling in here with concrete. That's always a bad sign." He pushed the prongs of his damp meter into what remained of the original beam, and explained that the needle should not record more than 20%. It shot up to 60%.

One way and another, it was quite a relief to get outside into the fresh air.

"What do you think then?" I said. "You can give it to me straight. Don't pull your punches."

"I never do," he said. "Of course, I'll be sending you a full report in a few days, but briefly I recommend you strip the whole thing down to the bare bones and start again. That way you'll really find out what you're in for."

He then announced that his estimate for restoration work had leapt from £30,000 to £50,000.

He asked me how much they were asking. I told him eighty-nine and a half. He whistled through his teeth.

"Offer them seventy-five," he said, "and you could be in business. Nicely done up, it could be worth a hundred and fifty."

Suddenly, from being convinced that only a mad millionaire would dream of turning what is obviously a derelict hovel into a country house fit for a successful man of the world and his family, I suddenly see myself less than an arm's length away from the property bargain of the year. I'm only sorry Mr Jarvis will not be acting for me in the sale. I very much like the cut of his jib.

Even JJ's runny nose and matching tummy could not wipe the metaphorical grin off my face this evening.

Sunday, December 23rd

Morning spent doing Christmas decorations. I cannot imagine there are many inner-city areas in Britain where one is unable to leave a Christmas tree in one's front garden without someone vandalising it during the night. Funnily enough, for once it was to our advantage, since B, in a commendable attempt to save money, had bought the top of a fir tree which cost half the amount of a traditional Christmas tree and, according to the man at the market, wouldn't shed needles all over the carpet the moment it was through the front door. Possibly for the very simple reason that its branches were so long we couldn't get it *through* the front door. Or at least not until the vandals had pulled the bottom branches off.

Borrowed a saw from the Harbottles, who are still showing no signs of moving, and cut six inches off trunk. Unfortunately, having cut thing down to ideal size, I trod on one of the top branches, bending it badly and completely ruining the proportions. Managed to straighten it up with Sellotape, but of course the moment B hung a gold ball on it, it bent again. Tried it without ball, but it looked completely ridiculous. Wood glue is obviously useless on living – or at least half-dead – wood, so at B's suggestion, slipped round to Mr Patel's to buy a tube of Superglue.

Unfortunately, the moment I snipped the top off the plastic nozzle, the stuff came shooting out all over my fingers and dripped through the branches. Was so anxious not to get it on to carpet that I did not realise that fingers of left hand had become stuck to branch in question. In trying to extricate self from foliage, slightly overdid it, and, as a result, the whole branch came away, leaving a glaring gap – not to say a small selection of pine needles attached to the end of both thumbs and forefingers. I agree that B's idea of turning tree so that gap is facing wall *is* a solution, and it is quite true that if one didn't know it was there, one would never even notice. The trouble is, I *do* know it's there, and no amount of trying to pretend it isn't will persuade me that black is white. Nor that delicate razorwork, followed by a good rub with a pumice stone, is the ideal answer to superglued fingers. On the other hand, lights a great success. I knew I was right to put my foot down over the ones that flash in time to Christmas Carols. Scandinavian angels less successful. Ditto, rather flashy so-called paper-chains that pull out like a concertina and don't quite reach to central light fitting.

We never seemed to have this trouble when I was a child. But of course, in those days, we had proper paper-chains that we made up ourselves with strips of coloured paper and paste.

Must have tried half a dozen shops last week but in none of them did any of the sales people have the faintest idea what I was talking about. In the end, had to organise makeshift extension from window catch to concertina, using length of ordinary string. But then that's this country all over. We come up with the most breathtakingly simple inventions, like radar and paper-chains, yet all too often we seem incapable of following them through.

When JJ woke from his morning sleep, B brought him through and I went to switch on the lights. I do not believe that even Crown Princess Sylvia of Norway can have felt more moved when she switched on the lights of the tree in Trafalgar Square than I did at that moment.

At last, for the first time in my adult life, Christmas has for me acquired some sort of meaning, and the look of excited anticipation in those little blue eyes brought home the Christmas message in a way that no amount of *Thoughts for the Day* could possibly hope to achieve.

"Ta ra!" I cried and threw the switch, and the whole room was filled with a glorious, almost supernatural, light. There was a moment's silence and then John Julius burst into the loudest screams I think I have ever heard from a baby of his age. Had imagined that it was simply a matter of shock and that he would quickly recover, but, if anything, he squawked even louder and finally became so hysterical that B had to take him out of the room. Oh dear, oh dear. What have we done to deserve this? I hope we haven't been landed with one of those children one hears about that won't go to parties and are fussy about their food.

In the circumstances, I think B is quite right to suggest that we ask Paula Batty to be godmother rather than Theresa, who is very sweet in her way, but judging from the *laissez-faire* way she is bringing up Yves, I don't think we can hope to rely on her help and advice when the going gets tough. It's unfortunate that I'm experiencing such difficulty at present dissociating P from her surname, but I daresay I'll manage in time.

After supper, made out my Christmas present list. Not an easy matter with bandaged fingers. Mother's nightie aside, I am still no nearer to filling in the blanks than I was when

B first raised the subject of Christmas shopping last August.

Am wondering whether I might not give B's father some wine. Possibly a couple of bottles of the Château Verdun from Mazzarini & Block's that I bought for JJ. I realise it might not quite match up to the rest of his excellent cellar, but of course it is still a very young wine, and a year or two on its side amid the Mission Haut-Brion and Ducru-Beaucaillou could result in something very interesting indeed.

Monday, December 24th

Was in Kippax's office bemoaning fact that I still hadn't a clue what to give Belinda, when he suddenly announced that he had been in exactly the same dilemma over Dorothy's birthday until someone had suggested this Mountbatten book there's been all the talk about, and apparently it had turned out to be one of the most successful presents he had ever given her.

In fact, had been thinking in terms of small piece of jewellery or a bottle of *eau de toilette*. On the other hand, a really nice book takes a lot of beating, and although B is not what you might call a bookworm and Mountbatten is not a name that features often in her conversation, Prince Charles certainly is, and his great-uncle was a man with whom she had a surprising amount in common. I think they'd have got on very well together. Rushed out to nearest bookshop only to discover that this putative relationship is now more academic than ever since the book in question is out of stock.

I said, "You don't mean out of print, do you?"

The man said, "I don't know what line of business you are in, but I happen to be a bookseller, and being closely involved with the world of words, I choose mine with care. If I wanted to say that the book was out of print, I am perfectly capable of expressing that fact clearly and unequivocally."

I said, "So it is out of print then?"

To my amazement, the fellow turned on his heel and started serving another customer. I wasn't about to take that sort of behaviour from anyone, literary or otherwise.

I said, "Excuse me, I wonder if I might have a word with the manager?"

The man said, "Do you mind? I happen to be serving someone."

"Yes," I said. "Me. Now then, I'd like to speak to the manager."

"There is no manager," he said. "I am the owner."

I said, "It may interest you to know that I am also in the communications business, and am equally aware of the power of words, especially when directed in the right ear."

He said, "You don't by any chance happen to be a publisher, do you?"

I said, "In a manner of speaking."

He said, "I don't know who you are or what firm you represent, but if you want to see your books on my shelves, I suggest you ring my secretary and make an appointment at a time that is mutually convenient."

I replied that the sort of people I was interested in in my business extended far beyond the narrow confines of a book-shop, and walked out.

Happen to notice that almost next door was a small shop selling second-hand books. To judge from the shelves full of brightly coloured dust jackets, some of them didn't look as second-hand as all that.

Slipped in while previous chap's back was turned and started browsing among shelves. Astonished to find that quite a few of the books had only just been published and that several of the titles rang bells from the literary pages of the *Telegraph*. And yet, there they were, being sold for only two-thirds of the advertised price.

When I asked the young salesman for an explanation, he said that these were all review copies which had been brought in by various Fleet Street literary editors and book reviewers.

I said, "So when they've finished with them, they give them to you?"

"Not give," he said. "Sell. Only the ones they don't want to keep for their own shelves or give to their friends for Christmas."

He told me that he paid them between a third and a half the jacket price.

I could hardly believe my ears.

I said, "Do you mean to tell me that there are people who give their friends review copies as Christmas presents?"

"Why not?" said the young man. "Who'd know the difference? As long as one remembers to take out the publisher's compliment slip first."

I said that it must be quite a lucrative sideline as far as literary editors were concerned, and no wonder authors made no money if half their books finished up at cut-rate prices in second-hand shops within weeks of publication.

"Sometimes even before publication," the young man said.

I said that since he was obviously so far ahead of everyone else in the game, the likelihood of his having a review copy of the Mountbatten book lurking on his shelves was presumably remote. He replied that, by a curious coincidence, one had come in only that morning.

"A reviewer with an unusually slow reading rate, perhaps," I said, with a laugh.

"I couldn't say," he said.

Had paid for the book when it suddenly occurred to me he might have a copy of the latest Alan Coren.

"I'll have to ask about that," he said, and going to a door at the back of the shop, he shouted, "Dad!" Whereupon through it walked the man I'd just had words with in the shop next door.

"It doesn't matter," I said, and fled.

Following a stupidly liquid lunch at the Coach and Horses, dashed to Marks & Sparks and by dint of what is known in the marketing world as "aggressive purchasing techniques" managed to buy a nightie for Mother. The assistant attempted to be helpful by asking what size she was and did I want the pink or the pale blue, but I told her she was wasting her time.

"Give me any size, any colour, any material," I said. "She's bound to change it whatever I get."

To toy shop next where I watched a man demonstrating a wonderful bath toy – a plastic fish with a large mouth, inside which was a small fish attached by its tail with a length of string. The action of pulling out the little fish wound up the big fish which then pursued the little fish by waggling its tail and finally ate it.

"It's almost existential, isn't it?" I said to the demonstrator.

"I wouldn't know about that," he said. "It says Made in Taiwan on the box."

Maddeningly, did not manage to get to Mazzarini & Block's, so will have to give the major his grandson's two bottles of Château Verdun for the time being and replace them later when all the excitement's died down.

Arrived home, tired but satisfied. What a joy it is at this festive and holy time to relax in the warmth and glow of family love with a large whisky and soda in one hand and a large helping of barbecue-roasted peanuts in the other. It all seems so right somehow, and so very much what the message of Christmas is all about that I can only curse myself at having wasted too many Christmas Eves in recent years, either in the flat watching Beddoes canoodling on the sofa with yet another in a long line of cheap doxies, or else in Kent with Mother watching Des O'Connor prancing around in a blazer looking pleased with himself.

True, I have always made a point of religiously tuning in to the *Service of Nine Lessons and Carols from King's College, Cambridge*, and the familiar words and the sound of the boy singing "Once in Royal David's" have never failed to move me in a strange and wonderful way; yet somehow I have always had this feeling at the back of my mind that this is not quite enough, that there is more to Christmas than a lump in the throat and a dampening of the eye, and that in some way I could never quite fathom, something was missing.

Now that I am blessed with a wonderful wife, a beautiful son, and a comfortable home, and know at last the joy of family life, just as Joseph must have known it all those years ago in Bethlehem – although admittedly in rather less congenial surroundings – I feel the least I can do is join millions of my fellow Christians all over the world in thanking God and singing loud Hosannas. I was only sorry that Belinda did not share my sentiments and that not only was she not feeling up

97

to joining me at Midnight Mass in Chelsea, but that she couldn't even face Clint Eastwood at nine thirty.

In fact, nodded off myself at one point and woke to find that it was eleven thirty and the televised service was already well under way. Leapt into the car and drove hell for leather to Chelsea. Arrived just as the last notes of "Oh Little Town" were dying away and made my way as discreetly as possible to a pew near the back. How reassuring it is to hear those familiar words again and how happy I am to find that there are still one or two churches left in this country that refuse to bow to the pedestrian and the hum-drum language of Series 3, and how right I was to plump for this church in which to introduce my son to the joys of Christian fellowship.

Quite apart from the service itself, the sort of people who worship there have that good solid, middle-class feeling to them, which is and always has been at the very heart of the Church of England as we know it.

Was particularly taken by a family a couple of rows in front and slightly to one side. The parents struck me as being the epitome of all that is best in English life – good looking, well-dressed, humorous, reliable: the sort of people you wouldn't mind being in the next seat to in the event of an airline disaster. The boy looked a bit drippy, but the girl was absolutely gorgeous. Very young still, and obviously a bit gauche, but with perfect features and a beautiful figure.

In fact the more I looked at her, the more beautiful she became in my eyes, and before I knew what, I was shocked to find that, instead of concentrating on the words of the service, all I could think about was what she would look like in bed without any clothes on. I suppose it's possible that I was not the only member of the congregation that evening whose thoughts were straying from the business in hand, but if so, they were certainly showing no signs of it.

My real concern, however, was not that any of them should wonder why I had gone so red in the face, but that God had looked into my heart and seen the wickedness therein and was even then dreaming up some way of giving me a sharp rap over the knuckles.

It is at moments like these that one finds oneself believing in the notion of original sin.

Tried desperately to drag my thoughts away from the girl and on to something more suitable, but however hard I tried, I was unable to do so for more than a second or two at a time before they winged their way back to those naked limbs in that bed.

Decided I was in no fit state to take Communion, but when my turn to go up, found myself setting off, as if compelled by some outside force. Realised with a shock that, by some strange logistical quirk, I was standing almost opposite the girl in the queue. She was even more beautiful close to. On a mad whim, decided that when both lines reached the altar, I would dart to my right and, with a bit of luck, would find myself kneeling next to her.

I cannot imagine how I thought I was going to make use of this cunning ploy: I would worry about that when the time came. In the event, there was a slight muddle, thanks to a couple on their way back to their seats slightly losing their way, and although as I knelt there, with my heart racing, I was convinced I could feel her presence beside me, when finally I plucked up the courage to turn my head and make some sort of eye contact, I found that I was smiling not at her but at her brother. What's more, he smiled back in a way that I can only describe as knowing.

Wasted no time in getting back to my seat and spent unnecessarily long time kneeling with my head in my hands, my mind a complete blank. Finally, looked across to find brother looking straight back at me and winking. Am beginning to wonder whether my previous estimate of the minimum age for church attendance may not have to be upped by several years.

Fortunately, got slightly caught up in the scrum leaving, and by the time I stepped out into the cocktail party atmosphere in the street, the whole family had disappeared.

Was driving home in pensive, not to say penitent, mood when suddenly a police car overtook me and waved me into the side of the road. Asked if I had been drinking, I could hardly deny it. To have done so would merely have compounded my sins. So I said that I had, but only Communion wine.

The policeman sighed. "Pull the other one, sir. It's got bells on." And he handed me the breathalyser bag.

"You're very lucky, sir," he said when I had finished blowing. "You're on the line. Take my advice. Go home and get a good night's sleep. Happy Christmas."

God certainly does move in a mysterious way, and so did I when I got home, wrapped my two presents, and slipped JJ's into the pillowcase at the foot of his crib and B's under the Christmas tree.

To bed at last with some strange and peculiarly un-Christmassy dreams.

Tuesday, December 25th

Three Christians awoke and saluted the happy morn rather earlier than most in SW9 when the dog took it into her stupid head to march into JJ's room shortly after four and attack his pillowcase. Not content with that, she then wandered into our room, jumped up onto the bed and proceeded to hump B's sleeping form in a persistent and most unattractive fashion. We all managed to get back to sleep again at last somewhere around six. B would happily have gone on sleeping till ten or later, had I not reminded her several times that the children's service at Chelsea was at nine thirty, and that unless we got there a good ten minutes early, we'd find ourselves having to stand at the back. As a result, not the most Christianlike start to a day I have ever known.

Set off after scrappy sort of breakfast at nine fifteen. Or rather, when I say nine fifteen, that was the time we closed the front door and started to get into the car. By the time we'd actually set off it was nine twenty. Realised there was by now no chance of getting to Chelsea on time, so decided to cut losses and made instead for St Mungo's, who, for reasons best known to themselves, had begun at nine fifteen. Arrived to find completely full church, so had to squash up alongside West Indian family right at back on far side and behind huge pillar. Managed to join in last verse of "Hark the Herald Angels" (why is it that *everybody* always refuses to sing it the way Mendelssohn wrote it?) and was beginning to relax when my worst fears were realised and suddenly, without any warning whatever, we were all being urged to embrace our next-door neighbours.

Luckily, B had the excuse of a sleeping baby in her arms and got out of it, so it was left to me to do honours with entire West Indian family who were clearly all for clasping me to their joint bosom, but had to make do with a polite handshake all round. They seemed rather disappointed.

As if that were not unnerving enough, we then realised that all the children in the congregation were supposed to have brought little gifts for their less privileged counterparts in the Third World, which they then carried up to the altar where they were to be blessed by the Bishop of Brixton. Was on the point of suggesting to B that it was time we were on our way when the West Indian lady handed a small packet wrapped in bright red paper with robins all over it. "We always bring a spare," she said. "For those who are not familiar with our ways at St Mungo's."

Quite how it came about that I found myself on my own, without JJ, on my way to the altar, the only adult in a stream of small children, I shall never quite understand. At all events could hardly be blamed if I did not join forces with rest of congregation in "Oh Come All Ye Faithful" with quite my usual verve.

Religion's a funny thing. Less than twelve hours earlier I was entering into the spirit of things in no uncertain terms, yet this morning I could not have felt less pious if I'd tried.

On my way home in car found myself humming tune of "He Who Would Valiant Be 'Gainst All Disaster". The words have never had more significance.

After coffee and slice of Christmas cake (bought, unfortunately, but then B has had an awful lot on her plate this year), we opened the presents. JJ seemed moderately pleased with his fish; ditto the thing full of plastic objects which are meant to hang on a cord across his cot, which was from both of us. I daresay he'll be a bit more enthusiastic when he has a cot.

Paula Batty's head in the shape of a tomato which plays "London Bridge is Falling Down" when you pull a string at the bottom and rolls its eyes at the same time, undoubtedly the pick of the bunch as far as he was concerned, followed closely by Bryant-Fenn's towelling-covered duck which makes a sort of quacking noise when you jiggle it up and down. It had a slightly second-hand look to it, I thought.

B expressed mild delight at JJ's box of assorted Olde English hand soaps, and genuine pleasure at the Mountbatten book. She said that she had once met him backstage at a theatre.

"Of course, he wasn't my type at all," she said, "but I've always been a great admirer of Edwina's. That biography of her is supposed to be marvellous." I'm only sorry I hadn't bought her that instead, especially in view of the publisher's review slip that fell out the moment she opened it. How I could have missed it I can't think.

Must admit, the possibility of her buying me a household toolkit was one that had never entered my mind. She said, "No self-respecting head of a family should be without one."

Whether this is meant to be a tacit sign of approval of my plans for Pear Tree Farm I am not quite sure. At all events, it is definitely a step in the right direction and I look forward to handling my ratchet screwdriver and claw hammer under field conditions at the earliest possible opportunity.

To Kent slightly later than we had anticipated.

Our arrival marginally uneasier than it need have been, owing to Vita insisting on attempting to roger Mother's cat. To my mind the cat was definitely egging her on, but Mother couldn't see it that way.

"That animal should see a psychiatrist," she said.

No comment.

Had imagined that the presence of her grandson would have been more than enough to ensure an atmosphere of peace on earth and goodwill to all men for the short time our visit lasted, but Mother unable to resist the occasional short sharp jab to the ribs, beginning with,

"Well, I don't know. Maybe my eyesight's not what it was, but I can't see anything of Simon in him."

B remarkably restrained in circumstances.

She said, politely, "I don't suppose you could see much of yourself in him at that age."

A rather chilly dry sherry was followed by a hot, moist turkey and all the trimmings, and a surprisingly good bottle of Côtes du Ventoux. Unfortunately, Mother is not what you might call a drinker and I felt it was the wine rather than a delicate desire to upset B that made her reminisce at quite such length about all the wonderful Christmases she and I had spent together over the years, and how B couldn't possibly understand it now, but what a blow it is to a mother when her children desert the nest.

She then rose unsteadily to her feet, lifted her glass and proposed a toast to "Loved ones far away."

"To Nigel and Priscilla," I said.

"And James," said B.

Whereupon Mother dissolved into floods of tears and rushed from the room. Fortunately, she regained her composure in time for the Christmas pudding which she had filled with silver threepenny bits – "Just as I always used to when you were a little boy."

How extraordinary it is to think that there are people now who have never seen a silver threepenny bit in their lives, let alone nearly broken a tooth on one.

After coffee, we all opened our presents. Soap and bathsalts for B, a Marks & Sparks pullover for me and a cheque for five pounds for JJ. Mother seemed moderately pleased with her nightie and said that the great thing about Marks & Sparks is that they're always very happy to change anything. JJ's Society for the Preservation of Wild Birds calendar and matching telephone note-pad and pencil also much appreciated. Ditto, dog's box of After Eights.

In fact the atmosphere, not to say the sitting-room, had warmed up to such an extent that when B looked at her watch at three and suggested it was time we were on our way, I felt almost as loth to break the party up as Mother.

Must admit that, as we drove off towards the M25, seeing her forlorn rather bent figure getting smaller and smaller in the rear-view mirror, a lump came to my throat and tears to my eyes. There were tears of quite a different sort when we found ourselves stuck in a huge traffic jam just outside Charing.

B's explanation that we were not the only ones visiting our families on Christmas Day, though possibly true, did not wholly account for the fact that so many of the families in question appeared to live along the A20. Fog on motorway near Wootton Bassett didn't help. It was well after five by the time we reached Stroud and nearly half past when we finally drew up outside Tebbit's Farm.

Alyson said, "Oh you've just missed tea."

"Never mind," said the major, "you're just in time for some of the cold variety" and poured me one of the biggest whiskies I have ever seen in my life. Tim looked as if he'd had several already.

By the time we'd unpacked, settled JJ for the night and changed into evening dress, it was time for more drinks.

The major was opening a bottle of Château Palmer when I came in. When he heard that I'd been helping B to bath the baby and put him to bed, he said, "Each to his own, but I wouldn't have called it man's work myself."

Dinner was first class in every department, despite the rather silly argument I had with Tim re shooting. But then he really was rather drunk by then.

Finally turned to the major and asked him to tell me how he could possibly justify the killing of beautiful and innocent creatures who have as much right to live as we do.

"It's very simple," he said. "I happen to like it."

Frankly there's no talking to people like that.

After dinner, we exchanged Christmas presents. The major said that he had never heard of Château Verdun, but that he would certainly accord it suitable treatment. Alyson said that the bath essence was her favourite, and Tim said it was a pity his doctor had made him give up smoking, but he supposed that a small Dutch half-corona from time to time wouldn't do him any lasting harm.

B was understandably pleased with her cheque; JJ's cuff-links, though slightly premature to my way of thinking, were much appreciated and I'm sure my game of Trivial Pursuit is going to afford us many hours of pleasure in the months to come.

"We thought it sounded rather you," Alyson said.

Am still not quite sure how to take it. Or the Pedalows, for that matter.

Wednesday, December 26th

Woke early with splitting headache and stiff neck – the result, no doubt, of one of the most punishing Christmas Days I have ever known, or wish to know. If this is any indication of family life, it's small wonder so many comparatively young men are dying from heart attacks.

The shooting party began to arrive soon after breakfast in Range Rovers etc. Six in all, with dogs and wives in head-scarves. (I mean, the wives were wearing the scarves, not the dogs.) Vita managed to hump a labrador and a springer before being collared and shut in the car.

Despite being one of the family, felt oddly out of place in my skiing anorak and Russian fur hat.

One wife of about Belinda's age, with a pinched angular sort of face you could open a beer bottle on, said, "We haven't met."

This was true.

The major who happened to be passing at the time said, "I'm so sorry. Deidre Potterton . . . Simon . . . son-in-law."

"Really?" she said. Then, "Tell me, where did you get that hat? Is it one of Belinda's?"

"As a matter of fact," I said casually, "I got it in Moscow."

"Oh," she said. "You're not a Commie or anything, are you?"

Was tempted to tell her I was a dissident who had spent ten years in a Siberian prison camp before being exchanged for an East German ballet dancer, but knowing how hopeless people are at recognising irony, decided to let it go.

Instead, I said, "I promise I'll tell you, but only if you first tell me your bra size."

She gave a lop-sided smile, which I took to be her idea of

suggestive, and said in a low voice, "Actually, I don't wear a bra."

I replied conspiratorially, "And actually, I am a Communist, but don't tell anyone and I won't tell anyone about you."

As she walked off to join her husband, I couldn't help reflecting that if this was any indication of the level of humour one could expect to meet in the country, then I could well imagine myself following the example of people like John Fowles and William Trevor and keeping myself to myself.

Since B was looking a bit peaky, decided to stay behind and join guns after lunch.

The major said, "I thought you probably would."

Spent as happy and relaxed a morning as I can remember in a long while, stretched out in an armchair in front of a huge fire, reading back numbers of *Harpers & Queen* and *The Field*.

Lunched alone with B and Alyson. Smoked salmon, sandwiches and Chablis. Afterwards, left them both comparing breast-feeding notes while I drove out to find the guns at Prior's Bottom, taking Vita with me on the lead.

Afternoon less happy than morning, owing to fact that Vita slipped her collar, and before I could catch her, had humped everything in sight, including a dead pheasant. Mother may be right. I may well have to see someone about her. I wonder if dog psychiatry comes under my domestic pet insurance? I also made myself rather unpopular with the major by cheering every time a bird got through the guns unscathed.

An extraordinary conversation took place at dinner. It seems that when Tim and Vanessa were first married, he approached the local vicar and bought two adjoining burial plots in the churchyard, one for himself and one for Vanessa. Now that they are divorced and she is living with someone else, he no longer wishes, quite naturally, to be buried next to her, but doesn't know quite how to get out of it. Should he sell his plot to his ex-wife's boyfriend? Or buy her plot and hang on to it on the off-chance he gets married again? Or sell both plots back to the vicar? Or what? Can burial plots be bought and sold like flats and houses, and if so, do they go up in value like other property? In which case, how much should he be asking, or paying, for Vanessa's plot?

What really worries him is that one of them might die unexpectedly before an alternative arrangement can be made and he could finish up next to her willy-nilly.

I'm afraid I wasn't able to shed any useful light on the matter, nor was anyone else. However, it gave the major the opportunity to enquire whether I had taken out a life insurance, and if so, for how much.

"Belinda is your responsibility now," he said. "And more importantly, so is young John."

"John Julius actually," I said.

He said, "I have never heard of anyone being referred to by both his Christian names. Is this some new London fashion that has yet to reach us here in the country? Perhaps I should now insist on Alyson calling me Claud Andrew every time she addresses me."

In fact, I'm really rather glad he brought the subject up. I have been only too painfully aware for some time that I have made no provision for my wife or son in the event of my sudden demise, and it is high time I did so.

Whether it was thoughts of mortality and the faint sound of time's winged chariot hurrying near I don't know, but have never felt quite so keen on Belinda as I did when we finally retired that evening.

To my delight, my feelings were more than reciprocated. It was just like that weekend at the Spread Eagle in Midhurst all over again. B said she thought it had something to do with being back in her old home and feeling she ought not to be getting up to things with her parents sleeping only a few feet away, but risking it anyway. I daresay Dr Freud would have something to say on the subject. All I know is that last night we took the dying embers of our physical relationship and coaxed them into flame in no uncertain terms. If this is the effect that sleeping under the same roof as one's parents can have on one's wife, perhaps we should suggest they come and live with us on a permanent basis!

Despite a rather shaky start, a very happy Christmas indeed!

Thursday, December 27th

A glorious day. Up early and off to the office, leaving B and John Julius at Tebbit's Farm for the rest of the week. The fresh air will do them both good. Tim has apparently decided to take the rest of the week off, and next Monday too, his argument being that since most of the people he deals with close up for a fortnight around Christmas and the New Year, what is the point in trying to carry on as if everything were back to normal? I said I didn't know who these people were whom he dealt with, but that I suspected they were very much in the minority, and that frankly if people like us, who had been brought up and educated at great expense to be the nation's leaders, did not give a firm moral lead and show a proper sense of responsibility, then we might as well all give up and go and jump in the sea. I think I made my point.

Despite heavy traffic and large crowds in the West End and along the Strand, area round the office comparatively empty and was able to find a meter opposite front door.

Astonished to find no sign of anyone. Nightingale and Hebblethwaite did warn me they might be late. Charlie, of course, is away in Wengen as usual, but I would certainly have expected to find Pam and Karen at their desks by ten fifteen.

Sat down to compose sharp memos all round when I happened to spot a note stuck in my typewriter. It said: "Came in at nine as requested, but as no sign of you by ten, assumed you have decided to take morning off. Possibly day. Have gone to sales with Karen. Will call later. Hope you had a happy Christmas. Luv Pamela."

Someone is heading for big trouble if they go on the way they're going.

Returned to my office and made a long list of people to be rung, starting with Ski Time. By eleven, I must have made at least a dozen calls, and yet not a single one of my clients appeared to be at his or her desk. Left a number of terse messages on answering machines where appropriate, and spent rest of morning trying to finalise press list for Les Vals.

Nothing from the girls all morning, so at twelve thirty locked up and went to lunch. Arrived downstairs to find street completely deserted, except for my car and Clamp Unit busy attaching device to my front wheel. Could not believe my eyes. I told them in no uncertain terms that it was a fine lookout for this country when a man is penalised for trying to set an example to others and putting in an honest day's work while the rest of the nation lounges around with their feet up in front of their television sets watching Tarzan movies.

One of the men said, "Was there a Tarzan film on this morning? If I had known I'd have got the wife to tape it on the video."

The other said, "I know there was a Sherlock Holmes on BBC. That one about the snake that comes down the chimney and bites the old geezer on the ear."

"You're not thinking of the one about the thumb, are you?" said the other.

I said, "It's *The Speckled Band*, and actually it came down the bellrope."

"The thumb did?" said the second man.

"Sounds more like Tarzan," said the first.

"Are you sure there was a Tarzan film on today?" said the second.

I said that if they'd be kind enough to remove the clamp, we could all go home and find out for ourselves.

The first man said he was very sorry, but once the clamp was fitted, he couldn't undo it again.

I said that I didn't see why not, since he had the key and it was surely a simple matter of reversing the procedure he had just carried out.

He said he was afraid it wasn't as simple as that at all, and that although, technically speaking, he was able to undo the lock, from a procedural point of view it was quite out of the question until the fine had been paid and the paper work put in order.

I said that I was perfectly happy to pay up there and then and reached for my cheque-book, but the man said that he was very sorry but he was not authorised to accept payment. His job began and ended with the actual clamp work, and that I would have to go to the Clamp Office near Marble Arch and pay the fine there, whereupon in due course another team would come and remove the clamp and I would be at liberty to proceed on my way.

I asked him how much the fine was. He told me twenty-seven pounds fifty.

"All right, then," I said. "Fifty pounds in cash, in your pocket, now, no questions asked."

The first man said, "You wouldn't be trying to bribe us, by any chance, would you, sir?"

"Call it a Christmas box," I said.

"I'd call it very naughty indeed," said the man. "And you're trying to tell us you were setting a good example to others?"

I pointed out that although he couldn't possibly have known it, I was co-ordinator of my local Neighbourhood Watch Scheme and that in a way we were very much on the same side, if not actual colleagues in the non-stop fight to keep crime off the streets of London.

At this, they both adopted a very different tone indeed and we were soon comparing notes on the effect of the clamp on illegal parking figures and chatting away with the same sort of easy camaraderie that I imagine you find in police stations up and down the country.

I said, "When you come to think about it, all this time you've spent dealing with this one vehicle you could have been in the West End really teaching people a sharp lesson."

The first man said, "What, and clutter the streets up with even more stationary vehicles?"

And with that he slapped a large sticky notice right across my windscreen and the two of them wished me a Happy New Year and drove off up the empty street.

By the time I'd found a taxi and struggled all the way up to Marble Arch and back, it was nearly two o'clock, and nearly three by the time they came and removed the clamp.

Had been planning to slip along to Lillywhites and see if I could find myself a decent pair of skiing gloves, but by that time I was so exhausted that all I wanted to do was go home and lie down.

Arrived back to find that Harbottle had parked his blooming great Volvo Estate slap outside my front door, yet again. As a result had to park the Polo on the other side of the road, risking a nasty donk on the wing from lunatics who will insist on using Valderma Road as a short cut. As an ex-coordinator of the local Neighbourhood Watch Scheme, he ought to know better.

Finally managed to relight boiler, using *ad hoc* spills made from sports pages of *Telegraph* and settled down with whisky and soda in front of TV, only to be confronted by comic film about traffic wardens. In the circumstances, even Tarzan would have been preferable.

Had a pork pie and a pint at The Cricketers and went to bed with mild indigestion and a longing for B that was almost unbearable.

Virtue has certainly not been its own reward today as far as I am concerned.

Friday, December 28th

Woke very early with a shock to realise that in all excitement of the last few weeks, I had completely forgotten to get in touch with the private health insurance people about claiming back maternity expenses on account of complications.

Rang their Eastbourne office shortly after breakfast to be greeted by very silly voice on answering machine informing me that the office was closed until Wednesday January 2nd, but if I'd like to leave my name and telephone number etcetera . . . Did so, adding sharp postscript to the effect that ill-health was not something that took advantage of public holidays and put its feet up, even if they did. I shall be interested to hear their reaction.

A messenger arrived soon after I did, bringing a belated Christmas present from Bryant-Fenn in the form of a book entitled *Families and How to Survive Them*, written by Robin Skynner and John Cleese, of all people. The paperback edition, needless to say. Imagine it had been sent to Hugh to review by one of the many obscure publications for which he "writes". To spend three pounds ninety-five voluntarily would be completely against his principles. Although I have no doubt that it was meant to be a gentle leg-pull on his part,

III

the fact is that the joke has rather backfired on him, since, despite the humorous cover, the book is a serious attempt to explain in simple, straightforward language how relationships work and what to do if they don't.

I could not be a happier or prouder father if I tried, and although B and I have never enjoyed what one might call a lovey-dovey marriage à la Philippe and Theresa, we do rub along fairly well, which is the main thing. On the other hand, there are one or two aspects of family life on which I am not entirely clear – to wit: the fact that I do not appear to be accorded quite the degree of respect to which I feel that, as *paterfamilias* and breadwinner, I am entitled. Indeed, there are times when I get the feeling that the dog takes me more seriously than my wife does. It's hard enough having to wrestle with the Pedalow family for a scrap of B's attention without also having to do psychological battle with my infant son.

Who better to help me along the road to a greater under-standing than the founder of the Institute of Family Therapy and author of *One Flesh: Separate Persons*, aided and abetted by the greatest comic genius *de nos jours*? I doubt I shall ever feel the need to submit to group therapy as John once did; I have never been a great believer in the "let-it-all-hang-out" school of behaviour, nor do I wish to spend valuable free time seated, having organised shouting matches with people: I get quite enough of that at home.

On the other hand, a man of John's intelligence and percep-tion who has had such a long experience of group work, can hardly fail to have a lot of interesting things to say on the subject.

Indeed, so much do they both have to say and so relevant is their every utterance to life at Château Crisp that although I had fully intended to spend all morning finalising the Ski Time press trip guest list, I was unable to drag myself away from the book for a single second. *Tant mieux*, as it turned out, since I got a call just before lunch from Valjean to say that they had been rethinking the press trip and had decided instead to run a familiarisation trip for a few selected travel agents; and that although they felt it would be useful for me to come along as well, it was the sort of event they would prefer to handle themselves. Saturday, January 19th to Saturday, January 26th are the proposed dates.

I am sorry that B will not be coming with me, but a few days on my own away from the pressures of family life, amid the grandeur and solitude of the mountains, could well provide me with a much-needed opportunity for quiet contemplation and a general recharging of batteries all round.

Saturday, December 29th

A letter from Beddoes to say that he is thrilled and honoured to be asked to be godfather to John Julius and that by a curious coincidence he and Bobby are coming to England on Friday, January 11th, and is there perhaps a chance we might be able to find a bed for them for a few nights?

It is, of course, a well-known fact that men who display an inordinate sexual appetite for women do so in order to conceal their deep underlying homosexuality. I had often suspected this might be the case with Beddoes, but until now I have come up with no concrete evidence to support my suspicion. I daresay many men in my position would, faced with a similar situation, reconsider the advisability of landing their son with a godfather who has so blatantly stepped out of the closet. I take a more liberal line myself. However, while I am perfectly prepared to overlook my old friend's predilections, even to the extent of allowing him and his friend to put up in some rudimentary way on the sitting-room floor for a couple of nights, I think it might be a wise precaution if he were not actually to kiss the baby. I must also warn B to give their cups and cutlery particularly vigorous attention in the washing-up bowl.

After washing up breakfast, doing a little light dusting in the sitting-room and giving the loo a good going over with Liquid Ajax, settled down with Cleese and Skynner and was just getting stuck into section on "Influence of the father" and the need for Dad to step forward and reclaim his place as husband and lover, when B rang to say that I would be down for lunch, wouldn't I, since the Gurney-Richards were coming in for drinks and were dying to meet me. I said I thought this was probably an exaggeration, but that anyway this pleasure would have to be postponed, since I had rather a lot on my plate with Neighbourhood Watch Scheme work and would almost certainly not be able to get away much before teatime.

Needless to say, B wanted to know exactly what I had on my plate. I explained that there were still one or two households that hadn't had their window stickers saying they were part of the scheme, and that since it was a well-known fact that more burglaries were committed over the Christmas holiday when people were away than at any other time of the year, it was imperative I distributed them as soon as possible.

She said, "If everybody's away, as you say, there won't be anyone at home to give the stickers to, will there?"

I pointed out that a) not everyone in Brixton is lucky enough to have parents with beautiful homes in Gloucestershire where they can retire for the festive season, and that b) burglars spend a lot of time sitting in anonymous-looking cars watching the comings and goings in a particular street, and if they see someone with a folder under his arm and a pile of stickers in his hand going round knocking on doors, they might well be scared off.

"On the other hand," she said, "they might think you're canvassing for the SDP."

I'm afraid that, despite my very best intentions, sharp words were exchanged at this point, the upshot of which was that if I wasn't down there in time to meet the Gurney-Richards for drinks before lunch, she couldn't answer for the consequences, and could I remember to bring down a new box of nappy liners? I'd find them beside the dressing-table in the bedroom.

Looked up various sections in Cleese and Skynner in hope of finding reasonable explanation for this unreasonable behaviour, including "Imbalance in personality", "Parental firmness", "Coping with change" and "Madness and extremism", but none seemed to fit this particular bill.

Could well assume self to be a classic case of a hen-pecked husband. However, whatever failings I have – and I certainly have my fair share – no-one could possibly accuse me of being

114

a man who "won't take responsibility, stand up for himself and look after his wife properly". *Au contraire.*

After a further bout of soul – not to say page – searching, finally found answer on page seventy-one, under heading "Demands of the baby". Skynner explains that before the baby arrives, a couple are both free to give each other emotional support, but that once the baby is around, the mother needs even more love and support from her husband than usual, but because she's dishing out so much emotion to the baby, there's nothing left over to give the poor husband in return. He's telling me.

Arrived at Tebbit's Farm at twelve forty-five after hair-raising drive to find Gurney-Richards had cancelled at last moment.

The major said, "We didn't press the point. We assumed you wouldn't be coming."

Following rather alcoholic lunch, attempted to explain to B Cleese and Skynner's thing about emotional demands of baby on marriage. All she said was, "There's not a lot to choose between them, but I'd say John Cleese is even more attractive than David Owen. In fact, I sent off my subscription to the SDP only this morning."

As clear a case of "madness and extremism" as I've come across in a long time.

Instead of joining her and JJ on walk to Lawson's Field, retired upstairs to study section on depression. Rather surprised to learn that sadness can be healthy. Not when accompanied by a corking headache, surely?

Sunday, December 30th

A potentially peaceful, life-enhancing family breakfast transformed into a bout of mental bear-baiting when the major suddenly took it into his head to grill me over the sausages on the question of life insurance. There's nothing more irritating than having one's wrist slapped over some matter that one knows very well one ought to have dealt with weeks previously.

Would never have believed it possible that a man so lacking in imagination could have dreamed up quite so many potential scenarios for my sudden demise. I agree, it's perfectly possible that I might reach across the table for the coffee pot and suffer a massive coronary: ditto that I might tomorrow trip and fall under a tube train at Holborn station. God forbid, as the major himself added at frequent intervals – though not perhaps quite as whole-heartedly as one might have hoped. On the other hand, with the best will in the world, I simply cannot believe that I shall end my days in the fierce embrace of a grizzly in Yellowstone National Park or the chance victim of a jousting accident.

At all events, assured him that I would do something about it first thing on Monday morning, thinking that would be an end of the matter. However, by now he had got the financial bit firmly between his teeth, and before I knew what, we were deeply embroiled in a hypothetical discussion concerning our future domestic arrangements in the light of our changed circumstances. He said, "Naturally I have made certain financial provisions both for my daughter and my grandson, but these need not concern you at this stage." I replied that, as a man who had made his own way in the world without any financial help from his family or anyone else, I had always been a firm believer in standing on one's own feet and not relying on anyone else, and had no intention of changing tack at this comparatively late stage of my life. He said he was glad to hear it.

Was naturally tempted to enquire as to the precise nature of these "financial provisions", but did not wish to appear too interested, so said nothing and reached for the coffee pot. Curiously enough, thought I felt a slight twinge in my chest, but it was probably just a touch of indigestion.

The major and Alyson seemed quite surprised when we said we were returning to London in the afternoon and not spending New Year's Eve with them. I reminded them that Monday was a working day and that we wanted to get ahead with plans for the christening. I thought they both seemed rather relieved.

As we were putting the last few bits and pieces in the car, the major came up and said, "I can't pretend to understand your way of life or your means of paying for it, but I suppose you know what you're doing."

I said, "It must be very difficult for a man to entrust his daughter into the hands of another, but I can only ask you to trust me."

"That's exactly what her last husband said," he replied.

Rang the Rev. Paul Niblock at Chelsea the moment we arrived home re the christening and he has suggested we all go and see him at the vicarage tomorrow evening at six.

Spent half an hour this evening studying the Public Baptism of Infants service. I hope this does not mean we can expect to be playing host to any Tom, Dick or Harry who takes it into his head to walk in off the street. Although it is some years since I last attended a baptism per se, the time-honoured words of the centuries-old service strike a familiar and comforting note.

Am wondering how the godparents are going to react to the vicar's question as to whether they are prepared, in the name of John Julius, to renounce the devil and all his works, the vain pomp and glory of the world, with all covetous desires of the same and the carnal desires of the flesh.

Paula Batty will doubtless have little difficulty singing out that she renounces them all, but a professional freeloader and *bon viveur* like Bryant-Fenn might find the words stick rather more awkwardly in his throat, and if Beddoes isn't made to look very foolish indeed, then he's a very much better actor than I give him credit for.

At all events, I feel totally confident that John Julius will manfully fight under Christ's banner against sinner, the world and the devil, and I simply cannot wait for him to become His faithful soldier and servant.

Monday, December 31st

The last day of the Old Year and one which lives on in my memory, and I daresay Belinda's too, as the most momentous in our lives. Yet for all the joy and comfort that family life has brought me in the last few weeks, and despite the fact that at long last I feel I know what it is to be a man, I'd be the last to pretend that I am without my occasional flaws and short-comings.

What better moment than the eve of a New Year to take stock of myself and my life and make a few serious resolutions as to how both could be improved in the months to come?

Attempted to draft out a working list when I got to the office, but was surprised to find that it was a great deal harder than I had imagined. Jotted down a few obvious things like watching less television, reading *Pride and Prejudice*, putting Pamela van Zeller firmly in her place once and for all, being more Christian-like, giving up coffee from the machine on the fourth floor etc, but thereafter became completely stuck.

Any further efforts sharply curtailed by the arrival – un-heralded, needless to say – of Pamela with a long list of her own, comprising suggestions for future promotions on behalf of Botticelli. Clearly her success at the Christmas lunch has gone to her head and this is her way of giving notice that she is bidding to take over the account herself. Could have disil-lusioned her there and then, but have always held that it is bad luck to put New Year resolutions into effect before January 1st. There'll be time enough to sort out the pecking order once and for all, and in the meantime, it won't do her any harm to *think* she's doing better than she really is.

To Chelsea after work to meet up with B and JJ at the vicarage. Mr Niblock a nice but rather wishy-washy type who, almost before we had sat down, had started on a lengthy set piece about the number of middle-class parents who ask him to baptise their children only because they think it's the socially acceptable thing to do and they've been pressurised into it by their families, and how very few of them bother to sit down and give serious thought to what baptism means.

He said that everyone nowadays is far too obsessed with making money, and the acquisition of material things to take account of spiritual values.

B assumed a suitably contrite expression and nodded solemnly throughout, but I'm afraid to say I took a rather different line. I said that that was a very sweeping generalisation and one of those old chestnuts that all vicars trot out without thinking, and that most young people nowadays were not obsessed with making money at all: it just looked that way simply because everything cost so much they had to keep their noses to the grindstone purely in order to make ends meet. What's more, he was quite wrong to suppose that the wearing of Babours and green wellington boots and the owning of pedigree dogs automatically signified a complete lack of interest in things spiritual. I myself took a keen interest in religion, had always considered myself a lively limb, albeit a rather minor one, in the body of the church and indeed had received the sacrament from his very hands only a few days previously.

Niblock duly chastened by this passionate and unexpected outburst and quickly started backtracking, saying that he was merely expressing a general concern etc etc. He finally recovered his composure sufficiently to enquire after the names of the godparents, whether they had all been baptised, if they were regular churchgoers, etc. Feeling that we were very possibly borderline cases in his eyes anyway, and not wishing to risk being shown the vestry door, I said yes to all of them, but at the same time firmly crossing my toes.

He then asked if we had any further questions. I said only that I had often wondered what baptism signified in pre-Christian times. After all, John the Baptist had obviously been baptising people long before Jesus came on the scene. Niblock replied that it was an interesting question and that quite honestly he'd never thought about it before and would obviously have to do a little homework before we next met.

I'm beginning to wonder if he's really the right man for the job. On the other hand, his heart appears to be in the right place and he obviously relishes the cut and thrust of intellectual debate which I have brought to the proceedings.

At all events, he has booked us in for three o'clock on Sunday week. I hope that suits everyone.

Had thought of inviting a few people round to see the New Year in, but thank heavens we didn't. A couple of hours on the sofa with my beloved wife, basking in the warmth of family life and the Cosiglow gas heater is worth a thousand paper hats and squeakers and ten thousand of Bryant-Fenn's dubious jokes.

January

Tuesday, January 1st

An unfortunate start to the New Year. I leaned across the bed with the intention of giving Belinda a friendly pinch and punch for the first of the month, but blow me down if she didn't choose that particular moment to move her position. As a result I finished up by sticking my finger hard into her right eye. Her vision is still rather blurred but the casualty people at Moorfields seem to think the damage is not permanent. I hope this isn't a bad omen for the year ahead.

The maddening thing is, I had hoped to slip round to all my Neighbourhood Watch people and make a list of the ones who might be interested in borrowing the invisible marker – when the police finally manage to get a new one. On the other hand, B's protracted visit to the hospital did enable me to spend more time on my own with John Julius than at any time since he was born. I am only sorry he should have thrown away the opportunity for the establishment of some important parent-child identification by squawking loudly and virtually non-stop for two and a half hours. Gripe-water completely ineffective; ditto jiggling up and down of fluffy duck, playing of musical tomato, rocking of cradle etc.

Naturally, the first thing B wanted to know when she got back looking like a female version of Black Jake, with a large patch over her eye, was what I had done to him. I suppose I should be used by now to the concept of the head of the family as universal scapegoat, but somehow it is a role that sits no more easily and happily on my shoulders now than it did on our honeymoon night at the Kinnock Hotel. Cannot somehow believe that Prince Charles submits uncomplainingly to the lash of his wife's tongue every time one of his boys decides to turn on the royal waterworks. Who knows, though? I'd love to get together with him one of these days over a cherry brandy or two and compare notes.

After a cold lunch and an even colder walk on Clapham Common, in the course of which Vita wrestled a Rotweiler to the ground and sank a remote-controlled speedboat on the pond, B and I settled to a trial game of Trivial Pursuit.

There's a quotation printed on the outside of the box, ascribed mysteriously to some anonymous carpenters, which says, "It's yesterday once more". It certainly wasn't as far as I was concerned. But then my yesterdays were not totally taken up with the ins and outs of the hit parade, the private lives of pop singers and the cast lists of popular TV comedy shows. I fared reasonably well on the literary and political questions and current affairs – eg "How frequently is Punch magazine published?" "Which POW camp was the subject of Airey Neave's *They Have Their Exits*?" "What British dependency voted 12,138 to 44 in favour of retaining British rule in 1967?" "What cricket commentator was awarded an OBE in 1970?" etc. But I'm afraid that questions like "What colours were the curtains in Cream's *White Room*?" and "Who played lead guitar on Led Zeppelin's 'Whole Lotta Love?'" and "What was Mr Clampett senior's Christian name?" had me completely stumped. So did the answers.

B on the other hand, seemed to know the answer to every single question that came her way; not only the fact that the line that follows "Boy, you've been a naughty girl" in *I Am the Walrus* is "You let your knickers down"; but Cheyenne's surname, the name of the late guitarist whose great grandmother was a Cherokee Indian, and the type of engine that the NSU Ro 80 was the first car to be fitted with in 1968.

It was only after she had won three games hands down that it occurred to me that the vast majority of the questions stemmed from the 1960s and 1970s and there was almost nothing of what might loosely be called *general* knowledge. When I pointed this out to B, she replied coolly,

"Of course. This is the Baby Boomer edition. For the under forties."

Why I had not noticed the words "Baby Boomer" printed all over the box and on the question cards, I simply can't imagine. I suppose because I wasn't looking for them. It is not an expression in common usage amongst the sort of people I mix with, nor am I entirely clear what it means now that it has been brought to my attention. I am even less clear as to whether there is an extra subtle layer of humour intended by my parents-in-law or whether they simply picked it up off the shelf in Harrods, without looking very carefully, assuming it to be the basic game.

At all events, told Belinda that while in no way wishing to cast aspersions on her deep and very real knowledge of the period in question, I could see little point in continuing to take part in a contest in which I suffered from the inherent disadvantage of having one hand tied behind my back from the word go.

Belinda said, "Why not admit you're just a bad loser?" Did not pursue the matter. After supper, sat next to her on the sofa and said how very happy I was and how much I had enjoyed our quiet New Year's Eve together. She said, "I don't think I've ever spent a more depressing evening in my life. The first minutes of the New Year should be spent celebrating with friends, not as a gruesome twosome." I seem to be in what is known nowadays as a "no-win situation".

Wednesday, January 2nd

The way my luck's running at the moment, the next 364 days cannot go fast enough for my liking.

The day began disastrously enough with a letter from Mr Jarvis of Price Feltwell saying that, after due consideration and taking into account the present structural condition of Pear Tree Farm, the possible costs involved in making good, the asking price and the level of house prices in the area, he did not feel he could honestly recommend our purchasing it.

This was followed by a phone call to the private patients

people who said that, whatever I had been told to the contrary, and no matter what other similar organisations did in comparable conditions, they did not consider that the use of forceps during the course of delivery constituted a complication, unlike, say, a birth by Caesarean section.

I replied that if they would care to get in touch with Mr Armstrong who had delivered the baby, he would confirm that the birth had been quite complicated. The girl at the other end said that she would *not* care to get in touch with Mr Armstrong, since their rules were quite specific on the point, and that even if Mr Armstrong had been obliged to call upon the services of a tractor and pulley to bring the child into the world, they would not pay a penny towards it.

A stiff note to the BMA might not go amiss.

As for Pear Tree Farm, I cannot believe that this is the end of the story by any means. Have rung the local Hampers chap and suggested he bang in a take–it–or–leave–it cash offer to the old ladies of £80,000. It's that or nothing. If that doesn't get them sitting up in their bed–jackets and taking notice, nothing will.

Have also put a firework under Loomis Chaffee's bottom with a thinly veiled threat to the effect that if I don't see some action in the next few days, they may well find themselves looking at a half-commission situation.

I am not a hustler by nature, but then can one ever tell what coals of hidden character one might not find oneself pulling out of the fire in the face of an emergency? I shouldn't be at all surprised to learn, for instance, that the late Colonel Carne VC of the Glorious Gloucesters was as timid as a mouse until he got to the Imjim River.

Thursday, January 3rd

Talk about swings and roundabouts. Yesterday, not a single letter or telephone call brought anything other than news of fresh disasters. This morning, on the other hand, within moments of getting into the office I had a call from Andrew Lord, of all the unlikely people, saying that it was ages since he and Melons had last seen me, and was there any chance I might perhaps get down to Exeter one of these days? If so, why didn't I have dinner and spend the night? By a curious coincidence he happened to be coming up to town tomorrow to see someone in Dulwich, and since he had to come practically past my front door, why didn't he pop in and see me for a few minutes?

Not having seen hair or hide of him since we all went skiing in Zürs fifteen years ago, I was naturally rather surprised to hear from him out of the blue like this. To have tracked me down to TCP showed determination and application of the highest quality, but to have discovered that I was married with a baby and living in Brixton smacked almost of the supernatural.

Still, I had always had a soft spot for Andrew. I knew him really rather well at university. I'm not quite sure why or where. I have a feeling I may once have taken Melons to an Eights Week dance at Keble. Or was it St Peter's? Even so, I can't imagine why he should have decided to get in touch after all these years; but does it really matter? The whole point about friendship is that it doesn't need explaining.

Friday, January 4th

Arrived home at six to find Andrew with a whisky and soda in his hand, bouncing JJ on his knee and generally behaving as if he were an old friend of the family. He and B were obviously hitting it off. I don't think I've ever seen her looking prettier and more animated. JJ gurgling away happily. Even the dog was lying across his feet. For a moment, I had the curious sensation that I had accidentally walked in on someone else's family!

I don't remember him being quite such a charmer in our undergraduate days. If anything he was rather a prickly type. At all events, we all got on like a house on fire this evening, and gossiped away like mad over several drinks. It was as if the years had dropped away and we were all back in the Trout at Godstow, planning our next youthful escapade amid the cry of peacocks and throwing beer mugs into the garden on the other side of the river.

I was very interested to see the snaps of his lovely sixteenth-century house in Exeter and Melons looking as voluptuous as ever, if a little greyer, and their two boys, Robin and Jason. I was sorry to hear that he had had such bad luck with his scheme for a mobile secretarial service and that he had had to take the boys out of prep school. However, he seems very confident that things will soon be back on an even keel now that he has finished his crash course in insurance selling. I feel sure he will find many ready customers among his West Country friends and acquaintances, and I am only sorry I was not able to think of anyone myself who might be in the market for some life cover. I said that even though I had not taken out a life policy *per se*, I felt that my wife and child would be quite well provided for one way and another, and that, of course, I'd certainly get in touch if I felt there was anything he could do to help me in that direction.

By the time we'd finished chatting, it was half past eight, and he seemed quite pleased when I suggested slipping round to The Silver Hake and bringing back haddock and chips. Even more so when I said I'd pay.

Belinda said, "How about your appointment in Dulwich?"

"Oh that can wait till another day," he said.

He left finally at eleven, saying that we mustn't leave it so long the next time. Whether he was planning to drive back to Exeter after all the Côtes du Ventoux he'd drunk was not entirely clear. Least of all, apparently, to him.

After I'd taken the dog for a wizzle and laid the breakfast table, B said, "I'm always amazed at how transparent these people are."

I suppose, now I come to think about it, that his friendly attitude towards her could be construed as flirtatiousness.

Saturday, January 5th

Vita behaved badly again this morning on the way to the paper shop. We were passing a young couple with a baby in a push-chair and a rather nervous-looking spaniel on a lead when, without any warning, V leapt at the unfortunate creature, causing it to squeal and the baby to scream. The couple, curiously enough, said nothing, leaving me to step in and separate the two contestants with fists and feet. When I'd finally managed to prise them apart, at the real risk of a nasty bite, the man said, "You want to keep that dog of yours under control." I replied that of course I was very sorry but, on the other hand, it took two to make a fight, and that I doubted if V would have behaved like that if his dog hadn't said something to her under his breath first.

The man murmured something that I didn't quite hear, but I decided to let sleeping dogs lie (or in this case snarling dogs) and proceeded upon my lawful occasion. The spaniel certainly didn't look as though it had suffered anything more than a nasty fright, but perhaps it will teach it not to go in for any more *sotto voce* growling.

To dinner in Bayswater with Vanessa Pedalow. I had heard she had done quite well for herself since divorcing Tim, especially since her mother died, and she'd met up with this high-powered international investment broker. Even so, I must admit we were both surprised and impressed by the size of her house and of the BMW parked outside.

Climbed front steps and rang enormous brass doorbell, whereupon door was opened by tall, grey-haired man, extremely well dressed and obviously successful in a quiet understated way.

B and I both shook his hand and said how terribly sorry we were to be late, but the baby had had a slight go of colic and the traffic had been diabolical, and on top of all that we hadn't been able to find anywhere to park and had had to leave the car four streets away and walk.

Suddenly realised we hadn't introduced ourselves, so we said who we were. He replied that he was called Charles and if we'd like to give him our coats, Mrs Pedalow and her guests were having drinks upstairs in the drawing-room, if we'd just like to follow him.

I must say, I do think if people must employ butlers for their dinner parties, they might warn their guests first.

A smaller party than I had expected. Philippe and Theresa, both looking ten years younger, with that yellowish suntan that is peculiar to the Alps, but not on this occasion with the odious Yves. Also an elderly American couple whose names I never quite caught: she rather lively and flirtatious, he dull – largely with drink, apparently. Murmured to Vanessa at one point something to the effect that somebody ought to be moving onto the orange juice, whereupon she explained that he had recently suffered a massive stroke and that many a lesser man would in similar circumstances have taken to his bed.

She also explained that "David" was very sorry he couldn't be there, but he'd been called away to Bermuda on urgent business at the last moment, and that someone called Roger Gomes had nobly stepped in at the last moment. Apparently he is quite a well-known poet. The name certainly rang a bell.

Having expected a vaguely Bohemian type, the large amiable figure who walked through the door looking like a successful stockbroker in his dark three-piece pin-striped suit came as quite a surprise.

Had hoped to have a word or two with him about the work of the late Philip Larkin, but unfortunately he was at the other end of the table. Attempted to buttonhole him after dinner, but all he seemed to want to do was tell dirty jokes. He said that he'd been in a cinema in the suburbs one afternoon recently, when right in the middle of a scene he'd overheard a woman in the row behind him saying in a loud voice, "'ere, where's yer manners? Tits first."

Interested to note that Philippe de Grande-Hauteville was the only person who didn't laugh. Try as he might, he will never become fully integrated into the English way of life.

Sunday, January 6th

Afternoon spent taking down Christmas decorations and helping B to go through cards for next year's list. First prize for ostentation goes as usual to Bob and Anthea, with

"St James's Park in the Snow from Horseguards Parade";
Bryant-Fenn gets the award for the meanest with "Robin on
Twig"; Nigel and Priscilla win the vulgarity cup for the third
year running – except that they do have the excuse of living
in New Zealand; the dullness prize goes to the manager and
staff of the Tiger Lee Chinese restaurant and takeaway; and
Maurice Valjean gets a special award for his picture of Father
Christmas on skis being followed down the mountain by his
reindeer, also on skis, and when you open up the card it plays
"Rudolph The Red-Nosed Reindeer" in a high-pitched electronic squeak. If this is a foretaste of what I can expect on his
forthcoming familiarisation trip to the Alps, I might seriously
have to start thinking of finding a suitable excuse and crying
off.

An even greater concern, however, is that this is the second
year running we have had a card from Donald, Prue, Dominic
and Arabella, plus full address in NW1 and message to say they
hope they'll see something of us in the New Year. Unfortunately, neither of us had yet remembered their surname, nor
the name of the account executive and his live-in girl friend in
Kingston where I first met them.

However, am enormously relieved that Miss Thatcher
should have taken the trouble to include both her address and
telephone number. The way things are going we may need her
services sooner than we think. The strain of motherhood is
obviously beginning to tell on B. This afternoon, she opened
the door of the dishwasher while the machine was in the
middle of its cycle and apologised to it.

Monday, January 7th

Am fast coming to the conclusion that my wife has married
completely the wrong man. Why else should she keep making
pointed references to how others would behave in particular
circumstances? This morning I was literally on my way out of
the front door when she said, "Some men I know take their
wives out to dinner from time to time." When I enquired
who in particular she had in mind, she replied that Philippe

makes a point of taking Theresa out to a restaurant or the theatre or a dinner party at least once a week.

I replied that that didn't surprise me a bit. It's a well-known fact that the French are not great home-lovers and that Parisian restaurants enjoy the highest ratio of table reservations per head of any population in Europe. I, on the other hand, like nothing better after a hard day at the office than a quiet supper on a tray in front of the TV and an early night with a good thriller. What is more, her cooking is so good that even Anton Mosimann at his best would inevitably be a let down.

Had assumed that she would take this little speech as the touching compliment intended, instead of which she launched into a long harangue about being stuck in the house all day and what a thoughtless, selfish, boring chauvinist pig I was etc etc. If that is really what she thinks of me, I can't imagine why she should want to have dinner with me or spend a minute longer in my company than is absolutely necessary.

Of course, I should have left there and then. Instead, made the fatal error of trying to press my point about the importance in this materialistic age of family life of a return to Victorian values of self-sufficiency and contentment with the simple things in life – songs round the piano, a quiet game of Scrabble, sitting on the sofa next to one's beloved, gazing into the fire in quiet contemplation.

Unfortunately, B chose this opportunity to lapse into one of her pedantic moods and point out that we didn't own a piano, that Scrabble didn't exist in Victorian times and that if there was anything less guaranteed to induce contemplation, it was a gas wall-fire.

This then led to further words, which in turn led to my leaving the house twenty minutes later than usual and having to travel to work in even more sardine-like conditions than usual. Arrived late for a Botticelli New Ideas Meeting, only to find that Pamela had presented all my stuff as if it were her own, including my "Great Artists of Italy" idea.

The ironic thing is, I had been planning to take B out to dinner tonight at the Bordelino, but obviously it would have been impossible to do so in the circumstances without looking as if I had been pushed into it.

Tuesday, January 8th

Am interested to note that since the beginning of the New Year, my diary entries have become shorter than they were. This is not because my life is any the less full or interesting; on the contrary, it is so packed with daily excitement that I am finding it harder and harder to find the energy late at night to write it all down.

Today, for instance, had planned to get into work really early, but suddenly remembered Vita's annual Parvo booster injection is well overdue, so had to rush to Dulwich and spend the first hour of my working day sitting amidst dogs with rheumy eyes, cats with boils on their bottoms etc.

Vita in unusually bad mood and attempted to savage Siamese through grill of cat basket. Apologised to owner, but she appeared not to be in forgiving mood, saying that dogs like mine should not be allowed into the vet's. I do see that a cat who is suffering from a dicky heart is unlikely to benefit hugely from the sudden appearance of a pair of baleful eyes and a set of bared teeth a few inches from its nose. On the other hand, I cannot help feeling that any animal which, for whatever reason, has to seek medical attention must expect to take its chances along with its fellow sufferers. After all, I have to sit next to people in Dr Aziz's waiting-room who might, for all I know, be carrying the most virulent, even deadly, germs, but I do not fly into a panic the moment the person on the next chair opens his mouth or asks me to pass him a copy of *Harpers & Queen*.

Suddenly noticed a young couple on the other side of the room, with a baby in a push chair. The wife was looking especially sorry for herself.

At one point, the nurse came out and said that she didn't have any definite news, but that if they'd care to hang on, Mr Ingrams would like to have a quick word with them.

At this, the wife burst into floods of tears.

The woman with the Siamese asked the husband what the problem was and he explained that he and his wife had been out walking at the weekend with their dog, when suddenly some brute of an animal had appeared from nowhere and, for no reason whatever, had attacked the dog with such ferocity that it was touch and go whether it would survive its injuries.

I'm pretty sure in my own mind that they were not the same couple with whom I had the ding-dong on Saturday morning. If they had been, they would surely have recognised Vita, even under the chair behind my legs where I had pushed her. On the other hand, their vision could easily have been slightly impaired by their tears. At all events, it was a very odd coincidence and one that definitely gave me food for thought – albeit of a fairly unconstructive nature.

Wednesday, January 9th

I am not a fanciful man, but when I am woken at five o'clock in the morning to be informed that Washington is on the line, and when I am asked if I am Mr Simon Crisp and say yes and the phone immediately goes dead, I think I can be forgiven for being very suspicious indeed.

B, whom I am seriously beginning to think has no imagination whatever, pooh-poohed my misgivings and put the whole thing down to another British Telecom technical hitch. All that happened was that Beddoes was trying to get through – probably to tell us what time he would be arriving – and he got cut off. What other explanation could there possibly be? What indeed?

Remembering Watergate, almost anything is possible. My reading of the situation is that Beddoes – though possibly not in the highest echelon of White House executives – is nevertheless subject to strict security checks and possibly surveillance by the CIA, especially when he is planning to travel abroad. I think it's quite possible that up till now my name has not featured on the files of the US security services, and my letter inviting Beddoes to be a godfather could well have been misunderstood in the light of this big clamp-down on the Mafia that is currently going on.

Is it my imagination, or is the dark blue Cortina that was parked opposite the flat when I came home from the office this evening the same one that I saw when I went off first thing this morning? And what is a man doing sitting in a parked car in a London suburb at six thirty on a wet January evening wearing dark glasses, I'd like to know?

Had been thinking in terms of a quick *tagliatelle* at the Bordelino, but in the circumstances decided to postpone it until all this had died down. Anyway, I doubt if Tessa Harbottle would have been able to baby-sit at such short notice. In fact, now she's taken up with this Old Etonian punk wine-bar waiter from No. 43, I shall be surprised if we'll ever be able to call on her services again. *Tant mieux*, as far as I'm concerned. I'm sure it is no coincidence that my last telephone bill was ten per cent higher than usual, and even B had to admit that when we came back from Vanessa's do on Saturday, there was a very peculiar smell in the sitting-room that is unlike any Virginia tobacco I've ever come across.

Thursday, January 10th

Relieved to discover on leaving house this morning that there was no sign of the Cortina. On the other hand, was approaching butcher's when happened to notice West Indian owner of Yorkshire terrier that Vita attacked a few weeks ago – or possibly ex-owner, since there was still no sign whatever of his wretched dog. I am not normally prone to bouts of paranoia, but am more convinced than ever that the animal has died, possibly as a result of the treatment it received at Vita's hands; or rather, teeth.

At all events, was in no mood for an ugly confrontation – not with a heavy Botticelli planning meeting scheduled to last all morning. So, as he approached on the far side of the road, arranged that my back should be turned towards him in the most natural way possible. I wonder what the odds are against kneeling down in order to give the impression that one is doing up one's shoe-lace and standing up only to discover that of all the possible spots one could have chosen to place the knee of one's newly cleaned suit trousers, one has picked one containing a small, freshly created smear of dog dirt? So incredulous was I at the callousness with which Dame Fortune had chosen to deal me this bum card that I actually rang up Ladbroke's when I got into work and asked them to quote me a price. The girl said she couldn't give me a precise figure over the telephone, but promised she would speak to someone who had experience of this kind of bet and call me back as soon as possible, since when I haven't heard another word from them. But then, of course, they are a very busy firm.

B rang later to say that she had been talking to Paula Batty about Vita, and Paula had given her the name and telephone number of a Mr Belfrage who is apparently one of the leading experts on mental disorders among domestic animals and has been interviewed on lots of chat shows and recently had a piece written about him in one of the Sunday magazines.

I must admit his name is quite unknown to me; nor was I aware that there were any experts of this sort for him to lead. And while I would be the last to make a snap prejudicial judgement against anyone purely on the basis of his name, there is something about the name Belfrage that makes it difficult for me to share B's wholehearted enthusiasm for the man.

Not that it matters two hoots what I think, since she has spoken to the Protect-a-Pet people who have said that we can claim it on our insurance and she has arranged for Mr Belfrage to come round and look at Vita at three o'clock tomorrow afternoon.

Friday, January 11th

A very curious thing happened this morning. Was wandering round the sitting-room with JJ over my shoulder, trying to bring up some particularly recalcitrant wind, when my eye was caught by a length of string hanging from one of the top catches of the window overlooking the street. Pointed it out to B, but she said she had never noticed it before and knew nothing about it. It may be nothing. On the other hand, one can never take anything for granted these days. Try as I might, I could not figure out any way in which it might be used to effect an illegal entry; but, of course, I was looking at it from only a semi-professional viewpoint. Were I a policeman or a burglar, the most seemingly innocent object might immediately assume considerable significance.

However, any further speculation halted when JJ brought up not only wind but most of his breakfast too. He would have to choose a morning when I'd forgotten to put a towel over my shoulder, not to mention the suit that's just come back from having the dog dirt removed at the cleaners.

Rang the office to say I might be a few minutes late. Is it my imagination, or did I read somewhere that you can always tell when your phone's being tapped because there's a funny buzzing noise on the line? Of course, it could just be a funny buzzing noise on the line. How to find out for certain, though? A discreet word with the Home Office could be the answer, except that they could easily be the ones who are responsible. On the other hand, it could be tied in in some way with the string. As co-ordinator of the Neighbourhood Watch Scheme, *and* an unwitting pawn of the British Secret Service, I feel it my duty to get to the bottom of this.

Rang the local station when I got to the office and had a word with PC Dunwoody who promised to pop round in the early evening and take a look.

Had in fact hoped to get away after lunch and watch Mr Belfrage in action with Vita, but at the last moment Hume Purkiss rang up to say he was passing through town and could he pop in and talk about my coming down to Norfolk to have a look at the Steamy Days set-up? Have made a provisional date for early February, although I cannot imagine that converted railway-carriages look their best in the middle of winter, even if they are very good railway-carriages.

By the time I'd found a taxi and picked up a case of Château Verdun and half a dozen non-vintage champagnes from Mazzarini & Block's and got caught up in terrible traffic round Westminster and finally got home, it was almost five; by which time Mr Belfrage had gone.

Apparently Vita is a highly intelligent dog who is suffering partly from stress at having been taken away from her mother at an early age, partly from a confusion over her sexual identity, due to never having known her father, and partly

135

from jealousy of John Julius. However, it's nothing to worry about. All that's required is some basic training using a firm but gentle hand. Belfrage has also suggested a spot of aversion therapy in the shape of a small squeaker, about the size of a breath freshener, which we are to let off near her ear whenever she attempts to mount anything unsuitable such as a football, a small child, a visitor's leg, or another dog of either sex.

By a happy coincidence, I have always been very interested in the art of dog training, and have long harboured a secret ambition to compete in the BBC 2 *One Man and his Dog* sheepdog trials. I'm only sorry I do not actually own a sheepdog. I suppose it might be possible to herd sheep with a terrier. I have never heard of it being done, but in every sport there is an exception that proves the rule.

Belfrage has also recommended a book entitled *How to Talk to your Animals* by someone called Jean Craighead George. I cannot wait to get a copy. I have always felt that Vita and I suffered from a severe communication problem and I shall be most interested to know if there is a way of resolving it.

It's a pity someone doesn't write a companion volume entitled *How to Talk to your Friends*, and include a section on the subject of being a house guest and the importance of letting your hosts know if you decide to change your plans at the last moment and not turn up at the time expected. After sitting up until one o'clock in the morning watching an old Peter Cushing double-bill while waiting for Beddoes and this Bobby person to arrive, or at the very least ring and tell us what is happening, I am seriously contemplating drafting out a rough synopsis myself and dedicating it to Beddoes.

It isn't the fact that all that moving round of furniture and going over the bathroom fittings with Dettol was for nothing that annoyed me so much as the total lack of respect that his behaviour so blatantly demonstrates. I somehow can't imagine him mucking the Reagans around like this when they ask him up to Camp David for the weekend.

Whoever it was who described "the mild dislike that exists between old friends" must have been feeling in a particularly genial mood at the time.

Saturday, January 12th

To Chelsea early to buy a copy of this talking to animals book, since it is obviously not the kind of thing they'd carry at our local so-called bookshop.

Who would have thought the day would ever have come when a paperback cost £4.95? Said as much to the assistant who replied that, considering it was impossible to order a round of drinks in a pub for under a fiver these days, £4.95 seemed to her to be excellent value for money.

I pointed out that, on the contrary, it was perfectly possible to order a round of drinks for under a fiver. It depended on what one ordered and for how many people. A couple of halves of bitter and a gin and tonic, for example, would come to around £1.50, and two orange squashes to less than a pound, and that's with a bag of crisps thrown in.

The assistant replied that she couldn't imagine how long it was since I last went into a pub, but that, judging from the mean and miserable attitude that I obviously had towards life in general, I might be very well advised to do so rather more often.

I reminded her that, contrary to popular belief, alcohol acted not as a stimulant but as a depressant.

She said, "In that case, I'd advise you never to touch another drop again."

I would have had no hesitation in taking the matter to managerial level had I (a) not been running rather late, and (b) remembered that I had left my wallet and cheque-book in my other sports jacket. In different circumstances, I might have suggested writing out a cheque for the amount on a blank piece of paper, which would of course have been perfectly legal and above board. But I daresay some footling objection would have been raised. Still, that's modern shops for you. No incentive, no imagination. I sometimes think they'd go to any lengths to avoid selling you something.

Arrived home to find a copy of the book sitting on the kitchen table. Asked B where on earth it had come from.

"From the local bookshop," she said. "Where else does one go to buy books?" And she disappeared off to Clapham to fetch the beef for tomorrow's christening lunch, leaving me in charge of John Julius, Vita *and* the breakfast washing-up.

In the circumstances, was barely able to scratch the surface of what is obviously a fascinating study by a fascinating woman. Am particularly interested to learn that because we humans have a poor sense of smell and hearing compared with dogs, and because our faces show our emotions more dramatically than theirs, we sometimes fail to notice their subtler expressions: but that, even so, we have much in common with our canine friends, not least in the matter of status.

The leader of a pack of wolves and the one that makes all the decisions and bosses all the others around is apparently known as the "Alpha". This is also used to describe a dominant dog. At the bottom of the canine ladder is the "Omega" who defers to everyone else. No points for guessing where B and I feature in this particular family pack.

Beddoes finally consented to roll up just as we were settling down to a late lunch of sausages and mash. To our surprise, and relief, Bobby turned out to be a girlfriend, or as Beddoes described her with his usual lack of *finesse*, his "live-in lover". I don't know why I should continue to find it so difficult to imagine anyone actually loving Beddoes, but there it is.

Not that she is the most obviously lovable creature I have ever set eyes on. When I think back to our days together in the flat and the succession of really quite attractive women who paraded in and out of his bedroom – not to say *our* kitchen and *our* bathroom – this short, dumpy, rather potato-faced woman, dressed in a shapeless bell-tent of a dress and wearing a fixed expression of curiously manic benignity, seemed an odd choice as the object of his affection.

Beddoes explained that they had hoped to arrive last night, but their plane had been diverted to Frankfurt because of fog and they'd had to stay there overnight. He may have been telling the truth or he may not. As anyone who has ever read a book by Len Deighton knows only too well, nothing is quite what it seems in the shadowy world of espionage.

They also declined lunch, which was just as well since there wouldn't have been enough to go round anyway, but said they'd love some coffee.

"I'm afraid it's only Nescafé," I said.

Beddoes pulled a face. "If that's really all you've got, laddie," he said. "I'd have thought you'd have reached an age by now when you could afford to treat yourself to a few of life's luxuries – beginning with fresh coffee."

I said, "As a matter of fact, Beddoes, I happen to like Nescafé."

Beddoes said, "I used to like cheap English cheroots until I discovered Havana cigars. And non-vintage champagne until I started drinking Krug '75. The shoestring life is all very well for the bachelor, or at least it is for some bachelors, but when you marry and have children, it's your duty and responsibility to give them nothing but the best. You wouldn't want young John there to grow up like you, now would you, laddie? Be honest."

I reminded him that it wasn't John but John Julius, and that since he had never been married, nor fathered any children, he was hardly in a position to comment on the behaviour of those who were and had. And since we were on the subject of duty, I did not ask him to be a godfather in order to preach the doubtful joys of worldly success. His task was primarily to ensure that John Julius was a good member of the Christian family, went to church regularly and learnt his catechism.

Beddoes said, "You'd be very upset if I didn't come up with a jolly good christening present and a healthy lob at Christmas and on his birthday, wouldn't you?"

B said, "Ralph and Bobby still haven't had their coffee."

I replied that we were discussing something that was fundamental to all our lives and that the coffee could wait.

B said, "Nothing is more fundamental to our lives than food and drink. It's discussion that can wait."

Stood up to make coffee and was on point of spooning freeze-dried granules into cups when Beddoes said, "I thought you said it was going to be Nescafé?"

"I meant instant, that's all," I said.

"Yes, perhaps, but what you actually said was Nescafé. Now if you'd said it was going to be Maxwell House . . . well, I mean that's a different thing altogether."

I couldn't tell whether he was trying to be funny or whether this was an example of transatlantic finickiness. At all events, it cut precious little ice with me, or apparently with Bobby, who did not utter a single word throughout, but stared intently at B to such an extent that I was seriously beginning to wonder if she might have designs on her. Finally she said, apropos nothing whatever, "Did you know your neck is completely out of alignment?"

B laughed and said that she had far too many other things to worry about without adding her own minor problems to the list.

Bobby said, "Why? Do you suffer from stiffness or headaches?"

B confessed that she did get headaches from time to time, especially when John Julius was in one of his moods.

"And what remedy do you take for them?" Bobby asked her.

B said that a couple of Veganin usually did the trick. And if they didn't, then a couple more.

Bobby said, "I thought as much. I bet your whole spine is one mass of knotted tissues preventing the blood from flowing freely to the brain. To compensate for these you have un-consciously bent your neck into a certain angle and it's remained that way ever since. I could help to relieve it, if you wished."

"Bobby is a trained physiotherapist," Beddoes said in a slightly smug tone of voice, as though implying he had personally trained her. "Her methods are a little unorthodox, but they are gradually gaining acceptance in Washington. She has already treated several state senators and is very much hoping to start work soon on Secretary of Defence Weinberger."

"Have you ever seen anything like his neck?" Bobby asked.

I shook my head and, as I did so, felt a tiny twinge that I had not noticed before.

B was obviously not at all keen to submit to Bobby's dubious fingertips, and once she has made her mind up about something, she is not easily swayed, as I know only too well. And yet, within a matter of minutes and with the washing-up still piled in the sink, she was flat on her face on the floor with

Bobby astride her back, her fingers beavering away at the base of her skull.

Half an hour later, B stood up and announced that she had not felt as well and relaxed in a year. She added that she thought I could benefit from a session too. It might help to make me less bad-tempered.

I do not hold with couples using their friends as a way of working out their differences, but I simply couldn't let that remark pass without putting up some sort of defence.

I said, "People who are not involved in the creative process can never understand the strains and pressures on those who are."

Beddoes said, "In my experience, public relations is about as far removed from creativity as Clement Freud is from psychoanalysis. You were bad-tempered as a flatmate and I have seen no evidence so far to persuade me that marriage has altered you for the better. If anything, you appear to be even more bigoted, middle-aged and bachelor-like than when I last saw you five years ago."

Ugly words might easily have been bandied at that moment had the door bell not been rung and all further conversation been made impossible as Vita hurled herself at the letter-box, treating it to her usual repertoire of high-pitched screams and Baskervillian snarls.

Decided this was the perfect moment to try out Belfrage's squeaker, so shouting, "Don't put your fingers through the letter-box whatever you do," I grabbed the thing off the kitchen table and rushed forward with the intention of letting it off as near V as possible. Unfortunately, caught my toe on the edge of the carpet, lurched forward and the thing went off within a few inches of B's left ear, causing her severe pain and temporary (at least, I hope it's temporary) deafness. It wouldn't have mattered so much if she hadn't just laid John Julius across her shoulder with a view to bringing up his wind.

I still maintain that she was overreacting when she accused me of deafening my child for ever and talked of his having to go to a special school and wear a hearing aid for the rest of his life.

Bobby was of the same opinion; ditto PC Dunwoody whose arrival had set in motion this series of unfortunate incidents. I am only sorry he could not be quite so positive about the piece of string by the window. He said that if it was some sort of subtle burgling aid, it was a new one on him.

At all events, he has taken a statement from me and from B concerning both the string and the suspicious Cortina, and made a little sketch of the string's relationship to the window-catch in his notebook, and has promised to make a few enquiries amongst his colleagues and come back to us as soon as possible.

In fact, so obviously absorbed was he by the whole problem that he did not appear to notice the constant sexual assaults that V made upon his right boot.

When he had gone, Beddoes said, "You didn't by any chance use a piece of string to hang your Christmas decorations?"

I replied that it was a remote possibility and that at all events it wouldn't do the Neighbourhood Watch team any harm to have something concrete to get their teeth into for once. It also afforded PC Dunwoody an opportunity to try his hand at some simple detective work. I shall be interested to see what sort of solution he comes up with, if any.

Had hoped to take Vita up to Clapham Common for some simple command work using the Flexi 2 extendable lead, while Beddoes got to know his godson, but before I knew what, the afternoon had disappeared and it was time for bath and drinks.

Bobby as silent during dinner as she had been during lunch – her only contribution to the festivities being the observation that my neck was, if anything, slightly more misshapen than B's. More out of politeness than from any real sense of need, I agreed to submit to a short bout of manipulation, as a result of which the tiny twinge that I had felt earlier developed into quite a noticeable pain and by the time I went to bed, I could really hardly move my neck in any direction without experiencing severe pain.

Bobby said that this was nothing to worry about. The

muscles were often a little bruised after manipulation and I should be as right as rain in the morning.

I hope she knows what she's talking about.

Sunday, January 13th

She does not know what she is talking about. I have never had a more uncomfortable night in my life and this morning my neck was such agony I had to ask B to lift me up from the pillow. What should have been one of the happiest and most momentous days of my life transformed into a new and subtle version of the Spanish Inquisition, and all because I didn't wish to hurt the feelings of a certifiable transatlantic quack. Is it any wonder that even the most respectable American doctors are obliged to spend thousands insuring themselves against possible patients' law-suits when they have to work alongside irresponsible paramedics who couldn't even take your temperature without giving you mercury poisoning?

To make matters worse, Bobby had taken it upon herself to bring John Julius a beautiful silver tankard as a christening present. Fortunately, she did not go so far as to have it inscribed, so I may well consider selling it to pay for the top man in Harley Street to put my neck right.

Beddoes had brought him a pair of cuff-links, which he was at great pains to explain were made by the Navajo Indians, using a special stone that is supposed to bring good luck to whoever possesses it. To me it looked like the garish sort of tat you see being sold on trays in Oxford Street. Possibly by Navajo Indians.

Generally speaking, though, everyone most generous. I should have thought that the modern-day vogue for plastic had pretty well knocked silver on the head as a feeding implement, but Paula Batty's fork, spoon and pusher was a kind thought nonetheless. I might well add it to the neck fund.

Why Bryant-Fenn should think that anyone, even a child, should ever feel the overwhelming urge to browse through his collected food articles for *Bedroom* magazine I cannot imagine. Though I'm bound to admit that Asprey's do know a thing or

143

two about book-binding, I cannot with the best will in the world believe that even the most exquisite hand-tooled leather can invest them with a literary and artistic quality they do not possess.

On the other hand, in the words of that great wizard of the written word, Anthony Powell, books *do* furnish a room, and, heaven knows, we could do with some decent furniture for the new house.

The major and Alyson donated an extremely generous cheque. I'm only sorry they cannot see their way to endowing their children's generation in the same way. That way we might be able to afford a new house. Mother gave a prayer-book. Tim sent his apologies and Miss Thatcher a matinée jacket which she had knitted herself. Using a pair of fire tongs by the look of it.

Lunch was a jolly and informal occasion, even though the smoked salmon was a little saltier than I had anticipated and the beef a little harder to carve. B said it was my fault for not getting the knives sharpened when the man came round to the door last weekend. I said, and I still say, it was the bit of gristle in the middle that was the nigger in the woodpile.

All I know for certain is that, by the time I'd finished serving everyone else, I was left with an extremely unappetising, unyielding and, as it turned out, inedible pile of scraps and gristle. Still, I have never been a wholehearted fan of the cow. Give me a nice leg of English lamb any day of the week.

The major and Alyson most complimentary to their daughter at every conceivable opportunity. Indeed, my father-in-law addressed me on only one occasion and that was when he enquired if the wine we were drinking was the same as the one I had given him for Christmas.

I replied that it was.

"Hm," he said.

It was impossible to tell from the tone of this muffled sound whether he thought it was a very good choice or a very bad one.

There was no doubting what Mother thought of it — although at the speed she was knocking it back, I doubt if she'd have known the difference between Château Verdun and cheap plonk. At one point I noticed she got a fit of the giggles and fell against the major's chest and had to be helped upright again.

She didn't seem particularly put out at being the only woman present not allowed to hold John Julius in her arms. He looked so sweet in his christening robe. Like one of those Victorian dolls you sometimes see in museums. Try as I might, I simply cannot imagine Alyson dressed up in it on her christening day.

Arrived at the church slightly delayed, owing to fact that the small procession of cars had got halfway to Vauxhall before anyone noticed that Mother had been left behind. Which reminds me, I *must* get that lock fixed on the bathroom door.

A simple, moving ceremony, made rather more muddling than it need have been, thanks to Niblock's insistence on abandoning the traditional prayer-book service in favour of grubby cards which were handed to us as we arrived. Not only was everything couched in that chatty style that everyone seems to adopt when addressing the Almighty these days, but it was often difficult to pick out the prayers and responses from amidst the multifarious instructions to parents and god-parents. At the end of one prayer, I distinctly heard Mother saying: "The prayers that follow are omitted when Baptism is administered at Holy Communion."

However, nothing could detract from the dignity, the grace and the wonder that this centuries-old ritual bestows on all who are privileged to take part in it. Listening to my two oldest friends declaring their faith, I felt strangely moved. No-one in his senses could call Hugh Bryant-Fenn a handsome man; yet standing there, his face glowing in the light of the symbolic candle, he seemed possessed of an almost ethereal beauty that quite took my breath away.

As for the actual baptism itself, when Niblock poured the water over John Julius's forehead and proclaimed the time-honoured words, I confess that I was very close to tears.

It was unfortunate that at the crucial moment Niblock should stumble over the name and baptise my son "John Jonas". I'm wondering if this means that we are now obliged to call him that willy-nilly.

145

I did mention it to B as we were leaving. She said, "Lady Di got her husband's name wrong at her wedding, but I've never heard anyone suggest she married the wrong man."

True enough, but of course the opportunities she has of addressing Prince Charles by all four Christian names are few and far between.

Niblock seemed very pleased with his envelope. I had assumed that the Baptism of Infants was very much part of the overall service offered by the Church of England, and the idea of tipping the vicar would never have entered my head, had I not chanced upon an article in one of the Sunday colour supplements on the subject of the black economy.

Had imagined that a tenner would more than fit the bill, but B insisted that this was not the moment for penny-pinching, and that twenty was the least one could give.

I can only hope he wasn't expecting fifty. His is not a church whose congregation are short of a bob or two.

As we were driving away, I could see Niblock out of my rear-view mirror obviously opening the envelope, but by then we were too far away to distinguish the expression on his face.

Tea was a comparatively brisk affair. A quick cuppa, a piece of B's home-made fruit-cake and a glass of bubbly to drink the baby's health.

I overheard the major saying to Alyson, "Is this non-vintage?" to which she replied, "I should imagine so." "Hm," he said. This time there was no doubting his meaning. There was an awful moment when I spotted Bobby treating the major to one of her looks, but fortunately, they were able to get away before she could take action. Mother, however, fell easy prey to her persuasive fingers and left for the station in a taxi saying she had never felt more relaxed and carefree in her life.

Funnily enough, I am feeling a hundred times better myself, despite having to spend an evening listening to Beddoes reminiscing about our life together in the flat in a way that constantly showed me up in a bad light. The older I get, the more I find myself believing in the existence of divine grace. As Jesus said, and I agree with Him, the meek *shall* inherit the earth. At least, I hope they will.

Monday, January 14th

Awoke this morning with the realisation that in all the years I have been friends with Beddoes, I have never *really* known what he does for a living. When we shared a flat, he was something in the City. Then he went to Brussels to be something in the EEC. Now he is something in the White House. But what exactly? Is he really as important as he would have us all believe? Who was the man in the Ford Cortina and why have the police dragged their heels over the matter? Are we to be the subject of heavy surveillance from now on and is every snippet of gossip between B and Paula and every restaurant booking to be recorded by grim-faced men in a closed van parked in Acacia Gardens? If so, the sooner we move to the country, the better.

Was certainly relieved to see the back of Beddoes after breakfast. Ditto his finger-happy friend. As they were waiting for their taxi, I couldn't resist remarking to Beddoes that I was sorry he had not more chance to tell us about his work in Washington, since it was obviously very important and we were still not entirely clear what it involved.

"No," he said.

I said, "Do you mean no, it is not important or no, we are not clear what it involves?"

He said, "Yes, it is important."

"Important enough to warrant interest from, say, Special Branch?" I said.

"It's possible," he said.

Would love to have pressed him further, but people who have signed the Official Secrets Act, or whatever the American equivalent is, are like friends of the Royal Family: you know you can go just so far with them and no further. Not that I have ever met anyone who knows the Royal Family. It's just one of those things one knows.

Anyway, at that moment the taxi arrived.

Bobby said, "You know, you're holding your head so much better than you were. You look much more handsome."

Beddoes said, "Hello, another to add to your list of admirers."

I gave a light laugh and bent forward to kiss Bobby goodbye. As I did so, an agonising pain shot down my neck and into my shoulder, and by the time the taxi had rounded the corner, I was scarcely able to move my head in either direction.

Was struggling into my overcoat when B asked casually, "Who are all these admirers then?"

I told her it was meant as a joke.

"Many a true word . . ." said B.

I told her she was beginning to sound like Miss Thatcher.

"So would you if you spent all day cooped up in a basement flat in Brixton with only a two-month-old baby and a sex-mad lesbian terrier for company. I couldn't love John Julius more but frankly his conversation doesn't exactly stretch the mind."

Oh dear, I do wish to goodness women would make up their minds exactly what it is they want. One minute they're singing the praises of single-minded motherhood and condemning women who put their careers before their children; the next they're grousing about being bored and making their husbands feel guilty for having an interesting job and working hard.

I blame Paula Batty myself, with her half-baked feminist ideas, her half-baked freelance journalism and, to my way of thinking, her half-baked husband, with his wishy-washy, *laissez-faire* views, who encourages her in the belief that carrying out interviews with second-rate actresses in local freeby magazines is more important than cutting up peanut-butter sandwiches for the children's tea. An *au pair*, even one as amply endowed and maternal-looking as their Gerda (or G-I-R-D-E-R, as it should rightly be spelt), is no substitute for a real mother, nor Grange Hill for tales of Blackberry Farm read out loud in the nursery.

The other day, apparently, Gerda caught Tom, aged four, sniffing Paula's roll-on deodorant with evident pleasure. And yet Paula laughed this off as "natural inquisitiveness" and "taking a healthy interest in the artefacts of everyday life in the latter quarter of the twentieth century". So much for this free and easy Montessori method of infant education that Paula is forever banging on about. The more I hear about it, the happier I am to have plumped for the state system.

Tuesday, January 15th

Telephoned comprehensive school with a view to making an appointment for a parental visit, only to be told by gruff-voiced man that, owing to unofficial action on the part of the teachers, all the pupils had been sent home and the headmaster would be tied up all day giving interviews to the TV and radio people. I said that I would try and ring back later in the week, but perhaps in the meantime he would care to send me a prospectus.

There was a long pause and then he said, "Oh I'm afraid we don't lend out laboratory equipment."

I said, "I hope I'm not speaking to one of the masters."

"You must be joking, mate," he said. "There are no masters here today. I'm the caretaker."

Not the most auspicious beginning to a child's educational career that I've ever come across.

Wednesday, January 16th

A rather larger post than usual for the time of year brings letters from the Battys and Alyson thanking us for helping to make Sunday such a happy and memorable day. I don't know about "helping". Without us, there wouldn't have been anything to celebrate in the first place.

Also a letter from Hampers' chap in Suffolk to say that he had now had a chance to consider my offer on Pear Tree Farm and that the old sisters have written to him from the nursing home to say that if it is a matter of taking it or leaving it, as I had suggested, they'd rather leave it. On the other hand, if I wished to come back to them with an offer that was slightly more in keeping with the asking price, they'd be very happy to consider it.

Whether *I* would, is another matter. I'll have to think about it.

Arrived at office to find memo from Ski Time giving details of flight times and travel arrangements on Saturday and listing names of my fellow guests. I cannot say that any of them rings an immediate bell. Interested to note, for no particular reason, that Tooting Travel is represented by a Ms Bubbles Macmahon. She sounds fun.

Arrived home to find Andrew Lord, once again ensconced in *my* armchair, drinking *my* scotch and bouncing *my* son on his knee. Not to say amusing *my* wife.

B wearing a slightly sheepish look, as well she might.

She said, "Oh hallo, darling. Andrew just happened to be passing by and thought he'd look us up."

I said, "Andrew seems to be passing by an awful lot all of a sudden. Dulwich again, is it? Or are you planning to give it another miss?"

I may look soft and malleable but I can be pretty sharp when I want and Andrew was obviously quite nervous.

He said, "I wondered if you'd had any more thoughts on that little matter of life insurance we discussed last time I was here?"

I said that I did not recall any discussions on the subject, beyond my saying that I thought I was already well provided for in that regard. "What you actually said," he said, "was that if you felt there was anything I could do to help, you'd get in touch."

I suggested that my silence spoke for itself.

Andrew, undeterred, said, "May I ask what particular policies you have taken out on your life?"

I said that I appreciated his interest, but in fact I had made a deliberate decision not to load myself with life insurance policies at this stage, but to go full out on a low cost endowment mortgage.

He said that, with respect, that wasn't quite the same thing, and before I knew what, he had talked me into pouring him another whisky, and while B bathed John Julius and put him to bed, I was compelled to sit there on the visitors' chair while he outlined the differences between Increasable and Renewable

150

Term Assurance, Whole Life Insurance with Profits, Endowment with Profits over a twenty and twenty-five year term, and Minimum Cost Endowment over the same two terms.

I do not believe I have understood less about anything since I made the mistake of attending an inaugural lecture by the Professor of Philosophy at university because I had always thought him so amusing on TV chat shows.

I finally had to tell him that although in fact I had been quite keen on the idea of a life insurance policy when he'd started, the more he'd talked, the more I'd realised I wasn't interested after all.

"I see," he said. "Well, in that case, I shan't delay you any longer. I'm sure you've got a lot of work to do. Don't go overdoing it, will you? Seventy per cent of heart attacks are caused by stress and strain, according to the statistics. And sixty per cent of those occur in males between the ages of thirty-five and fifty. I gather you're going skiing on Saturday. I hear they've had a lot of avalanche trouble this year."

Later, as he was putting the final touches to my proposal form, I said, "Selling life insurance appears to be money for jam. How can anyone refuse you?"

"Simple," he said. "By saying no. Fortunately, almost no one ever does. They invariably say something like, "they'll think about it", and then they're so surprised when I ring up the following week that they usually give in without a struggle."

I have suggested he pops the policy in the post. I don't want him dropping in again on some thin pretext while I'm away, and drinking my whisky and putting ideas into my wife's head, thank you very much.

All in all, though, it's a great weight off my mind to know that B and JJ will be catered for in the event of any unforeseen disaster: ditto that my moral overdraft at Tebbit's Farm has been marginally reduced. My only worry now is whether £50,000 is really quite enough.

Thursday, January 17th

To the office in unusually chipper mood, thanks largely to fact that, by dint of enormous patience, self-control and appalling bribery, I managed to lure Vita out onto the patio without her uttering so much as a squeak. As Eric Halsall would say of a particularly good bit of driving on *One Man and His Dog*, "Oh, she's going grand now, is Vita."

Unfortunately, she would definitely have lost points when she managed to snatch a copy of *Country Life* out of the postman's hands before he had even got it into the letter-box, pull it through in one single movement and hurl it halfway across the sitting-room before I had even found the squeaker, let alone given her a blast.

According to the author of *How to Talk to your Animals*, you can always tell if a dog is about to attack because it holds its tail straight out, horizontal to the ground. Unfortunately, V's is so small, it's often difficult from a distance to determine the precise angle of point. She also assures the reader that "An inviolable dog law is that anus sniffing is truce time. No one attacks." This does not presumably apply to postmen, especially when they are on the other side of the door.

At all events, we seem to be making some sort of progress, and it was in a mood of considerable optimism that I enquired of Pamela if she could recommend a restaurant that is stylish, lively, gastronomic, romantic and not too expensive.

"You're not too fussy then?" she said.

I replied that when it came to eating out I certainly was, and that since we hadn't been out since John Julius was born and I was going away for a week's skiing, I was looking for something pretty memorable.

After a lot of humming and hahing, she finally suggested a place called P'ong somewhere off the New King's Road. Apparently the cuisine is oriental and draws its inspiration from places as far apart as Outer Mongolia and Borneo. It has been designed in 1950s Samurai style with a hint of nomadic tentwork by someone called Sbigniew Ng, and is evidently a favourite haunt of top models, furniture designers and Channel 4 producers. It is run by two homosexual ex-advertising media buyers, one of whom likes to dress up as a geisha girl, but only on Tuesdays, Thursdays and alternate Saturdays, and only then if he hasn't had words with the cook, an ex-Vietnam helicopter pilot.

Had in fact been thinking in terms of somewhere like the Bordelino or, if all else failed, the Botticelli. On the other hand, B is always complaining that I never take her anywhere interesting, so drew a bow at a venture and rang for a table.

Phone answered by man with obviously pansy voice who said that, as it happened, he had a very nice table for two in the upstairs room, but as they were very heavily booked, would we be very kind and make it eight fifteen rather than eight thirty?

It couldn't have suited me better. I need all the sleep I can get if I'm going to acquit myself with any credit on the ski slopes.

B could not have sounded more delighted if I'd told her I'd decided to throw out my old school dressing-gown. Moreover, by some miracle, Tessa Harbottle happened to be available for baby-sitting.

Arrived at P'ong shortly before eight fifteen, as requested, to be greeted by the owner in full geisha outfit in totally deserted room except for a girl sitting at a table for four, smoking a cigarette. Could hardly believe it possible when we were shown to the table slap next-door.

Naturally, I asked if it might be possible to move to another table. He said he was sorry, but all the tables were taken.

"Not at the moment they're not," I pointed out.

"They will be very shortly," replied the geisha sharply, hissing loudly through his teeth.

I said, "Do you mean customers book particular tables when they ring up?"

B said in a low voice, "Please don't make a fuss." She looked up at the geisha. "Honestly, we're perfectly happy where we are, thank you."

I am not the sort of man who enjoys making scenes in restaurants, but I am of the opinion that unless we wish to see standards plummeting all around us, it is the duty of those of us who care about excellence to stand up and be counted; or in this case, sit and be counted.

I said, "I'm very sorry to have to disagree with my wife, but we are *not* perfectly happy where we are."

The geisha said, "Perhaps in the circumstances you'd care to try another restaurant?"

I said that another table would be quite sufficient.

B said, "I am going to take these chopsticks and push them up your nose if you don't shut up."

I'd like to have done something similar with the girl's cigarette at the next table. Either she was stone deaf, foreign, or in some inexplicable way part of this whole bizarre plot. For a moment I even found myself wondering if I had suffered severe memory loss and, though I didn't realise it, it was April Fool's Day.

At all events, by this stage I badly needed to go to the loo. This was situated at the back of the downstairs rooms, which were also completely empty.

Returned to my seat to be informed by B that we had been asked to leave. Am so unused to treatment of this kind that at first the news completely failed to sink in. All I did register was the fact that the girl at the next table had stopped smoking. Otherwise my attention was directed entirely towards the menu.

Was suddenly aware that B was coughing in a rather meaningful way. Looked up to see geisha standing beside my chair holding our coats.

"The evening has obviously got off on the wrong foot and I cannot see it recovering," he said. "I suggest you start afresh somewhere else."

I said, "I don't think that will be necessary. We couldn't be happier if we tried," and waved him away.

He had no alternative but to serve us. By now, however, chopsticks up the nose was the least of my worries. A pair in the back of the neck seemed far more of a possibility. It was the sort of evening when bang–bang chicken could suddenly have acquired a whole new meaning.

In the event, our punishment was comparatively light: casual service, indifferent food and wine that was confiscated after the first two glasses had been poured out and not returned until we had eaten our last spoonfuls of 'exotic' fruit salad.

I have long suspected that Pamela van Zeller is involved in a slow, subtle campaign to take over my job. After this evening, I am more sure of it than ever.

Friday, January 18th

The first post brings my return ticket to Geneva. Surprised and slightly shocked to see that I am expected to travel tourist class. I realise it doesn't make a lot of difference on short flights, but that is not the point. It is the principle that counts. I have not given myself grey hairs on behalf of Ski Time in order to be lumped together with a bunch of provincial tour operators to whom the company owe nothing and who in any case might not even do business with it.

Fortunately, remembered from previous flights that row 19, being next to one of the emergency doors, always has twice the leg-room of any other tourist class row, so rang my friend Ray at the airline and asked him if there was the slightest chance of my being able to book a seat in that row from London to Geneva. I told him I'd book my return seat at the other end. It's one of those curious facts, known only to regular air travellers, that it is easier to get exactly the seats you want in foreign airports than in London.

Ray's secretary rang back within the hour to say that I was confirmed in seat 19 C. It couldn't be more perfect. Like most seasoned air travellers, I never sit next to the window.

In the midst of a heavy morning, Valjean's secretary rang to say that in order that I shouldn't have to waste time on Sunday morning getting my ski pass, would I bring with me a passport-size photograph? That way the pass could be processed overnight and be ready by breakfast on Sunday.

Unfortunately, what with one thing and another, left the office rather later than expected. As a result arrived at home tube station shortly after five fifteen. Dashed straight to photographic booth in station to find a large OUT OF ORDER sign. Ran in pouring rain to nearest Woolies and rushed to booth at back of shop. Stuck in money, leapt onto

155

seat and combed hair etc as best I could. Also tried slightly different expression for each flash. I have always been a great believer in making a virtue out of necessity.

Made a mental note to point out to cashier that pictures here take five and a half minutes to develop, not four as advertised. However, waiting time of little significance since end result totally blurred and useless. Hunted for assistant who sent me to cash desk for refund. Further delay while cashier hunted for manageress to okay refund. Finally seized money and rushed back to booth, only to be beaten to it by ferociously ugly man of obviously foreign extraction who sat in booth for several minutes to no obvious effect before emerging and sending for assistant. She finally deigned to come across, whereupon she declared the machine broken and beyond repair for the fore-seeable future. Looking at the man's face, I'm not altogether surprised.

Saturday, January 19th

Woke much earlier than usual and worried for an hour about nothing in particular. Finally, at six thirty, decided I had better things to do than lying around listening to B snoring, so slipped out of bed, taking care not to disturb her.

Unfortunately, in my anxiety not to allow a whisper of cold air to infiltrate sheets, had failed to notice that the fool of a dog had crept in during the night and was stretched out next to my bedside table. As a result, stepped straight on to her head, setting her off and waking up the entire household. I know I'm not perfect, but I do sometimes think I am a man who is more sinned against than sinning.

Breakfasted uncharacteristically in pyjamas in hope of giv-ing B the illusion that this was just like any other Saturday morning, but her gloom at my impending departure was all too evident.

Suddenly realised as I was running my bath that I had done absolutely nothing in the way of pre-ski exercises. On the principle that every little helps, removed dressing-gown and tried a few pyjama-clad press-ups, only to find myself being mounted by Vita with a zest which, if carefully exploited, could earn her a fortune on the Rieperbahn.

Rather gratified to discover that I can still slip as easily into my ski pants as I did when I first tried them on in Moss Bros's winter sports hire department in 1959. Buying them outright at the end of that first holiday to Zell-am-See was one of the best investments I ever made. I daresay there are those, for whom fashion counts more than performance, who would say that black is not the most popular colour on the ski slopes these days and that the baggy look has had its day. That may well be so, but I do not remember Toni Sailer's downhill performances in the fifties being noticeably affected by the cut or colour of his trousers.

Nor have I ever been a leading advocate of the modern ski boot. True, my old Austrian lace-ups (another second-hand bargain) take rather longer to put on and take off than these clip-on types that are all the rage nowadays, and it's possible that they do not give quite such a degree of support to the ankles as some of these streamlined things that go halfway up to people's knees. On the other hand, I believe my stem-Christiania is second to none, given the right sort of snow conditions, and I'd like to see some of these young speed merchants trying to jive at tea dances without taking their boots off first.

Although the flight from Gatwick was not until two thirty, decided to make an early start. It can be a bit of a scrum down there at this time of year, and besides, B was beginning to look decidedly moist around the eyes.

As I was leaving, she said, "Make sure you behave yourself."

I laughed and kissed her tenderly on the forehead. "Some husbands spend most of their lives away on business trips," I said.

"Not in glamorous French ski resorts, they don't," she said.

Could not help reflecting on the way to Victoria Station that, in the circumstances, deciding not to become a career diplomat was one of the best moves I ever made in my life.

Arrived at station at eleven forty-five to discover there had been a derailment outside Redhill and that Gatwick passengers were being diverted to East Croydon where buses had been laid on to shuttle them to the airport.

As a result, arrived at airport with slightly less than an hour to go before take-off to find queues of wartime proportions at every check-in desk and absolutely no sign of Valjean and the rest of our party.

Another twenty minutes were to pass before I was finally able to heave my suitcase onto the weighing platform.

"Only smoking left, I'm afraid," the girl told me in an off-hand manner.

I explained that in fact I had already reserved my seat. She punched a few keys and stared at her computer screen.

"Are you Mr Cusp?" she asked.

To be recognised by a head waiter in a restaurant is gratifying enough, but to be addressed by name at an airport check-in desk, albeit slightly inaccurately, is, I think anyone would agree, some sort of indication that one has arrived, in every sense of the word.

I said that I was.

"Row 19, Seat C?" she said.

"That is correct," I said.

"You're with Mr Valjean's group, I believe?"

"I am," I said.

She said, "I understand that the whole group has been upgraded to Club class."

I said that I was very glad to hear it.

"However," she said, "Mr Valjean gathered you had made your own seating arrangements and since you weren't here at the time, he thought that you would probably be happier to stick to them."

To add insult to injury, Valjean and his travel agent cronies were even then, I discovered, enjoying hospitality and free drinks in the airline's VIP lounge from which I, as an economy-class passenger, was automatically excluded.

By this time, the flight was beginning to be called (though not, I daresay, for the privileged few) and I barely had time to buy my usual litre of Famous Grouse and the 200 cigarettes I always get for Mother (not that she smokes but the

Bossages next door do) before rushing to the departure gate.

Of course, it had to be out at the Satellite, which meant a further delay while the next monorail came in.

Finally scrambled aboard with minutes to spare, only to discover that not only was row 19 nowhere near the emergency exit, but that it appeared to have even less leg room than normal economy-class seats. *And* it was in the smoking section, right at the back, next to the lavatories.

To make matters even worse, the seat next to me was occupied by a man who looked as if he made a living out of winning pie-eating contests. Indeed, most of him appeared to be in my seat, if not in my lap.

Summoned stewardess to ask since when had they decided to alter the seating arrangements on their planes. She said they had been like that for as long as she could remember, and she'd been with the airline twenty years. And it showed, I felt like saying.

I said, "But Row 19 has always been next to the emergency exit. It's well known as having more leg room even than Club class."

"You must be thinking of the 747," she said, and told me to fasten my seat belt. With the Pie Eating Champion wedged up next to me, a seat belt seemed superfluous.

At that moment the pilot came on the intercom (always a bad sign when you're still on the tarmac) to say that unfortunately there was a bit of a traffic jam at Geneva, and that since we had been rather slow in boarding, we had missed our take-off slot and would therefore be subject to a slight delay. He couldn't give us an exact take-off time, but the way things were looking, he thought there was every chance we could be on our way by four thirty.

I couldn't believe my ears. That was two hours away.

But there was more to come. Because an empty slot might come up at any moment, he was sure we would quite understand if the cabin staff did not disembark us. In the meantime, they would be serving us lunch, which he hoped would help to pass the time much more pleasantly.

By the time my plastic tray arrived, was so hot and

uncomfortable, that the first thing I did was to tear open the little sachet containing the refresher towelette, and give my face a good wipe all over.

It was only when I had finished that I realised that it wasn't a refresher towelette at all but some kind of impregnated cloth for cleaning shoes, and that my face, far from being refreshed, was coated in a silicone substance that was very rapidly drying into a hard, shiny surface.

Managed to get the worst of it off in the loo, but still had that curiously tight feeling one gets when one has been too long in the sun.

Was wrestling with plastic wrapping on small portion of bright red farmhouse cheddar when Valjean hove into view to say how well I was looking, how sorry he was to have missed me earlier and how surprised that I should have gone to so much trouble to book what looked to him to be an unusually uncomfortable seat.

I told him that, for reasons I'd rather not go into, I only ever travelled at the back of aeroplanes. I also assured him there was nothing I needed, and that I was looking forward to meeting all the others at Geneva.

We finally took off at four forty-five and arrived in Geneva to find the baggage collection area looking like a scene out of *Exodus*. Fellow members of my party equally refugee-like and underprivileged. A man called Bob from Wolverhampton who looked curiously like Enoch Powell; a couple called Ken and Anna who bored for Birmingham; a tall, hideous man with thick glasses who did John Arlott impersonations; a man called Alec from Norwich who spoke with a stagey camp voice and walked with his hands clasped lightly over his stomach, as though he were pregnant – which for all I know he could have been; and a man with a mouth like a chicken's bottom called Bossage who was almost as boring as his namesakes who live next to Mother. I can only suppose the Bossages just happen to be from particularly boring stock.

The only ray of light is Bubbles Macmahon – a tall, well-built girl with the sultry good looks that so often go with a wall eye.

However, I was in no mood for social chit-chat, and since

my suitcase appeared almost immediately, I slithered off through the ice and slush in search of our coach which, needless to say, wasn't parked anywhere near where Valjean had said.

Threw suitcase into hold and climbed gratefully into seat directly behind driver's and nearest to heater. However, as there was no sign of the driver and no means of closing the door, by the time Peter, our brown-faced, heavily moustached, quite good-looking in an obvious sort of way, north country Ski Time rep., had finally gathered together all the Les Vals people, hunted for various missing items of luggage, checked them off endlessly against his list, and dragged the driver out of a nearby bar, a good hour and three quarters had passed and my feet were like blocks of ice. I had also developed a splitting headache.

However, succeeded, by cunning placing of various articles, to deter others from sitting next to me, and was congratulating myself on making up for the rigours of 19 C when at the very last moment, the door hissed open and who should come lumbering out of the darkness but the Pie Eater. And three guesses which was the only free seat on the whole bus?

Quite why I hadn't registered that the transfer from airport to resort took four hours, not including a stop in Annecy for coffee and rather nasty toasted sandwiches, I can't think; but it hadn't.

Finally arrived at hotel shortly before one – in my case, a mere fourteen hours after leaving home. I wouldn't wish such a journey on my worst enemies; on the other hand, an hour or two on that bus in the company of the Pie Eater might persuade some people I know that being a public relations executive is not all beer and skittles.

A light supper had been laid on in the dining-room, but I made my excuses and retired to my room. A blow-by-blow account of our journey, delivered in the style of a John Arlott Test Match commentary, was far too heavy a price to pay for the doubtful pleasures of an *assiette Anglaise* and a glass of *vin du pays*.

It was only as I was nodding off to sleep that I remembered I had forgotten to bring a passport-sized photograph of myself. Also my woolly hat.

Sunday, January 20th

A restless night, thanks largely to sexual antics of couple in next room. I had no idea people could keep going for quite so long. It might have been understandable if they'd been French.

Finally got off around two thirty, only to dream constantly and disconcertingly about Ms Macmahon. Woke at seven to a glorious alpine morning: the tips of the mountains on the other side of the valley pink with the rays of the rising sun; the sky a pale, cloudless blue.

Was on my way down to breakfast when the door of the next-door room opened and out stepped as unattractive a couple as it would be possible to imagine: she with protruding teeth and hips the width of the M4; he a weedy version of the famous mass murderer, Christie. Obviously it is not their fault that they look like they do, but I do think they might have the modesty to keep their intimate behaviour to themselves.

After breakfast, Valjean divided the party into two: experts and rabbits. He explained that each group would be assigned to an instructor who would take them off and show them the main runs, after which we were to *rendez-vous* at Charlie's Bar at the top of Les Crampons run for lunch with the Director of Tourism.

Unfortunately, had to forgo that particular pleasure, owing to spending half the morning queuing at photographic booth and fiddling about at offices of skilift company, trying to organise free skipass.

Interested to notice how, although it is several years since I last strapped a pair of hired skis to the bottom of my feet and launched myself off down the mountainside in a series of well-executed stem turns, it was only a matter of minutes before I was picking my way through the bumps as confidently and proficiently as if I had never taken them off. I was only sorry my talent for reading ski maps had not held up quite so well, since I got completely lost up by the heliport and instead of enjoying a delicious three-course lunch on a sun terrace, had to make do with a hot dog and a plate of chips, both very expensive, at a sort of glorified snack bar in the middle of nowhere.

Valjean obviously slightly put out that his PR man had apparently adopted such a high-handed attitude towards the Tourism Director, especially since he is our host. Enoch Powell, John Arlott and Alec also rather sniffy when we met in the bar for a pre-dinner drink. Bubbles, on the other hand, clearly rather intrigued by my maverick behaviour, and before long we were chatting away over a *kir royal* as if we had known each other for years. In fact, when she asked if I was married, I very nearly said no!

She was most interested to hear that they had a mixed sauna bath in the basement of the hotel and it seemed the most natural thing in the world to suggest we might give it a go after dinner. She seemed to think so, too.

Had rather more wine with my meal than I had intended, and it was that, as much as not wishing my motives to be misunderstood, that made me say to Bubbles over the coffee: "When I asked you to join me in the sauna before dinner, I didn't mean it in any sexual way, you understand."

To my surprise, she suddenly went very peculiar indeed and said she certainly hadn't taken it that way, and that on second thoughts, she was really rather tired and hoped I didn't mind if she went to bed early.

I'm still not entirely sure where I went wrong. All I do know is that, from that moment on, I have had the definite impression she has been trying to avoid me. The silly thing is, I really hadn't asked her out of any ulterior motive. Perhaps if I had, we might still be friends. Or even something more.

Monday, January 21st

Woke to heavy cloud, driving snow and almost zero visibility. Travelling up on a long double T-bar, I knew what Shackleton must have gone through in the Antarctic. The effect on my skiing was dramatic. From being a perfectly competent, if slightly slow, performer yesterday, I was reduced to a level slightly below that of a beginner. Celluloid images of skiers floating down through the deep snow, the powder flying up past their shoulders, rose up in my mind, but though the spirit

was willing, the flesh wasn't. At one point, I fell over just standing there. By some wretched stroke of luck, I happened to
land bang on my right thumb, bending it backwards and
causing considerable pain.

Lunched miserably off spaghetti bolognese in large, hot,
noisy self-service restaurant; told Jean-Claude and the others
that I was calling it a day, and headed off towards four-man
chair lift. Seeing an empty space between a young man on the
left and a middle-aged man and his wife on the right, I moved
forward, and as I did so, the middle-aged man moved to his
left, leaving me stranded. Was contemplating moving to far
right when chair came whizzing round, catching me under the
knees and carrying me forward, at the same time throwing me
violently backwards so that my head hit the bar behind me.
Had barely recovered from the blow when I realised I was
heading up the mountain with the middle-aged man sitting
firmly on my lap. I told him the least he could do would be to
apologise.

He said, in French, that on the contrary, it was I who should
apologise to him. His wife was not accustomed to this sort of
lift.

I replied, not in French, that in that case she shouldn't have
been on it then – certainly not with a face like a Marseillais
truck driver – and that it would look even uglier by the time I'd
been over it a couple of times with my Dynamic Omasofts,
and would he mind moving his fat French backside off my
legs?

And to think that when the Channel Tunnel opens in 1993
people like him will be in and out of England, polluting the
Kent countryside with their bad breath and, if we're not very
careful, buying up weekend cottages in Whitstable and love-
nests in Folkestone.

Arrived back in my room to find my anorak collar stiff with
blood and a hole the size of a silver threepenny bit in the back
of my head. This meant another wasted two hours sitting
about in the doctor's ante-room, flicking through old copies
of *Jours de France* waiting to have a couple of stitches in my
skull, plus an anti-tetanus injection. I told him that I was not
allergic to the stuff, but I think I may have been muddling it

with penicillin. At all events, felt so woozy in the middle of dinner that I had to go to my room and lie down. I may well have OD'd without realising it. *Tant mieux*, the way I'm feeling.

Dozed off to be woken at about one o'clock by sounds of another long, noisy, action-packed bout of *Sportsnight* with the Troilus and Cressida of Notre Dame. At one point they lapsed into coy, nursery language and threw themselves into an elaborate game of hunt-the-naughty-bits. This might have continued indefinitely had a man in a neighbouring room not suddenly roared out at the top of his voice, 'Oh, for God's sake, tell him where your little botty is and let's all get some sleep.''

Tuesday, January 22nd

As wretched a day as I have ever known. Heavy snow, splitting headache, throbbing thumb, overcooked boiled egg and non-stop John Arlott for breakfast, plus cold shoulder from Ms Macmahon.

Told Jean-Claude that, unlike the others in our group, I had important work to do and would therefore not be joining them on their ski safari to the nearby village of Fugeirolles for a traditional Savoyard mountain lunch with the mayor and a visit to a cheese-making factory before returning via the Col des Grottes in time for drinks and refreshments at Le Sunny, next to Les Marmottes chair-lift, with the Ski School Director, followed at six thirty by a presentation of the film *A Nous Les Jolis Valois* at the Maison de Tourisme, a demonstration of local lace-making by the nuns of the Convent of Sainte Marie des Avalanches, and a cocktail reception in the lounge of the Hotel des Invalides to meet ex-downhill champion and PR to the *Association des Hotels Valois*, Bernard Prost.

On the other hand, promised that if my condition did not deteriorate during the course of the day, I would certainly try and join them all for a Fondue Savoyarde at Mike's Place at eight thirty.

Quickly retired to my room before Valjean appeared and tried to jolly me into something I'd later regret.

Lay on my bed and read the new Charles Paris theatrical mystery by Simon Brett. I have a feeling I may have met the author at a party at Oxford. Or am I thinking of Simon somebody else?

Lunched moderately off *côte du porc Normande* in hotel restaurant, scrawled pc's to Mother, B, Charlie Kippax, etc, walked up to shops to try and find a little present for JJ, failed, returned to hotel and slept for the rest of the afternoon.

To Mike's Place for the *fondue*, but felt rather out of things. To hear everyone talk, you'd have thought the day had been one long round of hilarity. Perhaps it had, but I could hardly be expected to see it that way. Evening might have been more of a personal success if I had poured local white wine down my throat with anything approaching the same gusto as my so-called colleagues. However, decided in circumstances to abstain and drink water instead.

It is some measure of the contempt in which our Common Market *confrères* hold us in Britain that it wasn't until I had consumed several glassfuls that Valjean bothered to point out that one should never drink water with a fondue. Apparently it turns the melted cheese into a hard ball in your stomach and people have been known to die as a result. Wine, on the other hand, helps to digest the cheese. He didn't think there was any danger, but one never knew.

I can only think that this is Valjean's way of rapping me over the knuckles for cutting the day's programme. If so, he has chosen a pretty drastic way of doing so. I may well ask Kippax to take me off the account and hand it over to Pamela instead. Unless, of course, nature takes its course, in which case I may not have to ask.

To bed with a slight tummy pain and a raging thirst which, because I dared not attempt to slake it, gave me a virtually sleepless night.

Not a sound from Troilus and Cressida. Perhaps they've suffered a double heart attack as a result of their efforts. Feel curiously envious.

Wednesday, January 23rd

An astonishing turn of events. Woke up to a beautiful day, ate a huge breakfast and skied like a madman all morning. I didn't fall over once. Even Ms Macmahon was able to drag her eyes away from Jean-Claude on a couple of occasions, and sharing a T-bar with her at one point, she said, with a certain amount of awe in her voice, "You've obviously been skiing for a very long time."

I cannot pretend I wasn't flattered. "I've knocked around a few pistes in my time," I confessed.

"So have your ski-ing trousers apparently," she said. I laughed and said these modern nylon all-in-one suits were all very colourful, but that nothing kept out the cold more effectively than a good Babour, and a decent bit of English worsted. She said, "Have you ever thought of skiing in your overcoat?" I replied that the trouble with coats was that they tended to get in the way of your knees when turning. "Yes," she said, "and with the sort of turns some people do, their knees need all the room they can get."

Presumed she was referring to Alec and Bob in the mediocre group.

I'm so glad we're on speaking terms again, especially since we both speak the same skiing language.

To Le Ski Pub for lunch. Had barely sat down at plain wooden table on sun-kissed rustic terrace and begun to take in view when a voice said, in English, "What can I get you all to drink?"

Looked up and there, standing beside me with an apron around her jeans and note-pad in her hand, was Jane Baker! I simply could not believe my eyes: not least because she was looking so much slimmer and prettier than when I last saw her five years ago. The sun has obviously done her spots the world of good, and the contact lenses are a vast improvement on those terrible National Health type specs she would insist on wearing when we shared the flat together – and, for a short time, our lives.

Was so taken aback that I found myself ordering a *pastis*, a drink which I have never much cared for.

Obviously it was impossible to do more than exchange a few exclamations and pleasantries at that stage, but after lunch I stayed on and we sat in the sun drinking coffee and having a really good crack together.

Apparently her marriage to Hans had not been a great success. Being the wife of a handsome ski instructor was quite fun for a bit, and she was very happy looking after their little chalet and bringing up baby Anton. But the novelty soon began to wear thin. The sight of him setting off to work, dressed in the ski-school anorak and wearing the badge of assistant director on his left breast, never failed to bring a lump of pride to her throat. But somehow he never looked quite the same in his labourer's overall in the summer months, and really the bee-keeping had not been the success he had hoped for.

There was also the matter of the 'private lessons' he gave to the younger female members of his classes, which she tolerated for a couple of seasons, but which finally came to a head with a very rich, very tall, very slim, very beautiful American woman from Baltimore who infuriated Jane by always looking down her nose at her. "That nose," she declared "really stuck in my throat."

Finally, she had left Hans and gone to live in Innsbruck where she had scratched a living for a year giving English lessons. Then, when they had finally divorced two and a half years ago, she had met this young Frenchman called Bernard who was thinking of starting up a mountain restaurant in Les Vals and suggested she came along and helped him. She had a flat in the village, near the Office du Tourisme; Anton was at school in Les Beaumes, and she really couldn't be happier if she tried.

Surprised to detect in myself a faint twinge of jealousy, followed by sharp sense of relief when she revealed that she was neither married to nor living with Bernard, and that their relationship had always been on a purely professional footing.

Quite what my motives were for asking her to meet me for a drink after dinner this evening, I am still not entirely sure.

Although I do not believe that the chances of reviving old

168

love affairs are terribly high, I was in one of my devil–may–care sort of moods, and if something happened, then it happened. After all, I had known Jane long before B ever came on the scene, and just because I am married, it does not automatically cancel out everything that went before. To my way of thinking, old relationships should be seen as something quite separate from marriage and in no sense liable to the same rules.

In the event, the whole question was entirely academic, since I arrived at her flat to find that Anton had got a nasty tummy bug and such conversation as we managed to have was constantly interrupted by calls from the bedroom for "Mummy" and much to-ing and fro-ing with glasses of water, buckets, clean pyjamas, etc.

In fact, the nearest I came to making physical contact with Jane was when I leaned forward to kiss her goodnight on the cheek, Anton called out for the umpteenth time, she turned her head to answer and I banged my lips against the door-frame.

I'm bound to say that, all things considered, I was quite relieved. It was more than could be said, apparently, for poor old Troilus.

Thursday, January 24th

Woke to yet another glorious morning, feeling as if a huge burden had been lifted from my shoulders. Thumb still sore, but operative.

At breakfast, Bob told Alec that there had been a shortfall in per capita off-take with special reference to the Canary Islands. It was the first time I had seen Alec completely stuck for words.

Was in the bedroom Vaseline-ing my ankles when the phone rang. It was Jane to say that she was so sorry about last night, but that Anton was feeling much better and had insisted on going off to school, and since she had the day off, why didn't we ski together?

Told her I couldn't think of anything nicer and we agreed to meet in half an hour's time at the bottom of Les Bim-Boms bubble lift.

Unfortunately, had to watch five jam-packed *navettes* go by before I finally managed to squeeze onto one. Even then I had to travel with my nose an inch from the ugly features of a noisy German whose yellowish skin gleamed with Piz Buin and whose breath smelt like a Bavarian farmyard. Tried to hold my own for as long as possible at a time, but had to breathe in so deeply at end of each go that smell even more punishing than before. Tried twisting head away, but forced to desist owing to ominous twinge at side of neck.

Finally arrived at Bim-Boms feeling rather faint, only to discover lift out of order and several hundred skiers standing about in resigned fashion like expensively dressed sheep. Fortunately, bumped into Jane very quickly. She was looking very neat in her powder blue suit. Never realised before what a very nice bottom she has. Perhaps it looked like that when we were going out together. If so, it must have completely escaped my notice.

After standing about for quarter of an hour, there was still no sign of life from the lifts. Had imagined in the circumstances that the lift people might have had the common courtesy to address us over the loud speakers and explain the current state of play, but should have known better. Never apologise, never explain; that's the French motto. Never mind the stupid customers; they're only the ones who pay all their salaries and keep them in Porsche cars and Christian Dior underwear.

As one of the key figures in tourism in Les Vals, felt it my duty to find out who was in charge and what was going on. Unfortunately, by this stage, so wedged in amongst other skiers that I couldn't move an inch in any direction. Tried to push my way through, but of course everyone assumed I was trying to queue barge and there was very nearly an ugly scene.

In the midst of it all, the lifts suddenly started working, but even so, it was ages before the queue began to move. In a moment of exasperation, clapped my hands in front of me in a chivvying sort of way, saying, "Come on, come on." At that moment, the large woman in front of me stepped backwards and I suddenly found I was clasping several kilos of Gallic *gluteus maximus*.

I sometimes wonder if the French have any sense of humour whatever.

Still, I doubt if I have ever skied better than I did that morning. Jane also in marvellous form. I had never thought of her as a graceful creature, but watching her as she picked her way down the mountainside, I was reminded of a young chamois or perhaps a gazelle, so swift were her movements and so elegant her twists and turns. It quite took my breath away and made me wonder more than once why it was that we had never managed to put our relationship onto a sounder footing all those years ago.

It wasn't that I felt any the less fond of Belinda; but up there, in that brilliant sunshine and clean mountain air, swooping through the moguls and shussing down paths, she and John Julius and Brixton seemed an awful long way away.

In fact, trying to remember what she looked like when she smiled was probably what lost me my concentration, causing me to cross the tips of my skis and fall forward at high speed and finish up stunned, winded and flat on my face in the snow.

It wasn't until I was getting into my bath later that afternoon that I became aware of the full extent of my injuries: a very bruised rib – possibly even a broken one; a wrenched shoulder; a bruised cheek; and a stiff neck. The torn thumb and the hole in the back of the head seemed positively trivial by comparison.

Valjean peculiarly unsympathetic about my not feeling up to the fancy-dress evening, disco dancing and beer-drinking contest at Le Snowpub. But then that's the French all over for you. All macho on the surface, but softer than unsalted butter underneath. The slightest hint of a headache and sure as eggs he'd be prostrate in his room like the Dame aux Camélias.

Jane, on the other hand, as kind and thoughtful as ever I remember her.

Was lying on my bed after dinner, toying with Simon Brett, when there was a knock on the door and there she was with Veganin, half a bottle of Bells and a tube of linament which she proceeded to massage into my shoulder.

It was as much as I could do to restrain myself from pulling her down onto the bed beside me and crushing my lips brutally yet tenderly against hers.

While she was in the bathroom washing her hands, the phone rang. It was Belinda to say that she thought that husbands always rang their wives whenever they went abroad, but that I was obviously having far too good a time for the thought even to have crossed my mind.

I said, "Look, I'm in the middle of a business meeting. Can I call you back tomorrow?"

"By all means," she said; "but don't be surprised if I'm not here," and she put the phone down on me.

I do not hold a very strong brief for reincarnation, but in the event of it being an integral part of The Deal, the next time I come back, I'd like to do so as a gay orphan.

Friday, January 25th

Woke at six, more or less immobile. When I breathed there did not seem to be any part of me that did not hurt. Had a very hot bath and went down to breakfast feeling, and moving, like Frankenstein's Monster.

Was on my way to farewell drinks and buffet lunch at Office du Tourisme when I had a message my wife was on the phone. To my surprise, she behaved as if yesterday's conversation had never taken place.

She said, casually, "I thought you'd like to know. I've bought us a house."

For a moment I was rendered quite speechless. Then, suddenly, dozens of questions came pouring out.

Had the old ladies accepted our offer? Had she been looking elsewhere while I had been away? Gloucestershire perhaps? Kent?

"Tooting," she said. "Colliers Wood actually, Elwyn Road, SW19."

I reminded her that we had agreed that London was no place to bring up children these days and that, as I had understood it, we would be moving to the country.

She said that obviously I had understood it wrong. She had no intention, and never had had, of giving up her London friends, her London shops and her London hairdresser in return for a boring life in the middle of nowhere, surrounded by drab women in headscarves, quilted jackets and no make-up, driving round the countryside in a Volkswagen Passat estate on endless school runs while her husband grumbled continually about the train service and the rising cost of hay, thank you very much.

She added that she had had quite enough of my tiddling around England looking at houses that we couldn't possibly afford, in places that she didn't wish to live, and so, rather than risk further discussion, she had rung up Loomis Chaffee and told them to find us a house in south-west London, near a tube, with a small garden and not too far from a common, costing between sixty and seventy thousand.

They'd rung their people in Tooting who'd come up with half a dozen possibilities. She'd looked at three in one afternoon and decided this one fitted the bill. Three bedrooms, sitting-room, kitchen and breakfast-room and fifty-foot garden. The local agent, whose name is Hubert Smith, had assured her it was really exceptional for the area and for the asking price of £66,950. She had made an offer of £66,000 and they'd settled for £66,500 to include carpets and some curtains. That was on Tuesday.

On Wednesday, Julian Hankey-Barber showed the garden flat to a young Old Etonian stockbroker and his titled wife, who fell in love with it on the spot and settled that same evening for the asking price.

On Monday, someone called Richard something-or-other, whose name I didn't quite catch, is going to Elwyn Road to carry out a full structural survey, and on Tuesday, someone will be round to survey the flat.

She said she had spoken to her parents' solicitor who sees no reason why contracts shouldn't be exchanged on both properties in a fortnight and we should be able to move a week after that.

She had also been in touch with an agency in St John's Wood about getting an *au pair* girl. Apparently there is a whole bunch of them coming over in four weeks' time. Anyway, she had to go now, the baby was crying. She hoped I was having a good time and she looked forward to seeing me tomorrow evening sometime.

Women are all the same. You can't leave them on their own for five minutes. As for these so-called "financial provisions" that the major is supposed to have made for his daughter and grandson, they obviously do not run to a down payment on a house in a decent part of town.

In the circumstances, it is hardly surprising that the Farewell Barbecue on the terrace of the Mouton Agile mountain restaurant, followed by the torchlit descent of Le Mickey Mouse run, did not make as much impression on me as they might have done.

Felt it would be churlish not to join them all for a night-cap in the hotel bar. Ken and Anna rather nicer than I'd thought. Bubbles also more friendly than usual and even went so far as to enquire where I lived. I asked her if she knew London at all. She said that she and her sister had just bought a small house near Clapham Common. I said that, by an extraordinary coincidence, we were moving down that way ourselves. She was most interested to learn that we were to be neighbours and asked where exactly. When I told her Colliers Wood, she said, "Ah," and turned and started talking to Valjean about tomorrow's travel arrangements.

I cannot wait to get home. Or can I?

Saturday, January 26th

Astounded to be woken at six forty-five by a jangling telephone and the maddeningly cheerful voice of the receptionist reminding me that breakfast would be served in half an hour in Les Chamois restaurant, that I should have my bag packed and in the hall no later than ten past seven, and that the bus would be leaving at eight o'clock sharp.

I realise Les Vals is one of the more remote French ski resorts, also that the reps are keen to get everyone to Geneva Airport in good time to meet the next bunch coming in. Even so, to set off for a six thirty p.m. flight more than ten hours in advance was surely carrying caution a little too far.

Made my feelings known to Peter, the rep, in no uncertain terms over the *muesli*. He said that the traffic was so heavy in the valley on Saturdays, even in good weather, it could take at least four hours to get to Annecy, and that in snowy conditions like today's, five or six hours was not unknown. He added that if I wanted to blame anyone, I should blame the tour operators for organising all their holidays to run from Saturday to Saturday.

I said that I had every intention of looking into the matter when I got back to London, and that in the meantime a sharp word in Valjean's ear might not go amiss.

He said that Valjean was still asleep, but that he'd promised he'd try and get up in time to see us off.

I said that sounded suspiciously as though he wasn't travelling with us. If so, it was the first I'd heard of it.

Peter said he wouldn't know about that, and went off to check the luggage.

Not the most cheerful of departures I have ever known. Valjean very casual about leaving us in the lurch and muttered something about having to stay on and organise the bookings for next season.

I said that we'd doubtless be talking in London next week.

"We'll be in touch," he said, and shook me by the hand. "Goodbye, and thank you for everything you have done over the last year."

I laughed, and said, "Don't you mean *au revoir*?"

"No," he said.

I've said it before and I'll say it again, the French are queer fish. One might as well try and converse with Martians.

Set off in near-blizzard conditions and with sinking heart, which plummeted to knee level when, after crawling down the narrow, precipitous mountain road for less than five minutes, we came to a grinding halt behind a line of cars that wound away in front of us and below us as far as the eye could see.

Might have been able to take my mind off things by finishing Simon Brett, had a bunch of Sloaney types a few seats back not taken it into their heads to play Trivial Pursuit.

A young man called Rufus appointed himself question-master, a task which he performed at full volume. It wasn't the fact that his five companions felt it necessary to reply at similar decibel levels that very nearly drove me to the point where I seriously considered getting off the coach and walking to Geneva, so much as their utter ignorance and total stupidity.

The more I listened, the more I congratulated myself on having rejected the private sector of education in favour of the comprehensive system.

Partly for my own interest and partly because it might prove a useful piece of research for future students of sociology and English educational methods in the 1980s, here are a few random examples of their performance:

"Who called religion 'the opium of the people'?" Answer: John Lennon.

"What US city was named after British Prime Minister William Pitt?" Answer: Williamsburg.

"Where was El Greco born?" Answer: Barcelona.

"Whose diary was serialised on radio for many years?" Answer: Adrian Mole's.

"Who is Othello's wife?" Answer: Mrs Othello.

More often than not, their ignorance was concealed beneath a thin veneer of facetiousness, eg:

"What school did Billy Bunter attend?" Answers (amid screams of knowing laughter): Eton, Harrow, comprehensive, prep, cookery.

"What is the first Commandment?" Answer: Don't get caught.

"What was Sir Christopher Cockerell's uplifting invention?" Answer: the bra.

"What's the usual age for a Jewish boy to celebrate his *bar mitzvah*?" Answer: Don't know; never met one.

"What is a rhinoceros horn made of?" Answer: I know what mine's made of.

"What is man's most common pain?" Answer: Woman.

"What does the average American spend 710 days doing by age of 18?" Answers: Too many and too indistinct amid sounds of hilarity to note down, and mostly too unpublishable.

Their capacity for puerile humour appeared to be limitless; their concern at their lack of knowledge and their consideration for their fellow-passengers non-existent. Of the several hundred questions they attempted during the hour and a half it took us to get to Moûtiers, the one they all knew at once was "What shop's telephone number is 01-730 1234?" To hear them shouting out "Harrods!" at the top of their voices, one would have thought they'd discovered Halley's Comet or the law of gravity.

Finally, became so exasperated when none of them knew the name of the range of hills that runs through Oxfordshire and Buckinghamshire, that I could not restrain myself from calling out, "Oh for goodness sake. The Cotswolds. Don't you know anything?"

There was a stunned silence and then Rufus said, "The Chilterns, actually."

The stupid thing is, I knew the answer perfectly well. As I pointed out to them, I couldn't hear very well above the noise of the engine and thought he'd said Oxfordshire and *Berkshire*.

At one point in the journey, began to wonder if I would ever see either of those counties again, or indeed England, my wife or my child.

Finally, in a state of near physical and mental collapse, shuffled through front door of garden flat shortly before ten fifteen, to find Belinda deep in conversation on the telephone. Had naturally assumed that she would cut the chat short, gather me to her ample bosom and revive me with love and kisses and several large whisky and sodas. Was slightly surprised, therefore, when she merely looked up, remarked that she hadn't expected me so early, and returned to a long and, to my way of thinking, inconsequential discussion on the relative merits of various West-End hairdressers.

When she had finally shot her bolt and replaced the receiver, I asked her who she had been talking to.

"Paula Batty," she said.

I said, "Oh, and has she been away on a hard-working business trip too?"

"No," she said, "Why?"

"I just wondered," I said.

I noticed she didn't pursue the matter, so I rather think she must have got the point.

Slipped in to have a quick look at John Julius. How trusting babies are when they sleep and how lucky not to have to involve themselves in the hurly-burly of modern life. There are times when I would give a lot just to shed the years and return to the carefree warmth and ease of a carrycot and the simple pleasures of Cow & Gate.

Was naturally sorry to learn that B had been expecting me to come home bearing armfuls of large and expensive gifts for them all, but have promised to try and make it up to them in time. Meanwhile, I can only thank God for the joys and blessings of family life and ask His help in making me an even better husband and father than I am now. We can all of us only do our best.

Talking of which, I am surprised that B has made no comment so far on my injuries. Perhaps I should be relieved to know that they do not appear as bad as I thought. They certainly *feel* a great deal worse.

Sunday, January 27th

To Colliers Wood after breakfast to see the house. Had every intention of getting up really early and going to eight o'clock Communion, but felt that, in the circumstances, God would probably understand. In many ways I feel it was partly His fault that I was in the condition I was in in the first place. Or am I being a bit hard on Him?

In fact, I feel that one way and another my reborn commitment to religion has not been quite as whole-hearted as I had hoped. I may well have reached the age when either one goes the whole hog and becomes a Roman Catholic, or else one virtually gives up and hopes for the best. At least you know where you stand as a Catholic, and what's expected of you. In our church, if you miss the eight o'clock, well, that's it for another week. The RCs make absolutely sure you can't get out of it by laying on second houses at twelve and six in the evening, and sometimes more often than that.

The theatrical side of my nature is also very much attracted by the bells and smells side of things. You really do feel something is going on. Being an RC can also be a great advantage socially. I may very well have a word with the Varney-Birches on the subject and see what the form is about joining. Who knows, I may very well find it's just the thing for me. After all, a clever man like Malcolm Muggeridge would certainly never have embraced Rome if there weren't something in it.

At all events, it would really give the major and Alyson something to complain about.

In re the house: while I cannot pretend that SW19 is among the more sought-after postal addresses in London, nor ever likely to be, and although I am disappointed to find that in Colliers Wood the stodge of the fast-food joint has yet to be leavened by the yeast of the bistro, I must admit that this is not quite such a backwater of civilisation as I had imagined. Naturally I would have preferred the more solidly Victorian look of Tooting Bec or even Tooting Broadway and the rather greener feeling with which the presence of the Common seems to invest these two areas. On the other hand, Colliers Wood High Street, being slightly on the narrow side, does have a definite villagey feel to it – and Elwyn Road, though not the most distinguished in south London, is perfectly pleasant.

Am surprised to find that what is basically a three-up, two-down with a few extra grace notes in the shape of a certain amount of louvred woodwork and a faintly rural kitchen/breakfast-room should be described in the particulars as a "superb house" worth the thick end of £67,000. However, B assures me that this is not only rather more spacious than most in the area, but that there's nothing people go for more these days than a house that doesn't need any structural alteration, rewiring, replumbing, reroofing etc, and that they can move into straightaway and paper and decorate in their own time.

It is also rare, apparently, to find such a large garden so far out. And although I do not see myself following Harold and Vita's example and creating a miniature Sissinghurst out of

179

this suburban wilderness, it would be nice to have a bit of grass outside the back door instead of concrete slabs; possibly even the odd rose-bush.

Am naturally slightly alarmed at the prospect of increasing my mortgage from £15,000 to £25,000, but B assures me that this is pretty modest by today's standards and that she is prepared to sell a few of her British Telecom shares if I feel I can't manage it on my own.

In fact, by the time we got home, I was really getting quite excited about the whole idea and can hardly wait to move. I have always felt there was something of the pioneer in me, and I have a sneaking suspicion that in five years' time the streets will be lined with Passat Estates and Golf GTI's, and the High Street bursting with bookshops, wine merchants, French restaurants and gift shops, and our friends will not be able to believe the laughable price we paid for our £150,000 house. I am only sorry the owners, Mr & Mrs Dalrymple-Macintyre, were not there to confirm my suspicions.

Also that B has not made quite the strides with Vita's training I had anticipated. This evening she ate two nappy-liners and looked thoroughly pleased with herself.

I said to her, "You're a very naughty dog. I can see I'm going to have to take you in hand," whereupon she rushed off into the kitchen barking her head off and ate several dirty Kleenex's out of the rubbish bin.

B said, "I forgot to tell you. The psychiatrist said that one shouldn't look at one's dog too much. It makes them self-conscious."

I sympathise.

Monday, January 28th

Is it my imagination, or have we got through an awful lot of loo paper since I've been away? Mentioned it to B and suggested that perhaps the dog had been late-night snacking off it, as the Americans would say.

B said, "You really cannot at your stage in life start worrying about how much loo paper we're using."

I said that I wasn't worried, merely puzzled.

She replied that, to her certain knowledge, she had not been particularly heavy-handed in recent days. Since childhood she had used five or six sheets per visit, and saw no reason to start upping the figure at this stage in her life.

I said that, to my way of thinking, five or six sheets was extravagant. I had always managed perfectly well with one, two at the outside, and saw no reason why others shouldn't do so too.

"One sheet?" she said. "I call that positively unhygienic."

"Not if you fold it," I pointed out.

"Well I think it's disgusting," she said. "You ought to be ashamed of yourself."

I can't for the life of me see why. Anyway, I'm not.

My shoulder is, if anything, worse.

Tuesday, January 29th

Our purchaser's surveyor arrived just as I was leaving for the office. I said that I was sorry I couldn't stay.

"I'm very glad you can't," he said. "There's nothing worse than having owners walking round behind you breathing down your neck and trying to *explain* everything. We do do this sort of thing for a living, you know."

He seemed in rather a bad mood, I thought. I only hope he's not the sort of man who allows personal considerations to cloud his professional judgement. Also that B remembered to put the suitcases in the little cupboard, as I asked. I don't think that damp patch is anything, but there's no point in rubbing his nose in it.

Rang the comprehensive when I got in and spoke to Utkinson-Hill, the headmaster. He said he was very sorry he couldn't speak to me the other day, but really he did not think there was any necessity for me to look round the school at this stage, and that the way things were going under this government, by the time JJ reached school age there probably wouldn't be any schools left for him to go to anyway. He then laughed and said that he was only joking.

I replied that, of course, I didn't want to waste his time. We were both busy men. I had simply rung to ask a few basic questions, eg whether it was a soccer or a rugger school; what sort of cricket fixture list they had; whether they still did Latin – that sort of thing.

Utkinson-Hill roared even louder and asked if I was from *Game for a Laugh* or what.

When I told him that this was a serious enquiry, he replied that "quite seriously", they could barely afford a tiddly-winks board, let alone a games field.

Realised we were obviously slightly at cross-purposes and said that perhaps I'd better come back to him nearer the time, adding that I couldn't help noticing he spoke with quite a marked accent. Was he perhaps from Norfolk or Suffolk? "Neither," he said. "Trinidad."

Wednesday, January 30th

Paula Batty rang first thing to say that she and Roland were thinking of having a St Valentine's Day Party and would we like to go?

Before I could say a word, B had accepted.

As if that did not constitute one of the worst starts to a day in a long while, I then discovered it is to be a fancy-dress do. I may very well go as the Invisible Man.

To doctors *en route* for office to have stitches removed from head. Hope it is well and truly healed, otherwise I might genuinely have to resort to heavy bandages.

Had a long talk with Nightingale and Hebblethwaite over coffee re this business of the children's education. I said that although in principle I was all in favour of supporting the state system and that the more middle-class professional types who sent their children to state schools, the greater their chances of improving, I really wondered if I wasn't letting my heart rule my head and shouldn't plump for a private education before it was too late.

Hebblethwaite said, "The way things are going, you may have left it too late already."

When I asked him what he meant, he explained that there are so many people chasing so many private places in London nowadays that children were having to sit exams at the age of four in order to get into pre-prep schools, and that if one didn't have one's child down at birth, one could find oneself in deep trouble. In fact, he'd heard rumours that in some areas, children of two and a half were having to sit exams for local nursery schools.

Perhaps we have made a terrible mistake and we should have moved to the country after all. Rang B in a panic to find the phone engaged. Tried several times during morning but with similar results. I suspect Paula Batty. Just as long as it was *her* call. If my telephone bill gets any higher, I soon won't be able to afford to buy my son rag-books, let alone tail-coats and Eton collars.

Arrived home to find that the surveyor hadn't spotted the damp patch behind the suitcases, but that he'd found a much worse one in the cupboard where the suitcases used to be.

This is not my day.

Thursday, January 31st

Going up in the lift this morning, Charlie Kippax announced, that he had just had a letter from the secretary of his London club putting up the annual subscription by fifty pounds a year.

"It's getting beyond a joke," Charlie said. "If this is any indication of the way things are going, I may well have to consider resigning."

I feel for him. I, too, have seriously been thinking about chucking up my AA membership.

Shoulder marginally easier.

February

Friday, February 1st

Finally relented and invited Bryant-Fenn to lunch with me
at Botticelli. Pamela also there and looking very much in
cahoots with Carlo. I smell the beginnings of a palace revolu-
tion. Unless, of course, she and Carlo are having a bit of
a thing. I wouldn't put it past either of them after the cake
incident.

Hugh in unusually charming and amusing form. For all his
freeloading mentality and faint odour of BO, I'm really quite
fond of the old thing.

He was very interested to hear about the new house and gave
me a piece of advice which I think could be very useful. He said
that although surveyors are very good at telling you about the
actual condition of a house, no-one ever tells you the most
important thing of all, and that is what your prospective
neighbours are like and what sort of things go on in your road
during the course of a day.

He said he knew some people who'd moved into a house in a
very nice street in Kentish Town without bothering to check
first, only to discover that the man on one side of them kept a
hundred cats which he only ever let out at night, and the one
on the other was the lead guitarist in an amateur pop group
that used to come round and practise three times a week.
Moreover, at the weekends, a friend used to restore a Jowitt
Javelin which he brought round on a garage recovery trailer
which took up parking space for four cars.

Hugh suggests that I knock on each of my prospective
neighbours' doors on the pretext of needing to check the

184

party-wall, and have a quick look round. "You'll very quickly see what you're in for," he said.

He also suggests that I sit in the street in my car for a day and watch the comings and goings. As he points out, quite rightly, Elwyn Road could easily be used as a slip road by commuter traffic in the mornings; and I'd be jolly annoyed to find my hedge being pulled to pieces and my front garden being used as a litter bin by children on their way to and from the local school.

Why Hugh should be such an expert on these matters, I can't imagine. The number of empty crisp packets and used tins of Tab that get chucked through the window of his third-floor flat in Prince of Wales Drive could surely be counted on the fingers of one hand.

On the other hand (no joke intended), there's no denying that what he says makes very good sense indeed. I hope that in time John Julius will enjoy the benefit of his godfather's native wit. By way of a little joke, handed the bill to Hugh saying, "I have a feeling you owe me a meal here."

He didn't seem to find it at all funny.

But then no man who wears socks and sandals to lunch on the 1st February cannot be over-endowed with humour.

Saturday, February 2nd

Life seems to be one long round of surprises these days. Drove down to Elwyn Road with Vita in the middle of the morning and knocked on the door of No. 9. Heart plummeted when it was opened by a whey-faced creature in her early twenties, in black leather-jacket, short black skirt and black tights, with jet-black hair standing up all over her head like a latterday Bateman cartoon:

'THE PUNK GIRL WHO ANSWERED THE FRONT DOOR TO FIND A NORMAL HUMAN BEING STANDING ON THE DOORSTEP.' From the nether regions, pop music wafted down the narrow passageway like stale cooking.

"Grateful Dead?" I said.

She said, "Sorry, I don't give to charities."

I said, "I meant the music actually."

"Dire Straits," she said.

"Seven out of ten," I said with a light laugh.

She did not laugh. In fact, now I come to think about it, no-one seems to find my jokes very funny these days. I'm beginning to feel like John Osborne's Entertainer.

I said, "Actually, I just wanted to introduce myself. I've just bought No. 7, and I was wondering if I could have a quick look at your party-wall."

"Why?" she said.

I said, "It's just a formality."

At this point, a man's voice shouted from upstairs, "Who is it, doll?"

"Bloke about the wall," she said. "Says he's bought No. 7."

"I'll deal with it," said the man, and down the stairs, wearing nothing but a dark blue towelling dressing-gown, and holding a copy of *Campaign*, came my old assistant group head from Harley Preston, Colin Armitage.

I'm not sure whether I was pleased to see him or not. On the one hand, it's always nice to move into an unfamiliar area knowing that you are not completely surrounded by strangers. After all, as Derrick Trubshawe's nephew and my ex-fiancée Amanda's cousin, he is almost family, albeit the black-sheep end.

On the other hand, there are certain people one meets on certain rungs of life's ladder that one rather hopes one has left behind on one's progress upwards, and although I'm sure he is a very successful creative co-ordinator in Harley Preston and his live-in girlfriend Susie may well be the daughter of an earl, that still doesn't make me feel any easier about having them as neighbours.

I said, "When you went off to live with Jane all those years ago, I thought she told me you had bought some workman's cottage somewhere."

"Yes," he said. "Le voici! All of us come to it sooner or later, old cock." I said that, of course, what was yesterday's workman's cottage is today's exceptionally stunning semi-detached house in an ever increasingly popular area, as they say.

"I wouldn't know about that," he said. "I've been here seven years now, and I haven't noticed the green welly brigade fighting each other to gain a toehold."

It has never ceased to amaze me that a man with such little vision, imagination and style should have even been considered for the creative side of the advertising business, let alone finish up practically running it. But then, judging by the general run of TV commercials, I'm not so sure that he isn't ideally qualified. Still, one must look on the bright side. One never knows when one might not want to borrow a claw hammer or a bag of sugar, and if we have any trouble over the pop music, a word in Uncle Derrick's ear should do the trick.

It was only when I got home that I realised I had completely forgotten about No. 5.

Sunday, February 3rd

A busy day. Opened the colour magazine to find an advertisement inviting me to "Learn the secrets of successful property refurbishment." All I have to do is send off a cheque for fifteen pounds to an address in Bromsgrove and I will receive by return of post a ninety-page manual entitled *How to be Your Own Property Developer.*

Obviously I am not planning to make a business out of buying run-down houses, doing them up and selling them for handsome profits. On the other hand, it would be a foolish and near-sighted man who did not try and make the best of his new home and improve it in such a way that, when it comes to selling up, he is in a position to realise the best possible price: and the retired expert who has written this book reveals, apparently, just how one should go about this. Am particularly interested in the section on where to find cheap skilled labour and materials. B having worked, albeit only secretarially, in the interior decorating business, I have, of course, left the choice of wallpapers and fabrics to her. Although actually, I don't think the Habitatty paper in the sitting-room

187

and dining-room is at all bad and I could certainly live with the heavy textured cream paper in the hallway and up the stairs. Apart from anything else, it covers up all the lumps and bumps wonderfully.

Mentioned to B that although most of the shopping in the area is pretty undistinguished, there is a very good British Home Stores and a really excellent Marks & Sparks.

She said she was glad to hear it, but that she would probably be sticking to Peter Jones, as usual.

To Clapham Common after lunch with Vita. Her sitting and staying work has improved out of all recognition, but running still badly marred by excessive barking. I think the high-pitched whistle is helping to instil a sense of owner-authority; ditto the shepherd's crook, tweed cap and wellington boots.

A rather unfortunate thing happened during a run-and-stay exercise when V suddenly started chasing a Pan-Am 747 in the direction of Wandsworth. Very soon lost sight of her in small wooded area and finally caught up with her on far side of road near playground, where she was lying down, apparently guarding the wire compound, and preventing half a dozen small children from getting out. As I approached, the father of a couple of the children called out in a facetious voice, "Thirty-seven out of forty for the Drive, but she'll lose points on her Pen."

Pretended not to understand.

Monday, February 4th

Rang and left message on answering machine to say I was feeling a bit under the weather and would be working at home for the day, made an excuse to B about having to see a new client in Mitcham, and drove down to Elwyn Road and parked opposite and a little up the street from No. 7.

In order to avoid being spotted by Armitage or Susie, had taken precaution of wearing dark glasses; also of carrying pair of opera-glasses in briefcase along with Kit-Kat and individual-sized Um Bongo fruit drink.

It was unfortunate that the car-wireless should choose that particular morning to go on blink, since even Richard Baker and the *Start the Week* team might have helped to relieve the boredom.

Pleased to observe no noticeable increase in traffic during rush hour and only a sprinkling of school children, all of whom appeared to have a proper respect for the ecology of the higher SWs. Intrigued to see that, within a few minutes of Armitage leaving for work, a tall streak of a fellow with half-mast trousers, skimpy grey jacket and lavatory-brush hair strolled in through front gate of No. 9 and, with a shifty look in either direction, through the front door. Very soon afterwards, Susie appeared at the front bedroom window, looked quickly up and down the street and firmly drew the curtains.

Ho, ho.

Feel there must be some way in which I can make use of this information, but not quite sure what.

Apart from that, the only incident of any note was when the man from No. 5 – presumably the owner – stood by and watched with evident satisfaction while his poodle calmly walked in through our front gate and deposited a disproportionately big potty on our path.

Jotted down *aide-mémoire* on back of Um Bongo carton re fixing gate-catch.

Also to the effect that we are going to have to keep an eye on No. 5's parking habits. If he thinks he's going to be able to push his backside quite so far in front of our hedge, he's got another think coming. Was checking distances through opera-glasses when there was a tap on my nearside window. Looked up to find No. 9 standing there with a policeman who wanted to know what I was up to. Apparently, as co-ordinator of the local Neighbourhood Watch Scheme, he had noticed me behaving in what he considered to be a suspicious manner and had called the local station. Obviously did not wish to reveal to him who I was and what I was doing, so told officer that, by a curious coincidence, I was also a co-ordinator and that I was doing a little field research on behalf of my own area in various random parts of south-west London.

While I do not enjoy being arrested *per se*, I was nevertheless glad of the opportunity to see the inside of the local police station and to meet some of the counterparts of the men with whom I have been working in recent weeks. I was most reassured to know that we can expect to be in safe hands in our new home, and, as I told the duty sergeant, I shall be at their disposal to offer advice and experience as and when they may need to call upon it.

Which reminds me, I must tell Harbottle that he'd better start looking for a new co-ordinator. And a property-marking kit.

Tuesday, February 5th

It never rains but it pours. Arrived at the office to be informed by Kippax that he had been talking to Valjean and had decided the Ski Time account needed a fresh mind on it in the shape of Pamela van Zeller. However, he certainly wouldn't wish to lose the sound of my little piccolo from his big orchestra, and from now on, he wanted me to devote my energies whole-heartedly to a new account that had just come TCP's way. The product, as I understand it, is a gadget designed to turn the pages of piano-music without the need of an accompanist. Like all great inventions, it is, as Charlie was at pains to point out, ridiculously simple. The pianist merely presses his knee against a small rubber bulb concealed beneath the piano. This forces a jet of air through a rubber tube which points at the side of the music and blows the next sheet across at the appropriate moment. It is called the "Gerald Moore" and the inventor, whose name is Hoppit, is already having difficulty keeping up with orders in his workshop in Mitcham.

Charlie said, "I know you're an arty-crafty sort of chap at heart, and I think this could be right up your street. A personal letter to all the top concert pianists might not be a bad idea for starters – Solomon, Semprini, that little Russian fellow, and so on. It might also be worth getting in touch with *Tomorrow's World*, and Melvyn Bragg, of course. Anyway, I leave it all in your more than capable hands." I noticed he did not say anything about the Botticelli or Steamy Days accounts; nor did I feel inclined to ask. It never pays to appear anything other than confident in this game.

At all events, while not perhaps a step upwards, it is certainly very much a step sideways and one that I am only too ready to get my teeth into.

My shoulder worse than it has been for a long time. Am wondering if, given today's events, it might not be psychological.

Wednesday, February 6th

The morning post brings a letter from Jeremy Venison of Ackerman's the solicitors asking us if we would kindly answer the enclosed queries from the Gillespies' solicitor concerning the garden flat. Amongst other things, they want to know if we are leaving the TV aerial and whether the owners of flats 1, 2 and 3 have right of access in the event of repair work needing to be carried out on the rear portion of the building.

The answer to the latter is that I haven't the faintest idea; to the former that, even if we were planning to make off with an aerial and several yards of brown flex – which we're not, since we have a portable aerial which gives a perfectly satisfactory, if slightly fuzzy, picture, provided people don't walk around in the room too much – even if we were, I cannot believe that anyone who works on the Stock Exchange could not afford to buy himself a new one. Frankly, I'd have thought that the Gillespies were paying their solicitor a fat enough fee without his feeling the need to squeeze an extra bob or two with frivolous, time-wasting tactics of this sort.

A letter from the *au pair* agency encloses details of one Gisela Grütsch who is nineteen, lives in Luzern, is the eldest of five children, has experience of helping to run a delinquent children's care centre, loves babies and dogs, is a non-smoker, likes to cook, enjoys skiing, swimming and volleyball, has had three years of English at school, would like to spend six months with a family in London and could start towards the end of February.

If we think she sounds suitable, we are to inform the agency straight away, enclosing a cheque for sixty pounds, and write a letter to Gisela, formally inviting her to be our *au pair*, to do five hours a day of light housework and helping with the children and occasional baby-sitting, for which we will give her her own room, food, laundry, free weekends and twenty pounds a week pocket money.

Judging from the small colour snap, she is not exactly the most beautiful creature to come out of Switzerland since Ursula Andress. On the other hand, you don't have to be a Miss World contender in order to wash a nappy or push a Hoover; indeed, looks could be a positive disadvantage. A non-stop stream of telephone calls from heavily accented admirers picked up in Soho discotheques, rattling front door keys and heavy footsteps on the stairs at three in the morning are a heavy price to pay for the pleasures of a pretty face over the Rice Krispies and a fluttering eyelash over the ironing board.

Rang the mortgage people in the afternoon. According to a Mr Plank, there should be no problem bumping up my low cost endowment thing by £5,000, and would it be all right if their surveyor visited the house on Thursday or Friday? His fees were calculated on a sliding scale and shouldn't come to more than seventy pounds. I said that sounded an awful lot of money, considering I was also about to be charged an arm and a leg for a structural survey. Could the building society not use the survey that had already been done?

Mr Plank explained that the structural survey was done for my benefit, whereas the other was done for the building society's.

I said that, even so, both surveys had the same purpose – ie to determine whether the house was in a good state of repair.

"Well, yes and no," he said.

If I didn't have so much else on my plate, I'd seriously think about sitting down and writing a stiff letter to the *Telegraph* on the subject. Or possibly alerting Esther. I'd have thought it was very much her kind of thing. She is certainly very much mine.

Thursday, February 7th

Great excitement at breakfast with the arrival of the structural survey report on Elwyn Road. Am particularly interested in his comments re the condition of the sarking felt and the soffit boards. Like him, I was also rather suspicious of what the heavy, textured wallpaper might be concealing in the way of crumbling plasterwork, sub-standard wiring etc in the hall and up the stairs.

Rang Loomis Chaffee as soon as I got to the office and suggested that, in the circumstances, a reduction of a thousand pounds on the price might be in order. He said that, leaving aside the fact that I was talking to quite the wrong person on this subject, to start quibbling about a price that had already been agreed was both professionally unadvisable and morally reprehensible.

I'm rather sorry now that I even mentioned it.

Friday, February 8th

Was in the middle of drafting a rather witty "Gerald Moore" letter to André Previn, when I had a phone call from Julian Hankey-Barber to say that the Gillespies had just received their surveyor's report on the garden flat and were very concerned about the lack of a damp-proof course. They had taken advice from a builder who had quoted them a figure of a thousand pounds for a damp course, using the injection method. In the circumstances, they felt justified in asking that the agreed figure of £39,000 be reduced by a thousand. I said, "In my view this would not only be professionally beyond the pale, but morally reprehensible."

Julian said, "I quite agree, but time is running short and you presumably don't want to cause a hold-up and run the risk of losing the other property, do you?"

I said, "But your colleague in Tooting has just advised me against asking the owners of Elwyn Road to drop their price."

Julian said, "Yes, well, it's all swings and roundabouts in this game. Someone has to be flexible somewhere along the line, otherwise none of us would get anywhere, would we?"

Something has gone wrong somewhere, but I still can't quite work out what or where. All I know is that I am a thousand pounds worse off than I was this morning. And in rather more pain from my shoulder.

Saturday, February 9th

Am not saying anything against Belinda, who is in many ways an ideal wife and a wonderful mother, but I was interested to read in my *Telegraph* this morning that a Mr Knackerly of Kimbolton, who is today celebrating his 104th birthday, is a non-smoker, a teetotaller and a bachelor.

To Vanessa's for dinner, for the second time in two months. I'm only sorry that we have been unable to reciprocate, but one really isn't up to throwing glittering dinner parties when one has just had a baby. Also the garden flat does not have quite the same drawing power as Inverness Terrace: certainly not to people with expensive-looking cars. Whether the kitchen/breakfast-room in Elwyn Road will have London's glitterati hurrying across the river remains to be seen.

Belinda is such a good cook: I suppose taking the food to them wouldn't be quite the same thing.

During my bachelor days, had a reputation amongst London hostesses as the promptest guest on the dinner-party circuit, so the idea that, as a married man, I would count it a minor triumph to arrive at any social event less than an hour after the official asking-time never entered my head. But then neither had a lot of the curious anomalies that seem to go with married life: like not being allowed to listen to the *Today* programme in bed in the mornings.

Was so surprised, therefore, at finding ourselves turning into Inverness Terrace at eight forty-five that I immediately assumed something must have gone wrong. However, all seemed to be in order. B had managed to do all her fingernails at traffic lights along the way; I was definitely wearing my trousers; and my shave, although far from definitive, was certainly not likely to have fellow guests drawing back in horror and retching into their spinach *roulade*.

We even managed to find a parking space within a hundred yards' walk of the house.

Vanessa must have forgotten to get in touch with the domestic agency until the last moment, since the butler who opened the door to us on this occasion was not nearly as good-looking and well-groomed as the chap she'd had last time. In fact, with his stomach hanging over the waist-band of his crumpled, light grey suit, his straight greasy hair hanging over the collar of his mauve-ish shirt and his rather protruding eyes goggling at us from behind large spectacles, he looked more like a frog than a prince.

Remembering the unfortunate misunderstanding of the previous occasion and our embarrassingly gushing behaviour, we restricted ourselves this time to a curt "Good evening", handed over our coats and headed off upstairs with no further ceremony.

No Roger Gomes, I noticed, but a good-looking man with crinkly grey hair and a twinkling eye and a marked Scottish accent who looked like a better class of milkman, but in fact turned out to be a writer and broadcaster. Also a slightly mad-looking property developer who immediately made a beeline for B and engaged her in intimate conversation, as if he had known her for years, and his wife, a pale, faded beauty, who said she thought she had met me at the Hall-Porters – whoever they may be when they're at home.

Was chatting listlessly to someone called Antonia Large and thinking how extraordinarily well-named some people are, when Vanessa approached with frog footman and said, "I don't believe you've met my fiancé David. He only flew in from Washington this afternoon." Only just stopped myself from saying, "Hopped across the Atlantic, did you?"

But seriously, this is the second time in a row we've tackled the Melba toast in W2 feeling foolish. I'm beginning to wonder if Vanessa does it on purpose.

Sunday, February 10th

An otherwise hum-drum family breakfast enlivened by Sainsbury's croissants and an excellent profile of Alastair Burnett. Even after all this time, I still cannot get used to him being *Sir* Alastair. Am wondering how I am going to cope when my contemporaries start being recognised in the Honours List. Just for the fun of it, made out a list of people of my generation who are destined for knighthoods, if not more.

Bragg, certainly; Dimbleby; Branson; Puttnam; Archer, of course; Nunn; McKellen; Cliff Richard, I shouldn't wonder. I'm afraid my close friends and acquaintances are less likely to be weighed down with honours. Indeed, if we manage to rustle up an MBE between us, I think we can reckon we've done pretty well.

Certainly, I feel that at this stage I must reluctantly put myself out of the running. The public relations profession is not picked out as often for recognition as some, and Gordon Reece was very much the exception that proves the rule. It all depends, of course, who you relate publicly *for*. Am also of the opinion that there are certain names that lend themselves to knighthood more readily than others. Sir Geoffrey Howe, Sir Geraint Evans, Sir Monty Finniston, Sir David Lean . . . they all have a ring to them that Sir Simon Crisp could never hope to acquire, however often it was on people's lips.

Monday, February 11th

Venison rang this afternoon to say that contracts on both properties have been exchanged. While I applaud the speed with which he has pushed this thing along, I fear that his zeal will be more than reflected in his fee. No amount of pleading to the effect that conveyancing is a loss leader for the legal profession will make my cheque for £1,200 any the less easy to write out. I suppose I should be relieved that we do not have to scratch around and find the deposit. On the other hand, the knowledge that, thanks to their dubious bargaining methods, the Gillespies are there for nought, as they say on the golf course, is not exactly a cause for celebration. In the circumstances, the copy of *How to be Your Own Property Developer* which arrived this morning is somewhat superfluous. Indeed, were it not for a long central section entitled "Renovation Made Simple", I should even now be asking Karen to return the book in a large brown envelope, along with a stiffly worded letter demanding a full refund.

As it is, the writer is full of helpful, common-sense suggestions which might not otherwise have occurred to one – to wit: "It is important that you find a good plasterer to give you a finished job, especially in the kitchen and bathroom. If you can, hire a man who has done it a hundred times before. He may charge a little more than a less experienced man, but he will do the job that much quicker, and you can be sure that the plaster will dry properly and not leave nasty settling marks and unsightly cracks.'

I couldn't agree more.

Section on plumbing less sensible to my way of thinking.

B says that Paula Batty has come up with a decorator-cum-carpenter who could well be exactly who we are looking for. Paula's mother, Mrs Prickett, used him for years, and even though he did make rather a nonsense with her silk wallpaper at £100 a roll (apparently, because it shrinks as the paste dries, you have to hang it so that it slightly overlaps: otherwise you finish up with half inch strips of bare plaster all round the room – like Mrs Prickett) he is that perfect combination – experienced *and* cheap.

He is coming round tomorrow evening to Elwyn Road with his son to give us a quote. He is called Mr Cloutings.

Which reminds me, I suppose the Dalrymple-Macintyres are planning to move their stuff out eventually. I haven't seen hair or hide of them, and neither, it seems, has anyone else. Not even their estate agent.

Really, life is one long round of worry.

Tuesday, February 12th

Rang Hume Purkiss re firming up on a date for my visit to Steamy Days set-up in Norfolk, but he is away on holiday in Barbados and won't be back until the middle of next week. Since I am taking the whole of next week off, what with the move and everything, the chances of our getting together this month are beginning to look slim. Could not help reflecting that I must be one of the very few top PR men in London who has yet to manage an account that involves travelling to the Caribbean in the middle of winter. Am not sure if this is my fault or not.

Mr Hoppit of "Gerald Moore" also away. As for Botticelli, Pamela seems to have got things so well under control on that front that I appear to be almost redundant. Perhaps I *am* redundant. If so, how has this come about? Nothing appears to have happened that I can put my finger on, but at the same time, everything seems to be slipping away from me. I wonder if this is how Jim Slater felt when his empire crashed around his ears? Perhaps I too should consider taking up children's fiction as a profession. If JJ were a little older, I could start making up bedside stories for him. It's amazing how many children's classics started that way.

Mr Cloutings came at six with his son Terry. I couldn't make out if Terry had been drinking, had an unfortunate speech impediment, or had undergone brain surgery. At all events, his father treated him only slightly less harshly than the Squeers family treated Smike.

"What a pranny," he told us at one point. "Only tries to put up a cupboard over his bed, doesn't he? What does he do? Only forgets to tighten the screws, that's all. Only lands on his head at three in the morning, doesn't it?"

Not that Mr Cloutings is one of the world's towering intellectual giants. Small and vulpine, with a thin black moustache, he clearly thrives on tales of other people's disasters. There was not a room in the house in which he did not draw in his breath sharply and shake his head sadly at the naughtiness of the walls. The hall and staircase came in for especially gloomy comment.

"Oh dear, Mr Crisp," he said. "Someone's had cowboys in here. Dear, oh dear. You're talking trouble here, I kid you not. You could be talking . . . ooh, I wouldn't like to say what you could be talking. But whatever it is, it's trouble."

When I asked him what he thought might be involved, he replied, "I want to give you a first-class job, if you get my meaning, Mr Crisp. Not tip-top, you understand, like Mrs Prickett, but a first-class professional job that I'm going to feel proud of and you're going to feel proud of. What I'd like to do is have that wall right back to its bare essentials, then give it a proper skim, nice and smooth, then paper on top really nicely. Get rid of all those naughty bits."

I said I thought that that was that papering usually involved.

"That's what I mean," he said. "A proper first-class professional job. No messing. I think you're going to be pleased."

He certainly sounds a perfectionist, and although £450 for the hall, stairs, our bedroom and the *au pair*'s room seems a little on the steep side, to my way of thinking, I think that, as the refurbishment book says, it's worth paying slightly over the odds in order to ensure a really good job. Was surprised to hear that he could start as early as next Tuesday. I'd have imagined a man like that would be booked up for weeks ahead. Still, one mustn't look a gift horse in the mouth, as Miss Thatcher would doubtless say, were she still with us. Curiously enough, I'm quite sorry she isn't. We're going to need all the help we can get in the next few days.

Wednesday, February 13th

The removal people have confirmed next Monday as moving-day. I hope somebody has thought to inform the people at Elwyn Road. Left B wrapping glass and china in old copies of *Telegraph*. Pointed out that there is no point in paying the removal firm £750 plus insurance if we are going to do half the work ourselves. We might as well go the whole hog and take everything over bit by bit on the roof of the Polo. B said, "*You* are not doing anything, so what are you worrying about?" I

199

may be wrong, and I hope I am, but I strongly suspect that moving house does not always bring out the best in people. Harsh words could well be exchanged before next Monday evening is out. Cannot decide whether to be very much in evidence in the next few days or not at all.

As if I did not have enough on my plate, had to fritter away most of the afternoon in Parsons Green undergoing a rigorous medical for the life insurance people. Did not realise I possessed quite so many things that could possibly go wrong in quite so many out-of-the-way places.

Was afraid that the fact that I still cannot raise my arm above chest height might count against me, but the doctor didn't seem the slightest bit perturbed.

"Terrible bloody things, shoulders," he said. "Nothing to worry about. A year from now, you'll be as right as rain."

Could not believe my ears.

"A year?" I said.

"Shoulders always take a year to repair," he said. "Don't ask me why. It's one of those things."

As I was pulling on my shirt and letting out my stomach, he looked up from his desk where he was making notes and said, "So, you've just become a father. I think in the circumstances that's a cause for celebration."

I still cannot make up my mind if this was some sort of medical joke. Certainly little else was that I was forced to submit to that morning. Indeed, on the evidence of the probing examination of my prostate gland, I can only thank heavens I am not a homo.

Thursday, February 14th

Damn and blast. I knew today was St Valentine's Day. I wrote it down in my diary at the office; I tied a knot in my handkerchief; I even repeated the words "Valentine's Day" to myself all the way home on the tube, like a mantra. But even so, I forgot to send B a card.

To make matters worse, not only did I find one from her propped against my cereal bowl, but another one arrived for me in the first post. The postmark was W1, which offered no clue as to the perpetrator. The fact that it was of a humorous nature and showed a cartoon figure reeling beneath the blows from a huge heart-shaped hammer which an elephantine woman was wielding above his head, and the words: "YOU'RE A BIG HIT WITH ME," did not help to lighten the situation. On the contrary.

"Humorous cards invariably reflect some private joke between two people who know each other quite well," she declared. "I suspect that travel–agent creature you went skiing with."

She may well be right. I suspect an awful lot of people. But how to find out for certain? The culprit is going to deny it; the innocent are going to make me look a fool for asking. The truth is, as I told B, I have got better things to think about than wasting valuable time and money on supporting the British greetings card industry.

B said, "The truth is, you're about as romantic as a garden gnome."

I said that in that case we should perhaps seriously reconsider our decision to attend the Battys' St Valentine's Day party tomorrow night. I had a feeling that would make her change her tune. On the other hand, I am still no nearer thinking up what I am going to go as than I was a week ago.

B says she is going to look out all her oldest clothes, which she was saving for the Conservative garden party at her parents' house in June, and go as Shirley Williams.

If she really wants to make fun of the SDP President, I don't know why she doesn't just go as she is.

Friday, February 15th

It was Karen who, as usual, came up with the perfect solution when all others had failed. She said, why didn't I put on a pair of black trousers and a black roll-neck pullover and carry a box of chocolates and come as the man in the Milk-Tray commercials? I could even make a spectacular entrance, through the window or something.

By an extraordinary coincidence, the Battys have a pair of French windows leading out into the garden in their house in Hampstead Garden Suburb, so I could easily nip round the side when we arrive, let B go in on her own, and pretend I'd been held up "on serious business". Then after a moment or two, she could go across and open the French windows, whereupon I would come bounding through, singing the Milk Tray jingle.

Slightly to my surprise, B thought that was a brilliant idea, and we set off for the Hampstead Garden suburb in excellent spirits.

Had I known it was going to be quite such a cold night, I would definitely have put a vest on under the pullover, if not a couple. And my black gloves.

Indeed, had I known that B was going to swan in through the front door, set the whole place on a roar with her Shirley Williams impersonation, be rushed to the bar by Roland and given a huge glass of champagne, then come face to face with the de Grande-Hautevilles and become embroiled in a long conversation about schools and completely forget my existence, I would never have suggested the stupid plan in the first place.

As it was, after a quarter of an hour, could stand the cold no longer and was forced to call it a day and return to front entrance. Unfortunately, by that stage, the door was firmly shut and the party was in full swing. Whether their bell was out of order or what I don't know, but no-one answered my repeated ringing, and a further ten minutes were to pass before another guest, purely by chance, happened to open the door to chuck out a cigarette-end, and I was able to slip in.

Did not feel inclined by that stage to sing Milk Tray jingle, and even if I had, doubt if I could have moved my frozen lips sufficiently to do so.

When Paula finally deigned to greet me, all she said was, "Are you meant to be a burglar?"

I explained that I was the Milk Tray man.

"Who's the Milk Tray man?" she said.

"From the TV commercials," I said. "You know."

"Oh," she said. "I'm afraid we're not great TV fans. But well done anyway."

Am sorry I was not in a mood to reciprocate.

Saturday, February 16th

A slightly non-speaks sort of day, as a result of which I finished up on my own in the ABC Streatham eating a BA iced lolly and watching a Paul Newman film.

At one point, was aware of something rather more substantial than a cigarette packet or used ice-cream carton under my feet. Hoiked it backwards and picked it up to find it was a pair of skimpy girls' knickers.

Thought it only courteous to enquire of the girl sitting in the seat next to me if they happened to belong to her.

"Certainly not," she said. "Mine are in my handbag."

Sunday, February 17th

B in martyrish mood over packing of bed-linen, so after playing a little game with JJ and his teething ring, settled down to Sunday papers, only to be confronted by yet another snide article making fun of Sir Richard Attenborough. Am gradually being forced to the conclusion that the one thing we in this country – especially the so-called intellectuals and arbiters of taste – cannot forgive is success. Why it should be considered a sign of weakness and failure for a man to display his emotions in public, I simply cannot understand. On the contrary, it is a sign of great strength. I myself have been reduced to tears on more than one occasion, although admittedly not in full view of millions, and I certainly do not consider myself to be a lesser man for it. Rather the opposite.

The fact of the matter is that, for all the knockers and Weary Willies and Tired Tims of what we like to call our quality press, Sir Richard, or Dickie as he is known to his friends, is a man who believes in getting off his backside and getting things done. And frankly, if we had a few more people in this country

203

who were prepared to follow his example, we'd be in damned sight better shape than we are today.

Monday, February 18th

Had assumed, quite naturally, that what many people would consider to be one of the most momentous events of their lives – ie their first moving day – would be the subject of one of the longer and more thoughtful of my diary entries. And yet, I find that I can scarcely bring myself to put pen to paper – partly because I do not believe I have ever been quite so tired in my life, and partly because, far from my mind being full of memories and thoughts, it has never been emptier.

If I have any word of advice to offer my children and grandchildren on the subject of moving house, it is this: if you feel tempted to sit up until one o'clock the previous night working out a precise plan of what pieces of furniture are to go in which rooms, forget it.

Watch a bit of television, have a nice hot bath and go to bed early. Because the fact is, when it comes to it, it is the removal men who decide what is going to go where. And if the fridge finishes up in the bathroom and the spare bed in the kitchen, well that's just the way they happen to be feeling at that particular moment. One other important piece of advice: make sure that the first thing you do when you get the double-bed in place is make it.

The first night in your new home, trying to find the light switch is difficult enough, let alone the bed-linen.

At least if the bed's made up, you know you can fall into it at any moment and go to sleep. Even if you have forgotten where you packed your pyjamas.

Tuesday, February 19th

Our first day in our new home.

I cannot believe that the Prince and Princess of Wales could have felt happier and more fulfilled the day they moved into

Highgrove with their little chap than B and I did this morning when we finally managed to move the spare bed sufficiently to get at the cooker and make our first Colliers Wood breakfast. Thank heavens the previous people agreed to sell us that and the fridge. They are both far newer and bigger than the ones we had in the flat.

Was naturally slightly anxious at being forced to park on the opposite side of the road. Suspect this was done by No. 5 as a revenge for taking up so much space with the removal van. He couldn't wait to put his beastly little S-reg Ford Escort back in what he obviously sees as its rightful place the instant the men had driven away at five thirty.

It's all so petty-minded.

Fortunately, he drove off very soon after breakfast, so I was able to slip across and park the Polo firmly in front of *our* privet hedge.

B said she thought the front bumper was a little too close to the boundary for comfort. I reminded her that *close* is one thing, *over* is quite another. I am not one of these pedantic bores whose life is ruled by principles that have to be maintained at all costs; on the other hand, I have always believed in starting as one means to go on. Unless one establishes ground rules from the very beginning, one is simply being a fool to oneself. The phrase "Possession is two-thirds of the law" was not coined for nothing.

We were just clearing the last few packing-cases from the hall when Mr Cloutings arrived, bringing paint brushes, scraper, Polystripper, etc, but not Terry. He explained that he had dropped him off in Battersea Park Road to finish off a glossing job in a converted delicatessen, but that he would be along later in the morning.

We were standing in the bedroom shortly afterwards, drinking coffee and wondering whether to paper that, too, while we were about it, when I happened to glance out of the window and there, wandering up and down the pavement peering at the front doors was Terry.

"Isn't that your boy out there?" I said.

"No, no," said Cloutings. "I told you, he's in Battersea."

I said, "He hasn't got a twin brother by any chance, has he?"

Cloutings looked out of the window.

"What's he up to now then?" he said.

The answer was that Terry had gone to open the front door of the delicatessen, only to realise that his father had forgotten to give him the key. He'd tried to call after the Maxi as it drove off up Battersea Park Road but to no avail, so there'd been nothing for it but to run and try and catch it up. Once or twice he'd very nearly made it, but each time the lights had changed and the Maxi had once again been swallowed up in the traffic: so he'd had to keep running all the way to Elwyn Road.

I said, "But that's about five miles!"

"You're telling me," said Terry grinning.

"Why didn't you catch a bus or a tube?" B asked him.

"Nah," he said. "You can't rely on public transport."

"But you must be exhausted," I said.

"Bit out of breath, that's all," he said.

I said, "Perhaps you run a lot anyway. Marathons and that sort of thing."

"Get away," he said. "You've got to be mad to do that sort of thing."

While Cloutings drove Terry back to Battersea, B started unpacking John Julius's clothes and putting them in cupboards in his room and I began sorting the books.

Cloutings arrived back at eleven thirty saying he was very sorry to have taken so long but his car had broken down in Balham and he'd had to borrow some jump leads to get it going again.

Had rather hoped he'd finish stripping the hall paper by lunchtime, but had not taken into account the fact that he did not have his own ladder, nor that I should have to waste much of the first morning in my new home driving to Peter Jones to buy one. Actually, as it happened, B had remembered one or two bits and pieces she needed, and I doubt you can buy aluminium step-ladders anywhere cheaper than at PJ's – not even in SW 19.

Managed to fit ladder into Polo by opening hatchback and tying it with string, and arrived back just after one.

B said, "You didn't think to pick up Terry from Battersea on the way, I suppose?"

No, was the answer. I am not a mind-reader, nor do I run a taxi service for half-wits. Perhaps I should. There is obviously a big demand for both.

Cloutings said that since it was now his dinner-time anyway, and since he happened to have a little exterior paintwork job he wanted to check on in Clapham Old Town, he would pick up Terry on the way.

Following a makeshift picnic lunch, B took JJ and V to Tooting Common for a walk while I continued to wrestle with books. Cloutings and Terry arrived back and parked in our parking space. Did not say anything. It wouldn't do any harm to keep the spot warm until this evening.

Went out myself shortly afterwards to buy light bulbs, three-pin plugs etc. Also a bottle of white spirit for Cloutings. Arrived back to find them both hard at work stripping paper from hall walls which were turning out to be even naughtier than they had imagined. In view of the nasty holes, lumps etc, am quite glad the previous owners had the sense to run three-foot-high pine panelling along hall and up stairs.

Cloutings said, "I take it you do not want us to touch anything below dando height."

Presume he meant dildo height, but hadn't the heart to correct him.

Quite how Terry managed to cut through the electric wire on the landing I cannot for the life of me conceive. But then it's hard to imagine how anyone could have conceived Terry.

Fortunately, Cloutings knows of an electrician who, he feels sure will be able to sort it out without it costing us an arm and a leg. The loss of a limb could turn out to be the least of our worries.

Armitage looked in this evening bringing a Busy Lizzie and wanting to know if we needed any help. I told him not unless he fancied a spot of rewiring. He did not press the point and left soon afterwards.

To bed finally just before midnight. Had blown out candle when from somewhere down below there came the sound of dry plaster hitting aluminium. Thought about getting up to check, but couldn't face it and slumped back onto pillow.

I sometimes wonder if a Burmese elephant is as satisfied as I am after a full day's work.

Wednesday, February 20th

A rather more constructive day all round, although I am still irritated by the fact that yesterday evening No. 5 managed to be in his Escort and easing himself backwards before Cloutings had so much as pulled away from the pavement. He must have been sitting at his window waiting and watching our every move. Just let him allow his poodle to put one paw inside our gate and see what happens. Would not fancy its changes greatly with Vita in full throat.

For some reason Cloutings did not appear to have any other jobs on the go elsewhere in south London this morning, so he and Terry were able to give us their undivided attention, if not a tip-top job.

By lunch-time, they had reached the landing and had patched up last night's inexplicable mini-crater in the hall with some *ad hoc* spot-plasterwork. Even so, had hoped they might be a little further advanced by this stage. Gisela will be with us on Saturday and they haven't even made a start on her room yet. Have suggested they leave ours and concentrate on hers first.

Cloutings said it was all the same by him.

I said that if there was nothing else I could do to help them, I thought it was about time to knock off for lunch, adding for no particular reason that we would be having it in the dining-room.

"Right you are," he said.

Had barely settled down to a simple snack of toast, pâté and a small cheese-board, when Cloutings appeared in the door-way, rubbing his hands on his overalls and, to my amazement, plonked himself down at the table and started helping himself.

"Is that a piece of Brie I see over there?" he said, pronouncing it to rhyme with "sky". "A small saliver of that would go down very well indeed, if you would be so kind. I'm very partial to Swiss cheese."

Am not quite sure how this misunderstanding arose, but arise it did. I was no happier with the situation than B, but not all the face-pulling in the world was going to alter the fact that there was absolutely nothing that either of us could do about it.

Did attempt to make the point by saying, with a slight hint of sarcasm in my voice, "Terry not a cheese and pâté fan then?"

"Terry?" said Cloutings, laughing in disbelief. "Eat pâté? Our man Flint? I tell you, he is so ignorant he thinks adding tomato ketchup is the height of hoat quinine."

Clearly he does not have quite such high aesthetic standards when it comes to late Victorian architecture, to judge by the casual way he announced the accidental breakage of one of the rather nicely hand-turned banister rails. Cloutings said not to worry; by a happy chance, he happened to know where he could lay his hands on one exactly the same. When I asked him where exactly, he tapped the side of his nose and winked and said, "Ask me no questions and I'll tell you no porkies. Know what I mean?"

I don't know what the penalties are these days for receiving stolen goods. Slightly less for first-time offenders, I daresay.

As he was leaving, asked him if he'd managed to get hold of the electrician. He said, "Blimey, I almost forgot. I'll give him an ask this evening." I hope he will. Going up to bed with a flickering candle in a saucer tonight, I felt like Nickleby's uncle.

Thursday, February 21st

Up at seven with a view to making an early start on sitting-room shelves. B now finally resigned to my vision of rustic, open-planned effect, achieved with plain wooden planks supported by simple aluminium strips, to go with open brick-work of chimney-breast, thus giving the room a country cottage feeling. Had toyed briefly with the idea of buying an electric drill plus workbench, but decided there was nothing to beat a good hand-job, and what earthly use is a DIY shop if it can't cut a dozen planks of English beech to length? What I had not taken properly into account, however, was that in houses as old as this, a) it is very much touch and go whether a given point in a wall into which one is planning to insert one's Rawlplug is going to turn out to have the consistency of self-raising flour or the north face of the Eiger, and b) there is not a single wall, floor or ceiling that goes in a straight line.

It is one thing to hold six-foot-long aluminium strips up against the sides of a recess in a straight line and at the same time make marks through the appropriate screw holes with a pencil, without the slightest assistance from one's wife; it is quite another to drill the holes in a straight line. Where the wall is soft, the bit disappears like a hot knife through ice-cream; where it is hard, it assumes a will of its own and wanders off a centimetre to right or left, depending on how it is feeling at the time.

It also appears to be one of the unavoidable facts of DIY life that the tightest screws (and most of them are tight) are the ones that are right up against the back wall. This means that because you can't fit your fist between the screwdriver handle and the wall, you have to hold the thing at an angle, thus tearing open the slot on the top of the screw, and gouging holes in the wall. And that was on the side I could get at with my *good* hand.

Having the bad shoulder didn't help either.

As I said to B, if only she'd gone out for the day, as I suggested, she wouldn't have had to put up with all the concomitant shouting and swearing, but since she would insist on remaining within earshot, then I'm afraid she was asking for trouble.

It says something for the aluminium people that they are able to produce strips which, even though forced into a shape resembling a Fyffes banana, still manage to support several rows of shelves – even if one does have to drive one or two of them into the recess with a clump hammer. Personally, I think the dented edges add to the naturalness of the whole thing.

B less convinced.

210

To bed early with Cox's Orange Pippin and *Country Life* and, despite aching shoulder, a sense of real achievement at having made something with my bare hands that I have never felt from composing the most elegantly worded press release.

For all our sophisticated ways, we are most of us artisans at heart.

Friday, February 22nd

Cloutings arrived at nine-thirty, just as I was emptying the last packing-case of books, bringing with him his electrician friend Eddie – a stocky little man with a rather red face who exuded a curiously musty, slightly feral odour. Having announced that the rewiring job looked a doddle and that he would be finishing within the hour, had naturally supposed that Cloutings would finish papering the landing by the end of the morning and be able to make a start on *au pair*'s room, with a view to it being ready by the time she arrives tomorrow afternoon. However, for some reason that none of us could fathom, least of all Eddie, he was still hard at it by lunch-time.

Cloutings in the meantime announced he had to go and meet an Arab to discuss a major paper-hanging assignment.

"I'm talking real money, Mr Crisp. Know what I mean? I'm not blowing my own hooter but, believe me you, I've had this one handed to me on a silver spoon."

He arrived back at two thirty to find Eddie still trying to work out why, although he had replaced the wire, and the connection seemed perfectly good, the landing, bathroom and *au pair*'s room lights still wouldn't work. By this time he was decidedly rattled. His face became redder and redder and the smell got worse and worse.

"This just isn't my week," he said at one point. "Yesterday a vasectomy and today this."

Could not resist thought that perhaps he had mistaken the word lobotomy for vasectomy. They do sound fairly similar. Still, if this is the price one has to pay for safe sex, then I for one want nothing to do with it. In the circumstances, he remained remarkably cheerful throughout. At one point, the lights all came on and then abruptly went out again.

I said, "Have you ever come across something that goes for a while and then stops?"

"Yes," he said, "My wife."

Had I realised he would still be with us working away by candlelight at six fifteen, I would never have allowed Cloutings to make a start on stripping the *au pair*'s room. Still, they have both promised to come back first thing in the morning, and finish off. How lucky we are to be dealing with good old-fashioned types with a proper sense of responsibility towards their customers. One could so easily have landed oneself with a couple of cowboys.

Saturday, February 23rd

I'll kill Paula Batty. How she ever talked Belinda into believing that Cloutings was anything other than a cheapskate amateur with the mentality of a delinquent three-year-old I shall never know. I can't quite make up my mind whether Eddie was telling the truth when he said that he only knew Cloutings professionally and had no idea where he lived or what his telephone number was, but at least he had the grace to turn up, as he said he would, and finish the job. And although it must have been extremely annoying for him to discover that he had forgotten to check the fuse all the time, he still only charged us for half a morning's work.

Of Cloutings, on the other hand, we have had not a word. Nor indeed a new banister. It was B who pointed out that it was rather odd that if he was planning to come back in the morning, he should have taken all his brushes with him – not to mention my bottle of white spirit. That'll teach me to pay people for jobs in advance.

The Battys would have to go and choose this weekend, of all weekends, to take a winter break in Bruges. Am beginning to wonder if they suspected something like this might happen and did it on purpose.

Luckily, Gisela seems very relaxed and jolly about the

whole thing. Who knows, perhaps her bedroom in Luzern has half the paper hanging off and huge holes in the bare plaster-work, and this is home from home for her. And perhaps she really doesn't mind the fact that she is not going to be living, as she perfectly obviously thought she was going to be, within a stone's throw of the King's Road, if not Piccadilly. And perhaps she really did believe us when we assured her that although on the face of it Colliers Wood was not the prettiest area in London, it was very popular with young, middle-class, professional families and was very expensive indeed.

And perhaps she doesn't mind that her best friend Putzi is going to be living in East Finchley, and that the Wimbledon School of English, where she will be spending three mornings a week, is three-quarters of an hour away by bus, and that we do not know anybody else in the area that has an *au pair*, and that girls should never walk around late at night in this sort of area on their own, and that she doesn't have a TV set in her room. Who knows?

All I do know is that unless I find someone to decorate her room within the next few days, and buy her a small colour TV, and find her some friends in the area, and very possibly a car-hire company with a fleet of bullet-proof vehicles, we could soon be looking for another *au pair* girl.

As it is, I can only ascribe her air of benign acceptance to an instinctive and deeply ingrained sense of Swiss politeness, and hope that she will become so besotted with John Julius and his winning ways that nothing could persuade her to leave.

Little does our son know the weight of responsibility that will be resting on his tiny pink shoulders in the next twenty-four hours.

Gisela's mother rang after supper. Am slightly cursing myself that I did not keep up my German until at least O Level and slightly wishing we had plumped for someone from the French-speaking part of Switzerland. However, the general tone of her conversation seemed cheerful enough, even if I could not understand the actual words.

Can quite imagine that kedgeree was not quite what she was expecting as her first meal in England, but cannot believe it was anything other than tiredness after a long journey that

213

persuaded her to retire to her room quite so early. Am only sorry that she did not feel up to watching *Hi-De-Hi*. There is no better way of learning a language than by watching television, and this particular programme is really archetypally English. Not, of course, that I ever watch it myself.

Sunday, February 24th

Am becoming increasingly depressed by the quality Sunday press. It is so full of the news of clever people doing wonderfully creative things and being wildly successful that I sometimes think the editors must be involved in some cruel conspiracy to make the rest of us less talented, less well-connected, but nonetheless hard-working members of the human race feel like second-rate failures.

At the same time, I have long had the feeling that I was made for better things than trying to excite minor journalists about unimportant schemes and products in which they have no real interest, and today's latest parade of talent across the better breakfast tables of Britain comes as a timely reminder of the rewards and honours that await those who dare. Obviously it is unlikely at this comparatively late stage in my life that I will become a leading heart transplant surgeon, or direct Verdi at the Met, or score a try for England against Wales at Cardiff Arms Park. But that is not to say that every door of opportunity along the corridor of life has been slammed in my face once and for all. I feel I have as much to offer as the next man, if not more. But of what exactly? Like Churchill, again, I await the call. When it comes, I shall not shirk or turn away, but seize it gladly in both arms – even though one of them is not a hundred per cent perfect.

Tried to do something about the wallpaper in Gisela's room this afternoon, and failed.

Monday, February 25th

What an extraordinary way history has of repeating itself.

Seven years ago I was in the middle of a meeting in

Roundtree's office at Harley Preston, discussing the Barford project if I remember rightly, when Sarah, my secretary, rang through to say that someone from BBC Television was on the line and wanted to speak to me urgently, and before I knew what, I was having lunch with my Oxford undergraduate revue colleague and up-and-coming TV producer Nicola Benson and discussing my becoming the presenter of a major documentary series.

I can't remember now why they decided not to use me. Naturally it came as a bitter blow at the time. And yet, I had a feeling that it was only a matter of time before they'd be back knocking on my door. It was simply a question of matching the right person to the right topic and the right sort of programme format. So it did not come as a total surprise to me when this morning, almost exactly seven years later, Karen buzzed me through to say that someone called Miss Benson from breakfast television was on the line. Hearing her voice again, the years seemed to fall away and it was only a matter of moments before I slipped back into that relaxed, slightly bantering style of conversation that has been the hallmark of our long, if rather intermittent, friendship.

Being the professional she is, she had kept tabs on my career over the years, and although at first she couldn't find anyone at Harley Preston who had ever heard of me, personnel had been very helpful and had suggested she try Barfords, who in turn had pointed her in the direction of TCP.

She herself has moved around inside the industry since we last spoke, and is now something very important-sounding in the breakfast-time set-up.

I said laughingly, "So you've never been tempted to chuck it all up, get married, start a family and become a normal human being?"

"As a matter of fact," she said, "I was married for a while, to a news cameraman. Unfortunately, he was killed last year in Beirut."

She went on to explain that they were planning an item for tomorrow morning's programme about the Opposition's proposal that all the free travel, hospitality and accommodation that is offered to journalists, MPs and members of the

Royal Family should be automatically taxed as if it were income, and she wondered if I would be interested in coming along and being the mouthpiece for the public relations industry.

She wasn't sure who they would be having to speak for the other side, but there was a possibility they might be able to get the Leader of the Opposition himself.

This is the most exciting offer I have ever had in my entire career. In fact, this was the first I had heard of this proposal, but even so, I told Nicola that we in the PR profession were extremely concerned about it, and felt that it struck at the very heart of the free enterprise system on which the economy of this country has been based in the last fifty years or more.

"Good," she said. "That's the sort of thing I had in mind. If you feel happy about it, we'd love to have you."

I told her I was proud and privileged to be asked.

She said she was glad, and would it be all right if they sent a car for me at seven o'clock? The item was scheduled for the second half of the show.

I said that I could easily drive myself.

"No, no," she said. "We'll send a car."

When I told her that we had just moved to Elwyn Road, she asked where exactly Elwyn Road was.

"Colliers Wood," I said.

"Is that near London?" she said.

Obviously didn't want to make too much of a thing about it at the office and disrupt the hum–drum routine of everyday life, but felt professionally obliged to mention it to Pamela and Charlie Kippax, in case they wanted to alert any of their clients, tape it for the records etc. After all, it isn't every day one gets free PR for the industry in general and the company in particular. But then, of course, it isn't everyone in the business who has my sort of connections.

Asked Kippax if he had heard about this opposition proposal.

"Of course," he said. "Who hasn't?"

"Who indeed?" I said, and left the room.

He hasn't said much, but I think he's secretly rather jealous. B naturally very excited, if rather critical of my haircut.

Personally, I think it's just the right length: long enough to give an impression of creativity, but short enough to imply seriousness. I quite see there is a very good argument for wearing a suit. On the other hand, there's also a lot to be said, in televisual terms, for contrast, and feel the grey herring-bone jacket has a nice, unemphatic, breakfast-time feel to it.

Decided not to alert Mother. She has never watched breakfast television in her life and I don't want her getting herself stewed up unnecessarily. B says that she thinks it unlikely that John Julius will be able to recognise me, even if she were to hold him up close to the screen, which is dangerous anyway. Personally, I don't see any harm in letting him watch. There's no knowing the effect it might have on him in later years. After all, Sir Compton MacKenzie had vivid memories of being in his pram, and they certainly did his career no noticeable harm.

To bed rather later than usual as a result of watching *Newsnight* – a programme with which I rarely bother. Was most interested in the elegant way David Owen dealt with Norman Tebbitt.

Of course, an awful lot of television people have gone into politics, some of them with glittering results.

Tuesday, February 26th

Woken at six thirty by telephone call from TV people to check that I was awake and to confirm that the car would be with me at seven.

I wonder if Frank Bough has similar trouble waking up in the mornings. I suppose one gets used to it.

Car arrived on the dot: a Ford Granada.

Driver surprisingly chatty at such an early hour and told a hilarious story about Jimmy Tarbuck and the Kingston bypass. The girl in the angora sweater at TV reception seemed quite relieved to see me, although the "someone" who they said would be down to collect me was obviously rather less excited by the news of my arrival, since I spent the next fifteen minutes watching the programme on a television set in the far corner. It was strange to think that one moment one was just another anonymous face watching TV on a sofa in a reception area and that the next, one would be appearing in millions of kitchens and living-rooms up and down the country, being watched and listened to by millions of people as they buttered their toast and stirred their coffee, including possibly Prince Charles and Princess Diana. And why not? The subject, after all, concerns them as much as anyone.

Finally gathered up by a small, bossy girl with close-cropped hair who led me through empty studios up countless staircases and along dozens of corridors until we suddenly emerged at the back of the studio where the actual programme was going on. Picked my way on tip-toe amongst a small army of people standing around in the dark shadows on the fringes of the set, none of whom appeared to have any special function other than to hold clipboards and generally get in the way.

After stumbling over a couple of little wooden bridges covering some cables, I was shown into a poky room where half a dozen people were drinking coffee and watching the show on a television set in the corner. Vaguely recognised one who I think is a well-known union leader, or possibly a professional snooker player.

No sign, however, of Kinnock. Nor of Nicola. Presumed she was upstairs in "the box" as they say. Sat next to glum-looking man who had a banjo leaning against his chair. I said, "Hallo, are you going to be doing George Formby imitations?"

"No," he said.

After a few minutes, the girl came to take me to make-up. Surprised that I was in the chair for such a short time. The make-up girl seemed rather nice, too, and I was only sorry not to have been able to present her with more of a challenge. In the circumstances, a large wart or two or an ugly birthmark might have been a blessing. At all events, did not like to move my head while she was applying liquid with small sponge, but had definite feeling that man in next chair was Kinnock. He certainly had a gingery complexion. Mind you, so did I by the time the make-up girl had finished with me.

At all events, decided not to introduce myself, as I did not

218

wish to compromise our forthcoming conversation in any way.

Was finally shown across set by girl during newscast and welcomed by presenter dressed in expensive diamond-patterned pullover, and banjo man who turned out to be a leading income-tax inspector and my fellow interviewee. Asked in a low whisper what had happened to Kinnock.

"Who?" said the presenter.

Was about to have tiny microphone attached to my tie by young man in headphones, when he suddenly announced that my jacket was strobing and would I mind doing item in shirt-sleeves?

Replied that, in light of seriousness of topic, I would prefer to be fully dressed.

Would certainly have fallen in with his suggestion had I had the faintest inkling of the hideousness of the substitute jacket which was produced from wardrobe. Black and red and green specks simply isn't me. Still, time was very much of the essence, and before I knew what, I was wearing the thing, the income-tax man was stating his case and I was being asked for my reaction.

I began by saying that we in the public relations industry were deeply concerned and began to explain why.

Was fascinated to notice, as I was speaking, how very much more relaxed I was than I had expected, and how uninhibited by the lights and the cameras. I felt as if I had been working in television all my life. Indeed, so at home did I feel that it seemed the most natural thing in the world to lean back in mid-sentence and hook my arm casually over the back of the soft leather sofa.

Why my fool of a shoulder had to go and choose that moment to play up I shall never know. Off-hand I cannot recall anyone cry out with pain actually on camera, but then I doubt if any interviewee in the history of television could possibly have experienced quite such agony as I did at that juncture. The situation might have been retrievable had the relevant muscle not immediately gone into spasm, causing me to become locked in this quasi-relaxed, semi-supine position and, despite the efforts of the floor manager and two of his colleagues to relieve the situation, totally unable to move, speak or even think. Pain apart, was aware only of the fact that the director had cut away from me and that the income-tax man was having the entire interview to himself.

Finally, by dint of superhuman power, managed to wrench arm back into something approaching normal position just in time for presenter to thank us both for coming and cue in weatherman.

Everyone backstage very sympathetic and insistent that little things like this happen every day of the week and that really the item wasn't anything like as one-sided as it might have seemed. On the contrary, I had more than kept my end up in the short time available. After all, as the research assistant pointed out, quite rightly, it is mini-dramas of this sort that people remember far more than what the person involved actually said. Everyone remembers Bernard Levin being punched by the man from the audience on TW3, but who can tell you what he was rattling on about at the time?

She added that she didn't think that even the most experienced professionals in television could have coped as well as I did in similar circumstances.

She may well be right.

To Hospitality next for a cup of coffee and a croissant. Surprised that no-one there made mention of the incident. Perhaps they hadn't been watching at the time. Also that Nicola had not bothered to make herself known.

It might have been my imagination, but every time the car stopped at traffic lights on way from studio, I was convinced that passers-by were looking at me in a knowing way. Arrived at office expecting the place to be abuzz with talk about the broadcast, but of course they'd all been travelling to work at the time.

Rang B who said she was very sorry but JJ had been sick just as I came on, so she had missed the whole thing. I suppose that in the circumstances I cannot entirely blame her for recording over *Kind Hearts and Coronets*. I daresay they'll be having another Ealing season before long.

Spent the rest of the morning staring out of the window and feeling rather flat.

Mother rang just before lunch to ask what on earth I thought I was doing wearing that dreadful jacket? I explained that it wasn't mine and asked her what she thought of my performance.

"What performance?" she said. "I didn't think you got much of a look-in myself. I also didn't think much of your haircut. You really ought not to be wearing it quite so long at your age. If you're not careful, you'll finish up looking like that fool of a man Wogan."

This evening at supper, Gisela said, in halting English, "You were very good on television. Very handsome." And she went pink in the face and giggled.

I am beginning to find her strangely attractive in a bovine sort of way. I hope to goodness JJ is pulling out all the stops. I certainly will be from now on.

Wednesday, February 27th

A man sitting next to me on the tube this morning stared at me all the way from Clapham South to Waterloo. Finally, he leaned across and said, "Don't I know you?"

I said I didn't think so.

He said he was sure he did; my face was very familiar.

The situation was so classic that I could barely restrain myself from smiling.

I said, "I think you'll find you've seen me on television."

"I don't think so," said the man. "Oh, what is your name? Don't tell me. It's on the tip of my tongue."

Decided the time had come to put him out of his misery.

I said, "It's Crisp, actually."

"Who?" he said.

"Crisp," I said. "Simon Crisp."

The man shook his head firmly. "No," he said. "It's not that."

Did not feel inclined to argue with him further. The fact is that this is just one of the many little inconveniences one has to put up with if one is a media face.

Nicola rang in the middle of the morning to thank me for

coming and to apologise for not having been able to make contact. It hadn't been an easy morning. I said I was sorry about the silly business with the arm, but she said things like that can easily happen. Fortunately, not very often, I asked her if, apart from that, she thought it had gone all right.

"Fine," she said.

I said, "Perhaps we'll have a chance to work together again soon."

"You never know," she said.

Although she didn't actually spell it out, I have a feeling that the television studio could well become a second home for me before very long. They're notoriously bad at committing themselves, these producers.

Faced with an unusually empty diary, I spent a useful hour this afternoon updating my choice of Desert Island Discs. Have come to the reluctant conclusion that if it's a choice between the Vaughan Williams and the Elgar, the Vaughan Williams will have to go. The Schubert is obviously a must. So are the Cole Porter and the Mozart. I think that from the point of view of the actual programme, one could afford to include the Alan Bennett *and* the Woody Allen. Am still in two minds over Jack Buchanan. It's either him or Sonnie Hale. Otherwise, the list is as before.

Thursday, February 28th

Looking at John Julius lying on the bed this morning, gurgling and dribbling and kicking his little feet, I suddenly came to a very important conclusion concerning my life. The fact is, we are all sent into this world with a modicum of talent, and it is our responsibility to our fellow human beings, to our families and to ourselves to recognise that talent and nurture it and make the very best use of it we possibly can. I am still not entirely sure, even after all these years, what my talent really is. I believe I am a born communicator, and, as such, I have more to offer mankind than press releases about second-rate Italian restaurants, gimmicky holiday cottages and daft inventions for turning the pages of sheet music.

Have been thinking more and more about this programme I did yesterday, and frankly I feel I should be doing myself less than full justice if I were not to capitalise on my success. The fact is that some people are TV naturals and some aren't. It isn't something you can acquire: either the chemistry is there between you and the camera or it isn't. Frost, the Dimbleby brothers, Esther, Selina, Wogan, Raymond Baxter – they are all blessed with that special magic that lights up our screens the instant they appear and helps to make all our lives that much fuller and happier.

I believe that one day I, too, could count myself amongst their ranks. It's early days yet, but the Richard Dimbleby Award for services to television is by no means beyond my grasp and suddenly Sir Simon Crisp has a reassuringly solid ring to it. Ditto John Julius Crisp, Old Etonian.

From now on, I shall cease to waste my time and energies on people of little consequence and even less ambition. Think big: that will be my motto. And with a little luck, a lot of hard work, and the love and support of my dear wife and son, I will reach up into the skies, pluck down the stars from the firmament and bedazzle the world.

First, though, I must do something about this wretched shoulder.